THE
GUILT
WE
CARRY

Also by Samuel W. Gailey

Deep Winter

THE GUILT WE CARRY

A NOVEL

SAMUEL W. GAILEY

OCEANVIEW PUBLISHING

SARASOTA, FLORIDA

ISBN 978-1-60809-380-9

Cover Design by Christian Fuenfhausen

Published in the United States of America by Oceanview Publishing

Sarasota, Florida

www.oceanviewpub.com

10 9 8 7 6 5 4 3 2

PRINTED IN THE UNITED STATES OF AMERICA

For my two girls—Ayn and Gray

THE
GUILT
WE
CARRY

Sinclair had asked her what the sound was like, but she declined to answer.

Nobody—not her parents, her therapist, not even the police—had ever posed that question before.

But what would she have told them if they had?

The reverberation would prove to haunt Alice for the rest of her days. Nothing unusual in the sound in and of itself—it wasn't a chilling scream, or a wrenching cry, or the wail of a passing ambulance siren—no, nothing like that. Rather, it was a simple, repetitive noise echoing from far below; something seemingly innocuous. Like the pitter-patter of that night's rain, or the whirl of an air conditioner, or the hum of tires rolling upon asphalt. While this particular sound would merely be white noise to many, or a blip of irritation to some, Alice would never be able to block out the din and its fatal stamp on her memory . . .

CHAPTER ONE

MAY 2005

There was something about how water changed the very essence of sound. Everything muffled and distorted and far away. When submerged, Alice felt a deep, soothing comfort that gave her a sense of purpose and awareness. In the embrace of the water, nothing else mattered. The weightlessness allowed all distractions—the anchor of family, friends, school, boys—to disperse like tiny bubbles of water popping to the surface. It was home to Alice—a tiny sliver of the universe that was hers and hers alone, and there was no place she'd rather be.

Alice craned her head to the right, drew air into her lungs, then immersed her face once again into the warm, crystal blue liquid. She heard the beat of twenty feet and twenty sinewy arms cutting through the water behind her. Pounding, churning, thrashing. Getting closer. Her nearest opponent two, maybe three lengths back. The cacophony of sounds urged Alice to pull herself harder, faster, to keep ahead of the encroaching pack.

She focused on each stroke, exerting just enough energy to maintain her pace, but not too much as to deplete what little reserve she had left. The final burst would come soon, very soon.

Alice turned her head again. Exhaled. Inhaled. It was time to make her move, and her mind beat with the words *faster, faster,*

faster. Her body responded, legs kicking more urgently, arms torquing with more force. Water beaded off her pale, freckled skin. The racerback swimsuit, a second set of flesh, pulled tight over her athletic build—a perfect fifteen-year-old swimmer's physique. Her molasses-colored hair tucked under a latex cap; mirrored goggles cupped over her green eyes, everything an amber hue above, below, and everywhere around her.

Alice prepared for her final flip turn, spinning under the chlorinated surface, knees pulling tight to her chest, then a perfect kick-out against the concrete wall. She rushed forward, breaking the plane of water once again for another take of air. Then, as she always did, she closed her eyes for the final lap, trusting not only her instincts, but more importantly, her ears. She heard the muffled thrashing all around her. The swimmer in lane five, two lengths behind. Her opponent in lane three, four lengths back. Everyone else yet to make their turns.

Faster.

Her heart machine-gunned in her chest. Lungs burned. Arms and legs started to tighten and cramp to an almost unbearable threshold.

Alice dropped a curtain over the pain, pushed herself harder, not only wanting to win, but willing herself to shave off a few more precious fractions of a second. Winning wasn't enough—beating her personal best was.

Eyes pressed closed, swimming in utter darkness, nearing the finish line but not wanting to break stride just yet, Alice knew the exact number of strokes it would take to reach the wall.

Not yet, not yet.

Lane five closed in. One length behind her now. Alice came up for one final draw of air, eyes cinched tight. She could hear the frantic cheers and screams coming from the stands, could feel the repercussion in the water from thunderous clapping and stomping of feet on the fiberglass bleachers. Everything crescendoing to a frenzied climax—the kicks, the grunts of effort, the desperate sucking of air from the other swimmers.

Lane five pulled even closer. Half of a length.

Alice snatched at the fear of losing.

Faster.

She found the last bit of untapped energy, arms and legs working in unison for the final surge.

Faster.

At the last possible moment, she reached out, fingertips extended, until they grazed the dimpled concrete wall. She erupted through the surface of the water, pulled her arms up and over the edge of the pool, let her head fall back and took in air as if it could be her last.

Cheering and shrill whistles surrounded her from every side, echoing off walls and from the turbulent surface of the water. Alice didn't need to glance at the clock to know that she had eclipsed her personal best.

A smile creased her face, her eyes remaining shut as she savored the sounds of celebration and soaked in the fleeting moment of triumph.

CHAPTER TWO

It seemed as if her parents would never leave the house. Alice's mother kept finding things to do—she washed the dishes, sorted through the mail, changed her coat two different times. Anything to delay them from going out on their date night.

We'll be fine, Alice kept saying to her mother.

The cab outside honked its horn—for the fourth time.

"Go, already," Alice urged.

Her mother stared toward the door and chewed at her lip. "Are you sure you'll be okay?"

"Mom. Seriously."

Finally, mercifully, Alice and her father exchanged a silent look of understanding as her mother slipped on yet another coat, grabbed an umbrella, picked up her purse, and was ushered out the door. This was only the second time they were leaving Alice at home alone with Jason, her four-year-old brother.

Standing at the window, she watched her parents' cab pull out of the driveway and cruise down the street, and she let out a sigh.

Finally.

Her parents were going out to celebrate their twentieth wedding anniversary. They took a cab so that they could enjoy a few drinks at a blues bar after dinner—the same blues bar down on the Wilmington waterfront where they met twenty-one years ago.

A few months back, Alice had pleaded with her parents to not get a babysitter for the two of them. She was fifteen—way too old for a sitter. None of her friends had babysitters anymore and they had started to give her a hard time, calling her *Little Baby Alice*. She finally managed to convince her parents that she was responsible enough to take care of Jason and herself for a few hours. Besides that, they could give her half the money they paid to a babysitter—she could use the extra spending money. It was a win-win.

Alice proved herself reliable on the first date night, although her mom called her cell phone a half dozen times to check up on how things were going: *Was the front door locked? No scary movies for Jason. Make sure he eats his dinner. Don't forget it's bath night.* To which Alice had responded: *Yes. Okay. Jason had macaroni and cheese. No bath, but I'll use a hot washcloth.* Alice even managed to get him in bed by seven thirty after coaxing him with his favorite book, *The Gas We Pass.* Her parents arrived home to find Jason safely tucked in bed and Alice doing homework. Her mom and dad were impressed, even paid her ten dollars extra for the night. Total score.

Alice had successfully babysat once. What could go wrong this time?

She swung open the refrigerator door and poured her first Coke of the night.

* * *

One hour in and Alice was already wishing her parents were back home. Jason had gotten into her fingernail polish by minute twenty and decided to decorate her wallpaper with candy-apple red doodles. A *Jason* Pollock is what her parents would call it. Whether it was with crayons or ink pens scribbled on the walls or kitchen counters, somehow Jason's artwork proved to be nothing short of adorable or impressive to both her parents. *Oh, look at Jason's masterpiece,* her mom would say, hands on her hips, shaking her head and smiling like his doodles were the greatest thing ever. *He's going to be an artist when he grows up. A painter. Something creative, I just know it.*

Not only did Jason smear the fingernail polish all over her walls, he managed to splatter it on her shag carpeting, and on her new bedspread—a *brand-new* bedspread she had just gotten for her birthday. Alice's room was supposed to be off-limits to Jason because he always messed everything up and ripped through all her stuff. His last little exploit got him banned from her bedroom for good. *Supposedly.* In what her psychology teacher would call a Freudian move, Jason had collected all of her swimming ribbons and medals and flushed them down the toilet one by one.

When she had walked in and caught Jason painting her wallpaper, Alice completely lost it. She yelled at him. Grabbed him by the arm. Called him a little brat. Said a few other things that she regretted, and Jason had stared up at her with his big green eyes. For a second, she thought he might cry, but instead, his tiny face twisted in defiance. He glared at Alice, stuck out his tongue, then dropped the fingernail polish to the floor and stomped out of the room.

But despite everything—the tantrums, the constant need for attention, all his superhero toys scattered everywhere, and the inherited responsibility of watching over a little brother—Alice loved Jason. Alice was the one who taught him to swim, and like his big sister, Jason took to the water like a fish. Sure, there was an eleven-year gap between their ages, and their interests were night and day, but he brought an energy into the house that proved contagious. And, as much as she might hate to admit it sometimes, Jason broke up the monotony and generally made life around the house more unpredictable, which wasn't always a bad thing.

Alice was only halfway done scrubbing the doodles off the walls with rubbing alcohol—her hands raw and burning—when she heard a thumping from downstairs.

KA-THUNK. KA-THUNK. KA-THUNK.

The steady drum of rain pounded against the shingles overhead, but when Alice listened more closely, she heard a dull thumping noise that echoed throughout the house. The banging seemed to be coming from somewhere downstairs. Probably Jason lying on his back, kicking at the walls with his Keds—either pitching a little tantrum because she'd tossed him out of her room, or pretending to do karate. Whichever one, it didn't matter—he was being a brat, and the noise was annoying. Alice had never gotten away with behavior like that when she was four years old. Not that she had been an angel, but if she threw a fit, she'd get a time-out or a firm whack to the backside. But Jason always got away with temper tantrums. Little Jason, the *miracle* baby.

After Alice's birth, the doctors informed her mother that she would never be able to conceive again. Something about a scarred uterus from a difficult delivery made another pregnancy impossible. Her parents eventually came to embrace having an only child, heaping all their love and energy and focus solely on Alice for ten years. For those ten years, *she* was the center of their universe. Then, the impossible happened—her mother got pregnant again.

KA-THUNK. KA-THUNK. KA-THUNK.

The pounding was nonstop and almost defiant-sounding. Yes, Alice decided, her little brother was pitching a fit. Anything to get attention.

She stared at the spots of fingernail polish on the carpet and bedspread and knew that they would never come out. The bedspread was ruined.

KA-THUNK. KA-THUNK. KA-THUNK.

"Jason! Knock it off!" Alice hollered at the top of her lungs.

Almost seven fifteen, time to get Jason into his pajamas. The thumping kept on echoing through the house, and now Baxter started to bark like crazy. "Jason, I'm going to tell Mom and Dad if you don't stop it."

He didn't stop it. *KA-THUNK. KA-THUNK. KA-THUNK.* And Baxter barked even more frantically. Alice walked down the steps into the living room where the thumping and barking sounded louder.

"Jason?" She ducked her head into the kitchen, but he wasn't in there. Next, she checked the dining room and her dad's office—another room that was supposed to be off-limits, but only seemed to entice Jason that much more. Nothing broken or messed up in either room. No sign of Jason tampering.

She checked the living room again, then the downstairs bathroom. Still no Jason.

Then Alice noticed that the door to the basement was cracked open. Just an inch, but the sight of it made her heart skip a beat. The door was supposed to be latched so that Jason wouldn't venture down the steep steps and fool around with her dad's workbench. Sharp tools, chemicals, all sorts of stuff that Jason could use to hurt himself. She'd been the recipient of the *safety lecture* so many times she could recite it in her sleep by now.

Alice had gone down into the basement earlier to find the rubbing alcohol and must have forgotten to lock the door, and now Jason was playing in the one room in the house that she would get in the most trouble for letting him sneak into.

"Jason, if Mom and Dad find out that you're down there, they're going to go nuts."

Jason ignored the warning and kept banging away. Alice half-expected to hear him giggle, excited that his game had finally gotten her attention. Part of him thought that getting into trouble with his big sister or parents was all fun and games. Much like his other favorite activity: hiding from Mom and Dad when they were looking for him. He was a lousy hider. Couldn't keep quiet, giggling from his chosen spot in the closet or under a bed or behind the living room curtains. Except for now. No giggling or the excited pitter-patter of feet.

Alice spotted Baxter at the bottom of the stairs, the twelve-pound Jack Russell all worked up, running around in circles and issuing a constant barrage of high-pitched yelps. "Where's Jason, Baxter? Where's he hiding?"

Baxter kept barking and darted across the floor.

Alice came to the bottom of the stairs and searched the basement, partially hidden in shadows. To the left side of the room, her dad's work area. A six-foot-long workbench lined the far wall, neatly organized with all sorts of tools that Alice couldn't care less about, but that Jason found irresistible. A juice box perched on its side at the edge of the workbench, slowly dripping a steady flow of purple grape juice onto the floor.

"Jason. Dad's going to freak out if you stained the floor."

KA-THUNK. KA-THUNK. KA-THUNK.

Alice looked to the other side of the basement. Mom's domain. The laundry area. Boxes of detergent, bottles of bleach and stain remover lined up on a shelf out of reach of Jason's curious hands. An ironing board had a pile of her dad's work shirts stacked up, waiting to be pressed. Baskets of dirty clothes, carefully separated into darks and whites, sat in front of the washer and dryer. Baxter hopped into a laundry basket, then onto the top of the dryer. He clawed at the metal—whining and barking—then jumped back to the concrete floor. The dryer rattled and pitched side to side as its contents rocked the entire machine. It sounded like a pair of her dad's work boots were clunking around inside, but Alice didn't remember her mom putting any laundry in before they left.

Baxter continued barking and jumped up at the front of the churning machine, and Alice noticed that the dog's brown and white tail curled up and trembled between his hind legs.

"Baxter, no. Be quiet."

But Baxter didn't stop.

Alice sighed, trying to imagine what Jason might have jammed into the dryer. Stuffing things into toilets, sinks, any place that was off-limits happened to be another one of his favorite games. Then she saw the piece of red fabric sticking out from under the door of the dryer. It could have been anything—a red pillowcase or the tail of a shirt—but Alice knew exactly what it was. She'd seen Jason wear the red Superman cape a thousand times.

Her heart leapt, clogging in her throat as she reached for the handle of the dryer door. It wouldn't open. She yanked harder, but the door remained locked. She fumbled for the power button and shut the dryer down. The metal drum eased to a stop, and the thumping inside slowed like a dying heartbeat. She opened the door, lifted the red cape, and her hands slapped to her face. Her fingers still smelled of rubbing alcohol, but she didn't seem to notice.

Then Alice began to scream.

CHAPTER THREE

How BAD'S THE hangover?

Alice's eyes flickered and cracked open for a moment before fluttering back shut, and she waited. Waited to determine the degree of her hangover. That's how mornings rolled now, waking to the same question every single day—how bad were the aftereffects of another night of drinking going to be? Not what she had to do that day, or what to have for breakfast, or what errands to run. No, none of that. It was always the same.

Memories from the previous night swirled in a dull haze, smeared like a greasy countertop wiped down with a piece of wax paper, and Alice left the muddled remnants right where they were. She wasn't in a hurry to remember everything. Not yet. The memories would come bubbling back to the surface eventually, there to be pieced together, then regretted. Same kinds of mistakes, different sorts of circumstances. Rinse and repeat. Seemed like she usually ended up using remarkably poor judgment every time she got drunk, which was often. *Every day* often. In fact, she couldn't remember a sober day in years. Part of who she had become. Not so much embraced, but accepted. A tiger's stripes and all that.

She tried to cling to sleep a little longer, even for just a few more moments. Dreams were usually a better place to be—most of them, anyway. Reality would present itself eventually, and with that, the self-loathing would soon follow. It always did.

Alice had developed a rating system to determine what kind of toll the previous night of drinking would wreak upon her body and mind; a rating system that was hers and hers alone. Nothing to be particularly proud of, but when you put your body through a daily wringer as much as she did, the least one could do was devise a measuring stick to determine the effects.

She imagined other people awoke thinking about their upcoming day, facing tedious life decisions—what to wear to work, bills that had to be paid, whether to organize the garage, whatever. Others probably woke with visions and plans of how to accomplish their long-term goals and dreams—how to climb the ladder faster, toying with the urge to quit their jobs, to settle down and get married. And some people worried about their kids. Were they raising them right? Would they amount to something more than the parents who were rearing them?

But not Alice. She thought of none of those things. If she were able, she would probably embrace waking to mediocrity, whether it be copying and collating at Kinko's, or changing diapers and wiping noses all day. The thought of actually *overachieving* wasn't even on her radar—like going to graduate school, or working at a job that didn't entail either pouring some slob a cup of coffee or pouring some slob a shot of tequila.

No, Alice's first thoughts of the day were solely focused on the degree of her hangover. *That* was her reality. *That* was her state of mind. And the way things were looking, it wasn't about to change anytime soon.

The rating system was pretty simple. Five was the head-buster—a full-blown, temple-pounding headache. The kind where the dull pain started at the base of her neck, stabbing and probing and inching its way over the top of her head, eating up flesh and coursing through the veins in her temples. Any sudden movement or an attack of her smoker's cough meant sheer agony. As soon as she could manage to swallow two or three Motrin and chase them with a few swallows of whatever liquor was left over from the night before, Alice would stretch out on the floor, waiting for the painkillers to take effect, and all she'd think was *shit, shit, shit.*

Four generally required crouching beside the toilet and bringing up sour bile. She didn't eat much—not enough to puke anyway. Food happened to be an afterthought. Only when her body trembled, reminding her that she needed protein, something in her stomach other than vodka or whiskey or tequila. Sometimes four turned out to be just the dry heaves, but that was worse than vomiting, in her own expert opinion.

Three consisted of a class-A sour stomach that sat low and heavy in her belly like a loaf of bread, the stomach acid churning and bubbling, eager to absorb something other than high-grain alcohol. Milk helped a little, but she rarely had any around. Blame that on the absence of a refrigerator or the lack of foresight.

Two produced the fuzzies—her brain like a bag of wet cotton balls, leaving her unfocused and uncoordinated. The fuzzies were a half-dream state—a disembodied feeling that left her in neither the here nor now, like she temporarily hijacked some poor woman's body and beat the shit out of it. Recalling the previous evening's encounters took even longer to piece together. Trying to remember what she drank, where she drank, and with whom she drank. The latter didn't usually matter because she typically drank alone, even preferred to drink alone.

One stood at the bottom, the low man on the totem pole physically, but in many ways, it proved twice as brutal than the other four combined. One was the guilt hangover and resulted from not drinking enough the night before. Alice loathed the guilt. No Motrin, or milk, or *hair of the dog* could remedy that one. Feeling like a total failure for letting her life get so out of control and for attempting to drink her worries away. Drinking to forget all the mistakes she made over the years, especially the Big One. The Big One was what started all this in the first place. The liquor did what it was supposed to do at the time—numb her—but in the morning, regret was back. Back in a big way. The accident replaying over and over again, clear as if it happened yesterday.

CHAPTER FOUR

Alice felt the presence before actually seeing it. Beside her. Under blankets and sheets that smelled of sweat and something even worse. She glanced back over her shoulder, noticed the tangle of black hair spilling out from under the sheets.

Then, as she tried to recall what transpired the previous night, her eyes settled upon the ceiling. A powder-blue ceiling. A *different* ceiling.

A single light bulb suspended by wires hastily wrapped together with masking tape dangled from water-stained plaster. But it wasn't the light fixture Alice was used to staring up at in the morning in the crappy motel she had been staying at for the last few months. This place smelled different, too. Instead of the moldy scent her heater kicked off, the air reeked of cheap cologne and fried eggs, and the thought of fried eggs made her stomach hitch and churn. Flopped hard enough to get her into the sitting position to search for something to vomit in.

The room spun around her for a moment. A tiny bedroom. About enough space for the waterbed she currently rolled on top of, and the rocking sensation made the spinning and nausea that much worse.

Shit.

She was going to throw up. No doubting that. At the foot of the waterbed, she found a half-eaten bowl of popcorn, mainly un-popped kernels, a few pieces brown with butter. There were a couple of cigarette butts at the bottom as well. The bowl would have to do. Alice dumped the popcorn and cigarette butts onto the floor and let loose.

Christ.

Now the place smelled like cheap cologne, fried eggs, *and* vomit.

She glanced around the room, grateful that there wasn't a mirror to greet her. She avoided her reflection when she could. Hated the face staring back at her. Hated everything about it. Not that she was ugly. Far from it. Alice could be pretty if she wanted to be. If she actually gave a damn. A tomboy's face with a few freckles left behind from her teenage years, and a petite nose over lips that looked as if she had them injected with collagen, even though she hadn't. Her body lean and tight despite all the liquor she consumed. But it was her eyes that were the most striking and always a topic of interest to men—and a few women as well. Kelly green eyes that befit her Irish blood.

Beer bottles littered the floor—all of them American brands. Pabst Blue Ribbon, Miller High Life, Budweiser. Cigarette butts were stabbed onto small plates, dropped into coffee mugs, a few crushed into the carpet. A half-empty bottle of Jack Daniel's perched on the edge of the small dresser near the front of the bed. All the drawers partially opened, overflowing with T-shirts and blue jeans. The waterbed continued to loll under her as she stared at the tangle of clothes. Black T-shirts and faded Levi's. Men's clothes.

She was not only in some stranger's house; it was a man's place.

It was then that Alice felt her own nakedness—not a stitch of clothing on. Not even a pair of socks, and she always wore socks to bed, even in the hottest of summer months. She didn't mind sleeping in the nude, and often did, but felt vulnerable without something on her feet. She must have gotten good and hammered last night if she agreed to lose the socks.

The guy next to her didn't budge an inch. Sleeping like a log. *Good.*

She wanted to find her clothes and get dressed before solving the mystery of her bedmate. Her cheap thrift-store sweater, blue jeans, bra, and panties were all cast off in the corner of the room, lying in a hastily disregarded heap. Her jacket was missing, as well as the memory of shedding her clothes the previous night. The jacket must be somewhere. She wore it to work yesterday—*that much* she remembered. She stood too quickly, little stars flaring and zipping around the inside of her head, and she fumbled to put her clothes back on. The quick, abrupt movements launched a pulsating freight train inside her skull, roaring down the tracks.

Alice kept an eye on the sleeping stranger, searching through the muck clouding her brain, trying to figure out who the hell he might be. She tended bar last night at the Frisky Pony, a low-rent strip club in the industrial section of Harrisburg. An auto-body shop to its right, a scrap-metal yard to the left. An off-ramp of Interstate 81 dumped out right behind the Frisky Pony, causing the steady hum of tires to blend in with what passed for dance music. Alice would be lucky to pocket forty bucks on a good night, but the Frisky Pony was off the radar to cops, so it was the place to be for her. For the moment. She'd be moving on soon enough. Alice knew that. Could feel it in her gut, an internal clock that always served as her wake-up call for when it was time to move on. She'd been in Harrisburg for almost six months and that proved long enough. Things were becoming too familiar. Too personal. A few of the strippers at the Frisky Pony—Tia and Naomi especially—had been wanting to hang out with her, inviting her to parties, drinking with her after the club closed. That was always a sure sign to move on—when people wanted to get to know Alice better.

Tequila. Now she remembered. She got into the tequila last night. Sauza Hornitos. Never a good sign when she could recall the brand of tequila she drank, but not the name of the guy she slept with. Then, little by little, the alcoholic haze began to dissipate, and the memories started to unravel, revealing themselves in all their ugly glory. Tia and Naomi had been drinking with her, matching her shot for shot, then proceeded to kiss for a while and eventually invited Alice back to their apartment for a girls' night. *Thanks, but no thanks*, Alice recalled telling them.

Alice remembered Tia and Naomi dancing on the top of the bar, music thumping, both of them peeling off each other's clothing, trying their best to seduce her. She resisted. It wasn't the first time she got a private dance from the two girls. They were both nice enough, but dumb as hell. Alice got the sense that the two girls had absolutely no ability to see down the road a little. After a few more years and a few more miles on their tight bodies, flashing their breasts wouldn't earn them enough money to pay rent, buy food, and take care of themselves. They were blind to all that. Even though they were the same age, Alice had enough awareness that getting by with a firm ass would only last so long before reality hit. Not that Alice had everything figured out—far from it—but at least she wasn't grinding on a pole.

Alice remembered everything up to the point when both strippers got down to their G-strings, and that was about it. She couldn't remember leaving the Frisky Pony or how she got into the bed where she currently found herself.

A waterbed. God, she hated waterbeds.

She peered out the bedroom window. A trailer park. It was snowing a little. A fresh layer of white tumbled down on top of black slush left over from the last storm. A couple of kids were throwing stones at a cat. The cat shrieked as a rock connected with the side of its head and the group of snot-nosed boys let out a victory cry. Bullies. She hated bullies worse than she hated waterbeds.

Alice zipped up her jeans and searched the room again for her purse and jacket. Maybe she could get the hell out before her mystery man woke up. She'd be fine not knowing whom she slept with—some mysteries better left unsolved. No purse in the room. No condom wrappers either. She hoped that she hadn't been so drunk that she didn't opt for protection. That's all she needed right now. Getting pregnant or getting something worse.

Her big toe banged hard on the corner of the waterbed. "Shit."

But the sleeping man didn't budge.

She took a step closer to the sleeping man, but his face was buried under the blankets. "Hey. Guy. Rise and shine."

Nothing. Nobody home.

Alice watched the blankets, looking for a sign of life, but the man laid completely motionless. She watched him for another minute—still as a damn rock.

Alice picked up an empty beer bottle. Held it out in front of her, right over another empty beer bottle on the floor. She glanced back toward the bed and dropped the bottle. *CLINK. SMASH.* The bottle shattered into a dozen jagged pieces. It was loud—loud enough to wake the dead.

"Hello? Time to wakie-wakie."

But the guy didn't answer, and Alice had a sinking feeling as to why.

No, no, no.

The guy couldn't be dead. That didn't make any sense. You don't just wake up naked next to a dead man you don't even know.

Alice kept watching the sheets, waiting for them to rise and fall. Maybe the guy was a heavy sleeper. She waited for him to move. To cough. Sneeze. Moan. Anything. But he did none of that.

Black hair. Who did she know that had a head of thick, black hair like that?

Who cares? Doesn't matter.

Alice took another glance around the room for her purse, but the place was about the size of a closet, so it wasn't exactly like searching for a needle in a haystack. Must be in the living room. Or in the bathroom. Anywhere but in there.

But she couldn't help it—her eyes settled back on the sleeping man, who probably should be referred to as the dead man. Alice's hands were shaking now, rattling along with her thudding heart, and the surge of adrenaline wrung the hangover right out of her system. The tremor in her hands continued throughout her entire body, straight down to her knees, forcing Alice to take a seat back on the waterbed. The mattress gurgled like an empty stomach and the water rolled under the dead man, giving him the appearance of stirring. After a few seconds, the water settled and so did the dead man.

Screw it.

She stood up, reached forward, and yanked back the sheets.

The man was dead, all right. That much was clear. His eyes cracked open, pupils dilated, and both corneas smeared a hazy white.

Alice's heart jackhammered even harder as she jerked away from the bed, her feet getting tangled up with one another. She could feel the rapid thump in her chest as she stared down at the body—the second time in her life that she glimpsed death firsthand.

* * *

The dead man happened to be good looking. Or at least used to be, in that arrogant, white trash kind of way. Alice stared down at the face of the man she knew—Terry Otis, the manager of the Frisky

Pony. Terry *fucking* Otis, the coke-snorting, chauvinistic meathead that slept with all his strippers. Terry *fucking* Otis, that drank like a fish and strutted around the club like a rooster, throwing drunks out of his bar for touching the merchandise, then beating the shit out of them in the back alley. The big, tough Terry that drove a black Chevy truck on oversized tires, ironed his Levis, and kept his cowboy boots perfectly polished.

Now, Terry wasn't so tough or cool anymore, lying in a pool of his own vomit, naked and dead.

She kept staring at her deceased boss, trying to extract memories of the previous night from her booze-addled brain. She remembered Terry being at the Frisky Pony—he was always there—but she hadn't been drinking with him or paying him any attention. He was too busy snorting blow off the bar and watching Tia and Naomi grind against one another.

She'd never been to Terry's before. Not that he hadn't invited her to his trailer on more than one occasion. *Open invite anytime, honey,* he smiled and leered at her a half dozen different times. His breath always stunk from the dip of Skoal under his bottom lip. Always spitting into a beer bottle, half-full of brown spittle. *We'll have a good ole time whenever you're ready.*

Alice's stomach lurched, and she heaved but brought up nothing because her stomach didn't have anything left to give. Her face went red-hot and her pores opened, coating her face with a thin layer of sweat that reeked of tequila.

The room around her dimmed twice. Once from the sun tucking behind some approaching storm clouds, the other from slipping dangerously close to losing consciousness.

She pressed her eyes closed and dug gnawed-down fingernails into her palms hard enough to leave tiny crescent moons, and waited for her head to clear. It took a minute. Maybe two. When she opened her eyes again, she glanced around at the crappy, thin walls and flimsy door and the curtainless windows. Then she noticed the duffel bag stuffed in the corner of the bedroom next to Terry's side of the bed.

Terry's side of the bed. That seemed a stupid thing to think. Like they were a couple or something.

She kept staring at the Army surplus–style duffel bag. Olive green; a black serial number inked into the fabric. She glanced back over at Terry, whose head was tilted to the left and seemed to be gazing at the duffel bag as if he were keeping an eye on his property. It must have been the last thing he looked at right before his heart stopped beating.

Alice stared back at the duffel bag, zipped up tight. She wiped the sweat from her upper lip, scooted closer to the bag, suddenly very curious about its contents.

Need to call the cops.

But Alice didn't particularly want to call the cops just yet. That was something she didn't really feel like dealing with right now. There'd be questions. There'd be some digging into her past, a hornet's nest she didn't feel like kicking. Not now. Not ever, if possible.

She kept staring at the duffel bag—mesmerized like it was a piece of artwork. Something about a zipped-up Army surplus duffel bag begged to be opened. She would have to call the cops. Alice knew that. What choice did she have?

Maybe one peek into the bag. Terry, being dead and all, wouldn't give a damn. Alice rubbed at her face. She needed a few minutes to clear her head, drink some orange juice or whatever Terry kept in the refrigerator, and try and get her story pieced together.

And, *oh yeah*, to also look inside the duffel bag. That was going to happen. Like a free shot of whiskey sitting in front of an alcoholic, begging to be tossed back. It wasn't a question of *if*, merely *when*.

Alice tucked loose hair behind her ears, pulled the bag onto her lap, and eased the zipper open. No big surprise. No socks or blankets, no boots, no survival supplies. Nothing like that. Instead, it contained baggies full of coke. A lot of them. Alice was no expert in weight or the street value of cocaine, but she'd been around the stuff enough to know that there was probably ten, maybe twenty thousand dollars' worth of blow inside the duffel bag.

But that wasn't all.

Alice dug deeper and found a few bottles of pills. Amphetamines, Quaaludes, Vicodin. And one bottle of Rohypnol.

"God damn."

Alice didn't particularly enjoy partaking in pills—vodka, whiskey, or tequila suited her just fine—but she knew enough about them. Rohypnol. Roofies. Terry must have laced her drinks last night.

Alice glanced back over at Terry, her fear transforming into a wave of dull rage and disgust with herself for letting this happen. The thought of the scumbag being inside her made Alice feel like puking again, but her stomach was all tapped out.

White powder still clung onto his nostril hairs. Served the cokehead right. He got what he deserved. She noticed the cut on Terry's upper lip, swollen up and eggplant purple. He also had a nasty bruise under his left eye—a mark about the size of a set of knuckles. Despite her belly full of tequila and roofies, she must have fought him. Got in a few good shots before . . . *if* anything happened. Maybe the asshole OD'd before he had the chance to do anything to her.

Alice kept digging through the duffel bag and her fingers grazed against something else at the bottom. Another bag—a kid's brown lunch bag—jammed down under everything else. She pulled out the paper sack, about the size of a small shoebox. Taped up real nice and neat.

Alice ripped open the bag like a child tearing into a present on Christmas morning and stared at its contents. She licked at lips that went dry in a moment's time, and her heart almost felt as if it stopped beating altogether. Alice didn't budge for twenty seconds, and it was then that she noticed how deathly quiet the trailer seemed.

It was only when something hard whacked against the metal side of the trailer that Alice finally flinched. Another *thud*, then again, followed by the sound of juvenile laughter.

As Alice peered through the window, she clutched the paper bag tight between trembling hands and watched the pack of bullies sling snowballs at the dead man's trailer. The metallic reverberation went straight through her. She wanted it to stop. *Needed* it to stop. She hated that particular kind of sound—it triggered the awful memories of discovering Jason—but the kids were too caught up in their sadistic glory and had no intentions of stopping anytime soon. So, the sound continued, on and on, with no letup in sight.

Thud, thud, thud.

CHAPTER FIVE

NINETY-ONE THOUSAND DOLLARS.

Stacks of bundled twenty-dollar bills were spread across the kitchen table amidst a collection of beer bottles, a plate of cigarette butts, and empty cans of Skoal. As Alice fingered the crumpled brown paper bag, the amount of money kept repeating in her head. The number was truly staggering. More money than she had ever seen before, and would likely ever see again.

Alice stared at all that cash and sipped at a glass of Mountain Dew spiked with vodka. Terry didn't have orange juice after all, but plenty of vodka. Alice was currently on her second glass. The first had steadied her nerves and stopped her hands from trembling. The second cleared up her head a little and made her feel emboldened, and that was when she decided to count the money in spite of the fact that there was a dead man in the back of the trailer.

Ninety-one thousand dollars could sure get her out of her dead-end existence. Could get her back on her feet. A clean start somewhere. Anywhere. A new beginning. No more desperation jobs pouring cocktails for drunk assholes.

When Alice had searched the trailer earlier, she'd found her purse and jacket discarded next to the sofa, along with her boots that Terry must have been kind enough to remove. Now, along with the cash, Alice's purse sat on the kitchen table as well. Terry—true gentleman that he was—must have been *kind enough* to bring it from the bar. Not counting the change, there was exactly forty-three dollars in her purse. She knew. She counted it after tallying the ninety-one thousand dollars. Didn't take as long to add up the money in her wallet, though. Other than the clothes she owned—and those were nothing to write home about—Alice had no car, no credit cards, no checkbook, not even a driver's license. At the age of twenty-one, she was worth all of forty-three dollars and couldn't even legally drive a car.

Forty-three bucks barely covered two nights at the crap motel she'd been staying at for the last few months. The Comfort Manor—minus any degree of comfort and about as far from a manor as a cardboard box—did the majority of their business on a by-the-hour basis, but Alice had made arrangements with the front desk guy. Ernie What's-His-Name. She gave Ernie What's-His-Name twenty bucks cash every day and let him drink for free at the Frisky Pony a few days a week in exchange for the discounted room rate, no questions asked.

The Comfort Manor's walls were paper thin, giving Alice an unwanted front-row seat to the obligatory moans of prostitutes banging their johns in the rooms on either side of her. The roaches were the size of rats in the summer, and rats the size of cats in the winter. The only redeemable thing about the place was that everybody left her alone. No one bothered her or stayed around long enough to get to know her. No nosey neighbors. No one ever asked what her name was—no one except for Ernie What's-His-Name. The dude acted like a freaky little perv, but he seemed harmless enough. He would usually sip on a few Seven and Sevens on the same barstool, stare at the parade of tits up on the stage, too meek and afraid to speak to a soul, then go back home to wherever he laid his greasy head.

Alice wished she could remember more about the previous night. Beyond what Terry may have done to her—that didn't really matter right now. What she really wanted to recall was if anyone knew that Terry took her home. That was the ninety-one-thousand-dollar question: Could she be connected to Terry Otis?

The only reason she bothered to count the money and tried connecting the dots about what transpired last night was because she happened to be putting some pretty serious thought into taking the money and leaving Harrisburg behind her.

And why not? Terry OD'd. She didn't do anything to him. He snorted his way to an early grave. She just happened to be in the wrong place at the wrong time.

Or the right place at the right time.

It's drug money. Someone will come looking for it.

Alice drank some more of her Mountain Dew and vodka. A pretty good buzz started to kick in, right on the heels of the buzz she had woken up with.

She got drunk at the Frisky Pony. Terry was there. They left together. Tia and Naomi must have seen them leave. Unless Alice and Terry were the last ones at the club. But even if that were the case, the last time that Terry would have been seen alive was with Alice. Two dots. Connected.

Alice sucked down the rest of her cocktail and poured another.

The sensible way to play this thing was to call the cops. Tell them what she knew, stick to the facts and hope that they wouldn't try and blame her for Terry's death. Just tell them the truth. She got drunk, the sick bastard slipped her some roofies, and when she woke up, Terry was dead. That was it. The whole truth and nothing but the truth.

She topped the Mountain Dew with a little more vodka. Looked over at the front door. She could just walk. Leave the money behind and forget it ever happened.

The dots are connected.

For whatever trouble she would face for being involved with Terry, the shit would hit the fan ten times harder if she walked away from this mess and they eventually caught up with her. She was with Terry when he OD'd. The guy was in possession of rock cocaine and almost one hundred thousand dollars. Yeah, the police would want to talk to her, ask her some questions. Probably try and blame her somehow for what happened.

Alice sipped on her cocktail. Sipped it until the glass ran empty. She mixed another, even stronger than the first three. She kept drinking, thinking about using the victim card, playing out the conversation with the cops, but instead of feeling better about how this thing would shake out, she felt like she was slipping deeper down the rabbit hole.

*   *   *

Alice heard the crunch of tires pulling over the gravel driveway outside. Kind of a nice-sounding noise, like the slow drizzle of rain or popcorn popping from a few rooms away. She had collapsed on the couch and let her eyes fall closed a little while ago. Seemed like just a few minutes, but it could have been longer. Hard to tell, being as drunk as she was. She slammed another drink after she placed the call—or maybe it was two. She didn't give the dispatcher her name, or the fact that she possessed a duffel bag containing a boatload of drugs and cash. That would come later. Her voice had slurred a little. She even practiced what she would say beforehand, but she still slurred and hated the sound of her drunkenness. She informed the 911 dispatcher that she discovered a man's body in the trailer. Those were the only details she offered. Then she gave the dispatcher the address she found on an envelope from the kitchen counter—a bill from *Hustler* magazine. After she gave the dispatcher the home address, she hung up the phone, then left the receiver off the hook.

Alice ran out of Mountain Dew, so she drank vodka and water, heavy on the vodka. All the cocktails filled a recently emptied stomach, bringing forth a pretty intense buzz. She knew better. She found herself in a situation that wasn't exactly a normal everyday predicament, but she decided to tie one on before the cops showed up. It seemed like a good idea at the time. And if not a good one, one that she elected to do anyway.

Two car doors slammed shut and Alice's eyes snapped open.

Okay. Here we go.

She glanced over at the kitchen table. The pile of cash was gone. *Poof.* The nice neat stacks no longer there. Alice's first thought was that Terry must have taken it back. That he wasn't dead. That she was drunk and mistook the asshole for dead. He woke up and took his money back.

Alice stood up quickly. Too quickly. Drunker than she thought. She swayed on her feet for a moment before flopping back down on the sofa. She wasn't in any kind of condition to talk to the cops. She'd be lucky to string together a few coherent sentences.

Then the thud of a fist on the front door nearly made her head pound harder.

She tried again. Stood up and braced her hand on the wall for support. Put one foot in front of the other and managed to avoid tumbling over the coffee table. She stumbled back down the hallway and stuck her head into the bedroom. Terry was still in bed. Still dead. The duffel bag sat in the corner of the room where she found it in the first place.

Right. She put it back there.

The fist pounded on the front door again. Harder this time. The cops were impatient. She guessed that when they receive an anonymous call about a dead man in a trailer, they might want to get some pretty fast answers.

Alice staggered back into the kitchen, noticed the nearly empty bottle of vodka sitting on the kitchen table. She grabbed the bottle and tossed it under the sink.

The fist thudded again.

"All right. Jesus. Coming," she slurred and it sounded like, *Ahh it. Jeseth. Cummin.*

The panel window on the front door stood frosted white, so all she could make out were two large silhouettes. She glanced around the room again, tried to clear her head. No use. Screw it. She swung the door open to let the cops inside and get it over with.

Two men stood on the front porch. But they weren't cops. Far from it. They were both large, well-fed men. Both carried unkind faces; cold eyes that offered no mercy. The smaller of the two—his birth name was Clark, but people, including his parents, called him Pig—was a beat-up looking thirty, and wore an old-school track and field sweat suit, pumpkin-orange that matched his pumpkin-orange sneakers. His hair was parted down the middle, feathered carefully, and styled with hairspray. His left eyelid hung half-closed over a mud-brown eye.

The other man appeared much older and looked like he could be Pig's uncle—in fact, everyone referred to him as *Uncle Henry*. He had a buzz cut, accentuating the folds of neck fat that squeezed out from the buttoned-up collared shirt that he wore under a camouflage hunting jacket. His jowls were flushed red, more from poor circulation than the bitter cold outside.

"And just who the fuck might you be?" Pig asked. His droopy eye stared past Alice and into the trailer.

"Alice," she responded like it should mean something.

Both men slipped their hands into their jackets at the same time to conspicuous bulges.

"Okay, Alice. Where the fuck is Terry at?" Pig asked, eyes still searching the trailer behind her.

"Terry?" Alice repeated, tongue thick in her mouth.

"Yeah. The fucking guy that fucking lives here."

Alice tried to close the door a little before Uncle Henry's size-thirteen brown boot shot forward and propped it open.

"Uh-uh," Uncle Henry grunted.

"I'm gonna ask you one more time, Alice. Where the fuck is Terry?"

Alice noticed that Pig kept licking his lips like they were smeared with chocolate. "I don't know. He went out."

"Went out?" Pig jabbed his thumb over his shoulder toward the black Chevy truck in the driveway. "For a little nature walk, or did he forget his fucking truck?"

Alice tried again to nudge the door closed, but Uncle Henry's boot wasn't going anywhere. "He didn't really say."

"He didn't really say." Pig sighed and glanced over at Uncle Henry for a second, then glared back at Alice. "You Terry's fucking girl-friend or something?"

Maybe it was due to being drunk or maybe it was the fact that she woke up next to a dead man, but whatever the reason, Alice finally snapped. "Why don't you kiss my ass?"

Uncle Henry chuckled at Alice's quip, almost making him look harmless. Almost. Pig, on the other hand, didn't even crack a smile.

"Well, Alice, this ain't no social call. We got some things to dis-cuss with Terry, so either tell us where the fuck he's at, or take a step back and shut the fuck up."

Uncle Henry chuckled again and started to unzip his camouflage jacket.

Alice didn't budge. Just held her ground. "No."

"No to what?" Pig asked.

"No to both, asshole."

Uncle Henry stopped chuckling, and when his mouth drew straight, Alice felt her first twinge of fear.

"You got a mouth on you, Alice. Quite a mouth. You better be pretty fucking good in the sack to have to put up with that kind of shit. Christ. Have it your way." Pig's arm shot forward, and he slapped the palm of his hand over Alice's face and shoved her back with enough force to knock her flat on her ass.

Alice grunted and bit her tongue hard enough to draw blood.

Both men stepped inside the trailer, closed and locked the door behind them. Once inside, they withdrew pistols from inside their jackets. They were big, almost comically big, but Alice wasn't laughing. This was real.

Pig kept his good eye peeled on the hallway toward the back of the trailer. "Don't be a dumb bitch, Alice. Stay on the floor."

Alice couldn't pry her eyes off their pistols and decided to take Pig's advice to stay on the floor and keep her mouth shut. She didn't feel so drunk anymore. Adrenaline had seen to that.

Pig nodded to his partner—the two men communicating non-verbally—and Uncle Henry squatted down next to Alice with a grunt, knees popping from the effort of lowering his considerable mass. He pressed cold steel into Alice's ear and shook his head at her. "You're in the wrong place this morning, sweetheart," he whispered.

"Look. I'm—"

"Hush now, sweetheart. You've said enough. We'll take it from here."

Pig took a careful step toward the hallway, his pumpkin-orange sneakers sliding across the carpeted floor quite nimbly for a man so large. He pressed up against the television and stereo console, gun clutched in his hand. "Up and at 'em, Terry. Nothing funny. We got your smart-ass bitch with us. Come on out." Pig spoke clearly and calmly and waited for a response, but got none. He waited for another few seconds, listening for signs of movement from the back.

"Come on now, Terry. Stop with the bullshit. You knew we'd be swinging by to pay you a visit. Story didn't add up. We checked in with some people. We know what happened."

Still nothing. No sign of Terry. Pig sighed, kept the pistol in one hand, and shook a cigarette from its pack and clenched the smoke between his teeth. He lit up, sucked deep. "All right. Fuck it. I'm coming back, Terry. This ain't the way this was supposed to go. The boss-man ain't too happy. You know that." He winked over at Uncle Henry and grinned—Pig was enjoying this. "Uncle Henry will kill the bitch. You know that, too."

Alice peered up at Uncle Henry, and he stared right back, his expression dull and unreadable. As he pressed the pistol barrel tighter against her ear, one thought raced through her mind: *Where in the hell are the cops?*

With his cigarette tucked into the corner of his lips, Pig made his way down the hallway, the trailer's floorboards squeaking and groaning under his every step. He disappeared into the back bedroom and the trailer turned quiet except for Uncle Henry's labored breathing. Alice could feel the man's hot breath on her neck. Could smell the cigarettes and coffee and butterscotch candy.

Uncle Henry kept the pistol shoved to the side of Alice's head, his blue-gray eyes directed toward the hallway. His body tense. Rigid and waiting.

After a minute, Pig reemerged from the bedroom and lumbered down the hallway clutching Terry's duffel bag in one hand, his pistol in the other. He tossed the duffel bag onto the couch, then dropped down on the cushions beside it. He lit another cigarette and stared at Alice the entire time.

"Well, shit, Alice. Holy fucking shit. You gonna fill me in or what? Seems like we got a situation back there in the bedroom. You and Terry must have had some kind of night. Some kind of night."

Alice opened her mouth to say something, but the words weren't there yet. It was all a bit much—Terry dead; the fat men with guns; being too damn drunk when it was barely twelve noon.

Pig blew out a cloud of gray smoke and shook his head at Uncle Henry. "Fucker's dead."

Alice felt the pressure from the pistol ease off her ear, and Uncle Henry stood back up with a grunt, knees popping like fireworks. "Dead? Whattaya mean?"

"I mean he's stiff as a fucking board. Been dead for a few hours." Pig turned his attention back on Alice. "Okay, Alice. Why don't you start with who the fuck you are and what happened to dipshit back there? And if you start up with the games again, or the smart mouth, I swear to fucking God, I will fuck your shit up."

Uncle Henry found one of the kitchen chairs and plopped down. He placed his gun on the kitchen table, took a well-used handker-chief from his pocket, and cleared out his nose. "Sweetheart, you should give Pig here some good honest answers. You really should. Or he'll do as he says. I can vouch for that."

Alice scooted back against the wall and rubbed at her ear. She could feel an indentation on her skin. "I work at Terry's club."

Pig nodded like it was no big surprise. "No shit? Thought you looked like a pole dancer."

Alice shook her head. "I bartend. I'm not a stripper."

"Well, *oo-la-la*. Excuse the fuck out of me."

"I . . . I don't remember everything. Was drinking last night. At the club after it closed. Don't remember coming home with Terry. Don't remember anything. He slipped some roofies in my drink."

Pig worked on his cigarette and processed the information. "Roofies, huh? Sounds about like Terry's style. So how exactly did numb-nuts end up dead?"

"What do you think? The guy was a coke-head."

Pig nodded. "Got that much right. You fuck up his face?"

"I'm guessing, yeah. That's what happens when you try something with me that I don't want," Alice said.

Uncle Henry chuckled.

"What? You a muff-diver?" Pig asked.

"You're an asshole."

Again, with Uncle Henry's chuckling.

"All right, Alice. Jesus. Keep your panties on. We got what we came for and you saved us the trouble of what to do with Terry," Pig said.

Alice watched as Uncle Henry picked up the pistol and slipped his finger behind the trigger.

"But what to do with you? That's the million-dollar question we've got now."

"You got your money. Your drugs. I'm not involved with any of this stuff," Alice blurted. She didn't mean to, but her voice went up a few octaves, making her sound desperate and pathetic.

Pig dropped his cigarette in a half-empty bottle of warm beer where it fizzled and black smoke wisped from the glass neck like a summoned genie. "Well, you're wrong about that. You *are* involved whether you like it or not. How'd you know about the money anyways? You planning to skip town with Terry before he OD'd?"

"No. I worked for the guy. Poured drinks. That's all. He drugged me. Brought me back here. When I woke up, he was dead. That's it. That's all I know."

"But the money, Alice. How'd you *know* about that? Been snooping this morning?" Pig played with his pistol. Tossed it from hand to hand.

"Look. I don't care about the money. Terry got what was coming to him, if you ask me. I don't know you guys. I don't know anything. I just want to walk out that door and forget about all this."

As Pig shoved himself off the couch and towered over her, Uncle Henry followed suit at the same time, like it was a synchronized routine. They both stared down at her with their pistols dangling at their sides.

"Problem is you *do* know us. You know what we look like. That's the problem. You stink of booze, but I'm betting you're sober enough to ID us." He gazed over at Uncle Henry and the big man nodded in agreement. "Damn shame, Alice. I'm sorry about Terry slipping you some drugs and trying to fuck you and everything, but that's all done. Probably serves you right working at that kind of place anyways. We're all guilty by who we choose to associate with. *That's* the problem."

"Please. Just let me go." Alice hated the sound of her voice, the desperation, the pleading.

"And then what? It seems to me that you got a big fucking mouth. You really think that we can trust you keeping it shut? Sorry, Alice. No can do."

Pig's droopy eye went to Terry's stereo console that housed two massive speakers. "Looks like a new purchase. Fucker's been spending our money. Christ." He powered up the stereo and took a moment to peruse Terry's collection of CDs. His fingers drifted along the rows of CDs until stopping on one in particular that caught his eye.

He slipped the disc into the player and AC/DC's "Hells Bells" started to thump throughout the trailer. He cranked the volume loud enough that he had to shout to be heard. "Okay, Alice, let's do this shit."

Uncle Henry was on her before she had a chance to move—the obese man moved quickly despite his massive girth. He flipped her over, pressed his knee into her lower back, and shoved her head to the floor.

Alice could only groan as the wind squeezed out of her lungs. She fought him—kicked her legs, tried to push herself up—but he outweighed her by a good one hundred pounds. He was not only big, but strong as a damn ox.

"Hush now, sweetheart. This will be quick," Uncle Henry whispered into her ear, forcing his knee down even harder.

Brian Johnson shrieked the gravelly chorus to "Hells Bells," barely eclipsing the steady pulse of a bass guitar and rapid beat of the drums. Pig mouthed the words, well familiar with the song, picked up a dingy throw pillow from the couch, and shoved it over the crown of Alice's head.

Alice kicked and flailed some more, but it didn't matter. She grew still and thought about Jason and about her parents that she hadn't seen or talked to in over six years. Her mind raced with all the heartache and pain and loneliness she had endured for so long. Maybe it was better this way. To put an end to her pointless life.

As Pig pressed the barrel of his pistol into the pillow, another low-thudding sound joined AC/DC's explosive canon-fire chorus.

Alice's face smashed into the carpet that stank of dirty feet. She had a sideways, distorted view of the front door between Pig's sneakers. From under the door, she saw something move out on the porch. Somebody outside. She watched as the front door burst open, spilling a bright blast of sunlight into the kitchen. Two sets of feet wearing shiny, black boots with thick heels stepped inside the trailer.

Pop. Pop.

Pig slammed against the wall, one bullet obliterating his spine, the other entering through the base of his neck and exiting right below his Adam's apple. A spray of crimson showered down on Alice like liquid confetti, and she watched the man fold, dead before he hit the floor.

Uncle Henry pivoted, stared down the barrels of service revolvers held by two Harrisburg police officers. They shouted over the music, but Uncle Henry couldn't make out what they were saying. Not that it really mattered—their message was clear. *Put the gun down on the ground. Put it down now.*

Uncle Henry did just the opposite. He didn't appear alarmed or scared or caught off guard. In fact, he appeared remarkably calm. He squeezed off a round, catching the cop closest to him in the thigh, and ripping through the femoral artery. The man toppled backward, driving him and his partner back out the front door. Blood sprouted from the cop's leg like a broken sprinkler head.

Uncle Henry staggered to his feet and squeezed the trigger twice more. The injured cop's face morphed into a mass of flying flesh and bone.

Alice pulled into the fetal position, her screams barely audible over the next AC/DC track, "Shoot to Thrill." She covered her head, and couldn't look up—wouldn't look up.

Uncle Henry went after the second cop. He grabbed the man by his black boot and yanked him back inside the trailer, moving the two-hundred-pound police officer as easily as if he were dragging a bag of dirty laundry. The cop slid across the blood-smeared linoleum floor and smacked into the corner of the refrigerator. His head snapped back, scarlet leaking from an ugly gash above his nose.

Uncle Henry slammed the front door closed, his labored breathing growling from deep inside his throat. His lips pulled back over his teeth as he brought his pistol up. Aimed it directly at the cop's head.

Alice finally looked up. Saw what was about to happen. She took a breath and kicked out with both feet, catching the fat man in the shin. It was enough force to knock him backward, right into a growing puddle of blood. Uncle Henry slipped and came down hard on his wide backside as he squeezed the trigger. The shot went low and wide, missing the cop's head by a few inches, but instead, shredding his shoulder.

Uncle Henry struggled on the floor like a mammoth overturned sea turtle, growling and swearing. He still gripped the pistol in his beefy hand. A part of him. Not going anywhere. A few feet from his flailing arms and legs, the cop managed to get to the sitting position and switched his gun to his other hand—the one with the shoulder blade still intact.

Uncle Henry flipped over onto his belly, aimed and squeezed. *Pop.* The bullet ripped into the cop's stomach, leaving a ragged two-inch hole behind it.

Somehow, the cop still held his pistol and tried to aim it in the direction of the big man.

Uncle Henry leapt forward and dropped onto the man's chest— the cop's howls choked short as Henry wrapped his hands around the man's throat and squeezed.

Alice crawled away from the two men entangled in a death embrace. She saw the cop's eyes bulge, his face growing purple. The cop fought for his life but was quickly losing the battle. Too much pain. Too much blood loss. Alice screamed for it all to end, but Uncle Henry's primitive growls and the blaring music muffled her high-pitched pleas.

Another *Pop.* And a hole blew through Uncle Henry's back, lifting his camouflage jacket with a puff, and blossoming gouts of red dotted the trailer's ceiling. The big man went limp and slumped forward onto the police officer.

The cop sucked in air, and when he expelled ragged breath, red, speckled foam bubbled from the corners of his mouth. His breath quickened, his chest struggling to lift Uncle Henry's dead weight that pressed down on top of him.

Alice continued to push away from both men, crawling across the floor until she pressed up against the thudding stereo speakers. AC/DC kept singing as the pungent odor of gun smoke drifted into the air, plumes of black hugging the ceiling.

She felt wetness roll down her face. She wiped at it, thinking it was a mixture of all their blood, but when she stared at her palms, the liquid was clear. Across the room, the cop took a final few gasps, shuddered to a stop. The music faded to quiet and then the third track began to thump from the speakers. "What Do You Do for Money, Honey?"

CHAPTER SIX

Snow fell steadily. Thick white flakes tumbled down from a gray sky, making visibility limited. Alice had the truck's windshield wipers snapping at full speed, but it didn't help much. She could barely see ten feet in front of her as the tires chewed a path through the slush on the street.

Alice couldn't drive a stick transmission worth a damn. She eased her foot onto the clutch and ground the gear stick accidentally into fourth—missing third entirely—and the engine revved low, causing Terry's truck to lurch and shudder, knocking her forward and almost off the cold vinyl seats. She neglected to put on her seat belt. Wasn't exactly thinking straight.

"Christ, Alice. Keep it together."

The truck's momentum finally caught up with fourth gear. She slammed on the gas pedal and sped through a yellow light. She spotted the glow of the neon sign for the Comfort Manor up ahead on the right side of the street. Almost there. Once she got back to her room, she could think this thing through a little bit better. Think at all, for that matter. The vodka clung to her brain like a pile of wet rags and her ears still buzzed from all the gunshots.

The truck reeked of Terry's cheap aftershave and cans of Skoal that littered the floor, and Alice cranked down the window for some fresh air. The truck started to drift on a patch of ice, and Alice clutched the steering wheel with sweaty palms and finally managed to gain traction. She glanced down at her vise-like hands, dotted with spots of dried blood. Whose blood exactly, she had no idea.

When she peered back out the windshield, red taillights blinked back at her through a wall of white. She slammed down hard, locking the brakes and skidding on a section of black ice before stopping a few inches from the bumper of a blue Cadillac waiting to turn into a 7-Eleven. Her heart thudded even harder, the pounding ringing in her ears, reminding her that she had two hangovers sitting on top of one another.

When she'd made her hasty exit out of Terry's trailer, nobody had been staring out their windows at her, curious about all the commotion—the music, the gunfire, the cop car. Maybe everybody was at work, or maybe nobody really cared. Maybe the neighbors were used to loud disturbances and the police paying visits to Terry's. The important thing was that no one saw her spin out of Terry's small lot, kicking gravel against the trailer and barreling out of the trailer park like a house on fire.

At least she didn't think so.

The blue Cadillac in front of her appeared to be making a career out of their turn into the 7-Eleven parking lot, slowing down to an almost complete stop.

Alice pounded on the horn three or four times, then shook the steering wheel. "God damn it. Move already."

A hand extended out the Caddy's window and promptly flipped her the bird.

Alice wanted to slam on the gas and smash into the back of the Caddy. She wanted to plow through anything and anybody that stood in her way, but instead, she bit her lip, took a deep breath, and waited. Three or four seconds felt like an eternity.

Then, finally, mercifully, the Cadillac pulled into the parking lot, and the driver flipped her one more bird for the road. Alice jammed the truck back into first gear and lurched forward once again. She released the clutch too soon, and the truck rattled and almost stalled, then she gave it more gas and the engine leveled off. She had never wanted to get back to her motel room this badly before. She wanted to be in her room—water-stained walls, mildewy carpets and all—grab everything she owned, and go.

This is a bad idea.

Maybe it wasn't too late to turn back, call the cops—*again*—and let this thing play out the sensible way, the right way, but since when did she do things the right way?

She rode second gear into the Comfort Manor's parking lot, sparks flying from taking a speed bump too fast, and squealed to an abrupt stop in front of her unit. Lucky number seven. She grabbed Terry's duffel bag, dug her room key from her purse, and jumped out of the truck.

* * *

The room stood in complete disarray—just the way she had left it. Smelled of booze and cigarette smoke. Clothes everywhere, bed unmade. She didn't get housekeeping in her room—not for the rate she was paying, and that was just fine with her. She didn't want a bunch of maids snooping through her stuff. Alice wasn't being judgmental. She had done the maid thing. Vacuumed, mopped, scrubbed, and picked up after slobs for three months at a Motel 6 in Bethlehem. Or maybe it was in Lancaster. Either way, she did her share of rummaging through suitcases, toiletry bags, and dresser drawers, looking for cash or jewelry, stealing anything she could sell to buy food and booze.

Alice closed the door and leaned back against the flimsy piece of prefab wood. She took a few deep breaths and tried to steady her thundering heartbeat. Everything seemed to be spinning. The room turned and jerked in front of her, like she got hit on the back of the head with a brick.

Five men were dead. Two of them cops. The entire trailer splattered with blood. And what did she do? She walked away from all of it and stole ninety-one thousand dollars.

As for the drugs, she left those behind in Terry's trailer. An impulsive decision really. Besides, she had no use for them—she might be a drunk, but a drug addict she was not. She scattered the bags of cocaine and bottles of pills around the bodies of Pig and Uncle Henry. Maybe it would throw off the cops when they discovered the scene. Maybe the cash wouldn't be missed. Maybe the entire situation would go down as a drug transaction gone wrong.

Or maybe everything would get traced back to Alice. Trouble always seemed to follow her around. Like a puppy trailing after its mama. Never straying far. Always right at her heels. Nipping and nipping. And even if trouble didn't find her, Alice managed to find *it* instead. Didn't seem to matter where she was. The city or town never mattered. She always managed to be at the wrong job, associated with the wrong people, doing stuff that was stupid and dangerous and messed up. Being around people that never failed to make bad decisions and kept digging themselves deeper and deeper in a hole. She made all the choices. Hers and hers alone. Couldn't blame anyone else. She thought that once she got off the streets, life would get better, but she had been wrong—dead wrong.

Someone moaned in the next room over. The box spring squeaking like a cage full of rats. Kind of early in the day for that kind of business, but Alice figured that there were worse things to be doing in the middle of the day. Like watching a bunch of people kill each other.

She peered around the room for a moment. The motel room had been what she called home for the last few months. Pathetic. Depressing. Disgusting.

Another moan from the next room. Louder. More urgent. Then the box spring settled down and someone started to cough.

She cleared out the dresser drawers of all her clothing—not that she had much of a wardrobe. She owned two pairs of blue jeans. No skirts or dresses. She hadn't worn a skirt or nice dress since she ran away from home six years ago. A handful of shirts—one of them was Elton's T-shirt that he gave her all those years ago that she could never part with. She stared at the blue shirt, thinking about sweet Elton and his little house. It was the last time she felt safe and protected and appreciated.

Alice stuffed the T-shirt and everything else she owned in a red suitcase that had seen better days, then went about cleaning out the bathroom. No makeup to speak of. Not really her style. Some shampoo and tampons, a toothbrush and toothpaste, a hairbrush. It had always been this way. Packing light, keeping only what she really needed to get by.

There was a half a pack of cigarettes on the back of the toilet. She grabbed those, too, and wished she had something to drink. Her buzz had lost its footing, and she could really use one right about now. Her eyes fell on a can of beer at the edge of the sink. It felt about half-full. Then she noticed some cigarette ashes around the lip. Desperate, but not that desperate.

It seemed like she had always been in some kind of trouble and on the run, but not like this—not with a bunch of dead people behind her. She'd been caught shoplifting twice before. The first time for stealing an egg salad sandwich at an A&P grocery store in downtown Baltimore. She had been living on the streets for about six months; she was hungry, desperate, and didn't know what else to do. She didn't have any money and couldn't bring herself to beg—that seemed even worse for some reason.

Before running away from home, Alice had never stolen anything. Shoplifting seemed like a federal offense back then. But hunger trumped everything else. She stuffed the sandwich into her pocket and got as far as the parking lot before a security guard caught up with her. Just an egg salad sandwich, but the store manager insisted on calling the cops and pressing charges. And she didn't even get a bite of the damn sandwich.

The second-time shoplifting turned out to be a little less innocent. She shoved a watch in her pocket at a Kmart. She had intended on selling the watch on the street or at a pawnshop. She needed the cash, but it wasn't for food. By that time, she had developed quite a taste for alcohol and she was jonesing for a drink.

Both times she got arrested, Alice didn't have an ID of any kind. No driver's license. No library card. Nothing. And the cops don't like that at all. The first time she got caught, Alice was stupid and gave them her real name. She was barely sixteen and didn't know any better. But for some reason—maybe the supervising detective didn't feel like doing the paperwork or he didn't like dealing with runaways—the police didn't call her parents. Alice walked out of the police station, free and clear, but she officially had a record for stealing an egg salad sandwich. Alice O'Farrell was alive on paper.

Alice stepped out of the bathroom and fought the overwhelming urge to jump in the bed, close her eyes, and drift away. Maybe if she fell asleep, she'd wake up and none of this mess would have happened. Maybe she would just wake up with a lousy hangover, and as she always did in the morning, she would rate the degree of her condition from one to five. That would be nice. Nothing on her mind except for a hangover. Funny how sometimes in life you can suddenly look forward to one of the things you thought you hated the most.

Alice yanked all the sheets off the mattress and stuffed everything inside one of the pillowcases. She didn't want a single trace of herself left behind. She'd dump the crappy sheets somewhere and be doing the motel management a favor at the same time.

Alice checked her watch. Twenty minutes, she guessed. Twenty minutes since she bolted out of Terry's. How many of those minutes had been occupied by the discovery of all the bodies? Five? Fifteen? Didn't matter. Nothing she could do about it now.

She hauled the pillowcase out to Terry's truck and tossed it into the back. Just getting this stuff out of her room and into the truck made Alice feel a little better. It was progress.

"You ain't stealing our sheets are you, Alice?"

Alice looked over at Ernie What's-His-Name, who stood out in the snow, clumps of white sticking to his greasy head. He worked on a banana that was more brown than yellow, and a piece of half-chewed gunk stuck to the corner of his mouth. He grinned at her and it made him look stupid. He wore the same bright red, button-down sweater he always wore. The sweater had to be a Goodwill special, and judging by its stretched-out cuffs and floppy waistband, he'd been wearing it since high school. The kind of sweater that Mister Rogers wore with pride as the kindhearted and soft-spoken host on television. But those sweaters had looked good on Mister Rogers. Not so much on Ernie. Ernie was all of one hundred and twenty pounds soaking wet, his tiny frame swimming in the crappy sweater and a pair of cinched-up pleated khakis peppered with old coffee stains.

Alice forced a smile and jammed her unwashed, blood-splattered hands into her jean pockets. "Hey, Ernie. No. Not stealing the sheets. Thought they were overdue for a washing."

Ernie gnawed on his banana, mouth smacking open and closed. "Could let you have the maids wash them for a few bucks if you want."

Alice glanced over to her room. Door wide open, Terry's duffel bag sitting on the floor for the world to see. "That's okay. Probably should wash them myself. My time of the month kinda caught me by surprise this morning."

Too much information for Ernie. His eyes darted away from Alice and stared up at the falling snow. "Really coming down."

"Yeah."

"Supposed to get around eight inches."

"Is that right?"

"I like snow." He glanced toward her room and gestured at the duffel bag and red suitcase. "You leaving us?"

Alice chewed on the inside of her cheek, ready to crawl right out of her own skin. "No. I mean, just for a day or two. Going to see a friend."

"Oh. Okay." He kept staring toward her room. "Can I still come to the club tonight? You know. If you're not there."

Fuck, Ernie. Fuck.

"Why don't you wait until I get back? I'd like to be able to take care of you myself. Terry doesn't exactly know about our arrangement."

Ernie nodded, unable to conceal his disappointment. "Oh. Okay. When you coming back?"

"Saturday," Alice lied.

"Oh. I thought you were just going for a day or two."

Alice restrained herself from the urge to scream at Ernie. To shake him by the shoulders and tell him to leave her the hell alone. "Well, I got a friend over in Allentown that's in some trouble. Might take a few days to sort through it."

"Oh," Ernie said. "That's too bad. What kind of trouble?"

"It's nothing. Just a little trouble."

"Like with the law or something?"

"No. Nothing like that. Marriage problems," Alice said.

"Oh. That's a shame. She leaving her husband? Something like that?"

Alice heard a phone ringing in the motel office. An old-fashioned ringer. Loud and obnoxious. If Ernie heard it, he chose to ignore it.

"Your phone's ringing."

Ernie glanced toward the office and shrugged. "Yeah." He pointed what remained of the banana toward Alice's truck. "That new?"

The phone kept ringing, and over that came the sounds of sirens. Police sirens.

"It's a friend's," Alice said.

"It's nice. I'd like to get a truck. I'm tired of taking the bus."

Alice tried to inch her way toward her room.

"Whose truck did you say it was?"

"Just a friend's."

"Geez, Alice, I didn't know you had so many friends."

"I don't. Just. I don't."

The sirens got louder. Alice looked out toward the street and watched a police car whiz past. That was followed by an ambulance, then another two cop cars.

Ernie didn't seem to take notice. He stuffed the banana peel in his back pocket and kept looking into Alice's room. "I was wondering. At the club. You know. About the private dances. I was just curious. Like, how much are they?"

Alice finally stepped toward her room and stood halfway inside it. "I just pour drinks, Ernie. I gotta go."

The office phone started ringing again.

Ernie nodded. "Okay. But, like, the private dances—are they more than twenty bucks?"

"I tell you what, Ernie. I'll talk to Tia when I get back. See if she'll give you a private for twenty."

Ernie's face went a dark shade of red. "Oh. Tia? Really? I don't know." He picked at one of his burning ears. "Like, what happens in a private dance? You know. Like if you pay more than twenty?"

"I really got to go, Ernie. I'll see you when I get back."

"I'll probably just come in for a few drinks. When you get back. I don't know about the private dance with Tia."

"Well, think about it."

"Okay. Saturday, right?"

"Saturday."

"Good. And you sure about the laundry? I'm sure the maids won't mind washing them. They're women and everything, and they get their thing once a month, too."

"I'm running late, Ernie. I'll see you around."

And Alice closed the door. Through the curtain, she saw Ernie linger out on the sidewalk for a second, looking from Terry's truck and back to her room. He picked at his ear, wiped the finger on his khakis, then made his way toward the office.

Alice glanced around the room. All the trash gone. No more bottles of booze.

Her eyes drifted to a small pink scar on the inside of her forearm, about an inch in length. She traced her finger over the raised skin a few times, pushing down the welt like the effort would make the blemish disappear, and all Alice could think was, *God, I could really use a drink.*

CHAPTER SEVEN

OCTOBER 2005

The stains on the comforter still clung stubbornly to the fabric. It had been washed a few times, but the fingernail polish wouldn't come out. Light red spots near the foot of the bed. Might just as well be bloodstains. The first thing Alice saw in the morning, the last thing at night. Constant reminders.

She tacked a poster over the fingernail polish doodles on the wallpaper. Gwen Stefani and No Doubt's *Rock Steady* covered Jason's last attempt at wall art. Alice thought it might help to cover up the scribbles—to hide them. But it didn't. Not really.

Her mom had added a small throw rug to cover the spots on the carpet. A rug she bought at Target that didn't match her room at all—dark brown, and it stood out like a pimple on the tip of her nose. Alice's dad brought her a different comforter from the linen closet, but Alice put it right back. They all made an attempt to cover up and replace what really couldn't be covered up and replaced.

Jason was gone. A poster, a rug, and a different comforter wouldn't change that.

His room hadn't been touched since the *accident*—the only word used when referring to what had happened to Jason—like it had been contaminated. A toxic place barred from entry. The bed still unmade. Toys scattered on the floor. Legos, an electric racetrack that didn't work anymore, an Oscar the Grouch puzzle that was missing a few pieces, three or four Superman figurines. A USS *North Carolina* T-shirt hung over the bedpost. A Star Wars night-light continued to glow orange in an outlet.

Alice sat on the edge of her bed, dressed for school in a pair of jeans and a red blouse. She showered that morning as she always did. Combed and blow-dried her hair. Brushed her teeth. Applied some makeup. All the stuff you were supposed to do every day. All part of the routine of getting ready for school.

She didn't really want to go to school, but didn't want to stay at home either. Both places were equally unbearable. Everybody at school knew what happened. *Everybody.* A lot of the kids steered clear of her, staring at her and getting real quiet when she passed them in the hallways. Hardly anybody said anything about the accident. Not many of the kids, anyway. What were they supposed to say? *Sorry your brother's dead. Sorry that he died in a dryer. Sorry that you were the one that was supposed to be watching him.*

Mr. Houck, her swimming coach, said that he felt awfully sorry about everything. Tragic. Just tragic. He even got a little teary-eyed. Asked if there was anything he could do. Told her that it was okay if she didn't participate in the upcoming swim meet if she wasn't feeling up to it. Alice knew that part of him didn't mean that—she was not only team captain, but the team's best swimmer as well, and without her in the water, they would stand a good chance of losing the meet.

Alice kept up with her homework though. She studied for all the quizzes, handed in reports, even read Thornton Wilder's *The Bridge of San Luis Rey* for English class. Better to keep busy, she thought. She participated in swim practice after school each day, drawn to the sense of freedom that she could only find in the pool, the silence and solitude under the water cherished commodities.

Her best friends, Shelly and Rhonda, still ate lunch with her and walked to class with her, but even they were uncomfortable and a little weird around her. Yesterday, on the bus after school, Shelly started talking about her little brother, Barry. What a pain in the ass he was. How gross he was. Barry had walked in on her when she was getting out of the shower and saw her naked. He stared at her breasts, pointed at them and laughed. Shelly said that he was so lame and stupid, that she hated her little brother, then suddenly stopped in the middle of her story when Rhonda gave her a look. Shelly got all quiet and awkward. Her face turned red and she didn't say anything else the whole bus ride home. She wouldn't even look at Alice when she got off at her stop.

Alice stared down at her shoes. The laces weren't tied yet. She really, really didn't want to go back to school. It was only Wednesday. Three more days until the weekend. Three more days until she had to sit around the house the entire weekend and try to avoid her parents.

She could stay at home. Her parents would let her. They were both wallowing in their own private cloud of grief and didn't seem to care what Alice did on a daily basis. They were all supposed to go see a family psychiatrist the following week. Someone that specialized in helping families through tragedy. A grief counselor. Alice's parents wanted her to sit and tell a stranger how she felt about Jason dying. *It'll help you come to terms with what happened,* her mom said. *And help with the guilt.*

But staying home from school didn't seem like such a great idea either. Her mother usually slept most of the day because she didn't sleep at night. Alice could hear her moving around the house in the middle of the night. Walking up and down the stairs, moving from room to room. Doing what, Alice had no idea. She didn't really want to know.

Alice finally stood up. Grabbed her books and notebooks from her desk and stuffed them inside her backpack. She walked down the hallway, forced to pass by Jason's room. She tried not to slow down or look inside, but when she heard the gurgle of the fish tank, she stopped at the threshold and stared inside at her little brother's room, at four years of his life and at what used to be. She wondered how long it would take for someone in the family to finally gather the fortitude to pack up all of Jason's belongings and either store them in the garage or donate them to charity, and how long it would take to strip the room down entirely and remove all semblance of the fourth member of the family.

She watched three goldfish circulate in their tank, scanning the surface of the water in the endless search for food, and she thought that Jason was probably the last person to feed them some pellets.

She stepped into the bedroom and it smelled of Jason. Baby shampoo and graham crackers and dirty socks. Her eyes began to burn and everything around her blurred as a twisted knot lodged and expanded in her throat and made it painful to swallow. She crossed over the shag carpeting and sat down at Jason's play table. Dried chunks of red and yellow Play-Doh scattered all over the surface, along with scraps of construction paper and felt markers and a pair of kid scissors. She flipped through a stack of Jason's drawings and sketches, pictures of cats and dogs and what appeared to be a cow. Then she came to a drawing of a stick-figure family. A mother, father, and two children, one bigger than the other. A boy and girl. Alice wiped the tears that leaked from her eyes and noticed a piece of the Play-Doh had been molded into a shape of a head, complete with eyes, a mouth, and long hair.

The fish tank bubbled behind her. She picked up the container of food and dropped in a pinch of flakes. She watched the goldfish swarm the food for a minute, and wished that she were in the water with them.

Then she stared back down at the Play-Doh bust for a few moments until her vision blurred once again and she didn't bother to wipe away the tears. Her fingers found the pair of kid scissors and she turned them over in her hand a few times. She felt along the blade of the scissors, pressed her index finger against the steel edge hard enough to leave a mark.

Her mother's words about meeting with the grief counselor echoed in her mind. *It'll help you come to terms with what happened . . . And help with the guilt.*

But how could it? How could someone help remove the paralyzing guilt that squeezed at her from the inside out, slowly crushing her? That pain would never go away. Never.

She placed the blade against the tender skin on the inside of her wrist, closed her eyes, and pulled back with a hard yank. She could feel the sting as the steel sliced open the skin, then she pressed down harder and did it again. And again. Her forearm felt as if it had caught on fire, the pain rippling all the way up to the shoulder. Alice kept her eyes closed as beads of blood rolled down across her palm and off her fingertips, but for a few brief moments of time, the anguish of Jason dying leaked away as well.

CHAPTER EIGHT

Alice had always imagined that riding on an Amtrak train would be a little fancier than traveling on a bus, that the seats would be bigger, more comfortable, and that the service would be warm and friendly, the staff striving to make sure everyone's travel experience was pleasant. But it wasn't. Not even close. The seats looked and smelled dirty. The material a tropical pattern. Blue, green, yellow, and orange. All the colors faded and worn, covered with grime, coffee stains, and old pieces of pink chewing gum. The windows were smudged by the hands of children and uncovered sneezes, the headrests stained by greasy heads.

Alice lost count of how many Budweisers she consumed. She knew she finished off two before they arrived in Philly, had a couple more during the layover, and a couple more since pulling out of the 30th Street station.

She glanced down at her one-way ticket to Wilmington, North Carolina, clutched in her hand and noticed that she still had stains of red dotted on her skin. When she had stepped up to the ticket kiosk, her mind was blank, not having any real clue of where she was headed. All she knew was that she needed to get out of Harrisburg. The ticket woman had to ask her twice what her destination city was. Alice stared at the woman, then to the screen behind her that listed all the various destinations, and a name entered her mind like a slap to the face—*Elton*. Her eyes wandered to the last city listed on the board: Wilmington, North Carolina.

Go to Elton's, her inner voice instructed. She didn't second-guess it as she paid for a one-way ticket to Wilmington. From there, she would have to take the bus down to Shallotte. She didn't really like the fact that she was going back home—or where home used to be—but Wilmington would only be a quick pit stop before heading to Shallotte. She wouldn't stay in Wilmington. She couldn't.

Get to Shallotte. One decision down.

Alice managed to keep the seat next to her empty as most of the others filled up around her. Maybe it was the toxic cloud that loomed over her. Or maybe it was obvious that she just walked away from a trailer containing five dead men.

The beer performed its purpose. With its mellow buzz, she felt a little calmer, a little more resolved. She would get things figured out in Shallotte. Once she got down there, Elton would help her sort things through and decide what to do next. Everything would be fine. Alice drank some more beer. It was still cold and tasted pretty good.

* * *

Alice watched as a young girl—maybe fifteen—hustled into the car with her head down, shoulders bunched up under her chin like she wanted to disappear. The young girl didn't make eye contact with anyone as she searched for an empty seat. Any empty seat. Alice could smell the girl's desperation, but the young kid wasn't traveling alone—maybe she wanted to be—as a middle-aged burnout sporting a long blond ponytail, carrying two cans of Budweiser, trailed after her. Like a lot of guys wearing a ponytail, his hair was pretty thin on top. Wouldn't be long before he was bald. The man stood tall and rail thin, like a good gust of wind would send him down on his ass. His jeans and green work shirt were well worn and dirty, and his construction worker boots were caked with old mud, the color of mustard. A name patch was stitched above one of his shirt pockets: *Buddy*.

Buddy followed the young girl to the seat in front of Alice like a cat tracking a mouse, alert and curious and ready to pounce. The nature of their relationship appeared to be newly acquainted, if you could call it that.

The young girl was pretty. Caramel-colored complexion, free of acne or blemishes of any kind. She looked like she could be the next Noxzema girl. Big blue eyes, almost too wide for her face, gave her a cartoonish appearance and a look of complete gullibility. Her jaws worked on a pink wad of bubblegum and she didn't speak in full sentences. Mainly *uh-huhs* and *uh-uhs* when Buddy asked her a question or made a lame attempt at levity. As the young girl became more and more withdrawn, Buddy got more and more confident, sipping on his can of Budweiser. This back-and-forth went on for a half hour or so, but Alice kept watching anyway—a train wreck waiting to happen.

Buddy leaned in close to the girl, and she, in turn, pressed up as close as possible to the smudged-up window. "Fuck. I hate Philly. I really do. It's a real shit-hole if you ask me."

The girl didn't respond. She just kept snapping her bubblegum. *Chew, chew, snap. Chew, chew, snap.*

"Hope I never set foot in that city again, you know?" He stretched his arms over his head and cracked his back, thereby invading every inch of the girl's personal space, but didn't seem to care. "Born in Philly. Grew up in Philly. Served my time. I'm done with it. You?"

The young girl nodded her head. Not really an answer, but that was all she offered.

"Yeah. Got a construction gig all lined up down in Fort Myers. Construction work in Philly is a pain in the ass. Dickheads always stealing your tools. Homeless people and druggies breaking into work sites and camping out, pissing and shitting everywhere." He proceeded to play with his ponytail now. "Florida's nice, man. Ever been?"

"Uh-uh," the girl answered, wide eyes staring out the window. She looked like she wished that she was anywhere else.

"Yeah. It's fucking nice. Warm twenty-four seven. No shit weather. I mean, they get rain, but I like the rain. What about you? You like rain?" He didn't really give the girl a chance to answer. Just kept on yapping. "Yeah, people down in Florida don't go sticking their nose in your shit either. They leave your shit alone. Go about their own goddamned business. The blacks are different down there, too. No offense, but the blacks in Philly are assholes. You know? Down in Fort Myers, they're just black people. No attitude, like the whole world owes them shit."

"Uh-huh," the girl said.

"What's your deal? You look like you're half and half. Is that right? Half black, half white?"

"Uh-huh," the girl repeated.

"Yeah, that's the way to do it. Best of both worlds, right? Black people like you. White people like you. Shit, your mama must be pretty."

The young girl just nodded this time.

"Yeah. That's cool." The guy took a sip of beer, kept playing with his ponytail, stroking it like a pet ferret. "You want a beer?" He held out one of the cans of Budweiser.

The girl shook her head.

"You sure? You don't drink or what?"

The girl gazed around the train car. She appeared too scared to get up and move, and too scared to stay put. Her big blue eyes rimmed red, on the verge of losing it altogether. The girl glanced back at Alice for a moment, fear and desperation eating up her face, then looked away quickly, too uncomfortable with direct eye contact.

Alice knew what was going on with the girl. Pretty obvious. Alice had been living it for the last six years. Running from a life that didn't work and had nothing left to offer. The young girl was scared—just like Alice when she made the decision to run. But after months, or years, of being trapped in a situation that seemed unfixable, all the daydreaming and planning didn't prepare you for taking the big leap. *Running.* Leaving all the misery behind and living life as a runaway, knowing in your heart that it wasn't going to get better, so why not pack up and take your chances on your own? Alice had been convinced that her life was unbearable. That it couldn't get any worse.

Alice almost felt bad for the young girl. Almost. The kid was starting a journey that would rip her apart, piece by piece. Life on the streets was soul-crushing. But she wasn't Alice's problem. Alice sipped on her beer even though it wasn't that cold anymore.

"Man, you wouldn't say shit if you had a mouthful of it, would you? Christ. Lighten up, already." He drank the Budweiser like water. "Shit. I don't bite or anything."

The young girl nodded. Kept peering out the window.

Buddy emptied the beer down his throat, produced a foamy belch, then wiped his mouth with his sleeve. "Where you headed to anyways?"

The young girl stared down at her hands and squirmed closer to the window. "I have someplace to go."

Pffssst. He cracked open the other Budweiser. "I say bullshit to that." His playful, optimistic tone melted away a little. "You got no place to go, do you?"

The young girl clutched at her purse and moved to stand, but Buddy slid a rough hand on her thigh and kept her in place. "Come on, honey. Don't be like that. Just trying to be friendly and shit. You don't got a problem with someone just trying to be friendly, do you?" He kept his hand on her thigh.

"I think I'll move. To another seat," the young girl answered, more of a plea than statement.

He grinned and patted her inner thigh. "Nah. You're fine. What's your name anyways, sweetheart?"

The young girl shifted under his touch. "Please. I'm sorry, but I just want to move to another seat."

Buddy chuckled and kept his hand right where it was. "Nothing to be sorry about. Just tell me your name. No harm in telling me who I'm sitting next to, is there?"

The young girl hugged her purse like a stuffed animal. "Delilah," she whispered.

"Shit, that wasn't so hard, was it? Now come on and have a beer with me." He took the young girl's hand and pressed the cold can of Budweiser into her fingers.

The girl recoiled from the can like it was a bag full of dog shit and snapped to her feet. The Budweiser tipped over and doused his blue jeans with an eruption of white foam.

"What the fuck?" He grabbed the can and held it out in front of him, beer suds leaking all over the floor.

The girl skirted past him, stepping on his work boots, and rushed down the aisle with her head held low, knocking against armrests and elbows as she made a reckless retreat.

"Goddamn." Buddy stared at the mess on his jeans and boots and shook his head, jaw grinding. "Fuck this shit." Then he stepped into the aisle and followed right after the young girl.

In the seat behind them, Alice watched the guy storm off, still mumbling and swearing under his breath. His fists clenched at his sides and his long, greasy ponytail snapped back and forth like a cat's tail. Alice knew where this was headed. Guys like that hated rejection. The scumbag was immature, insecure, intolerant—just to name a few. The kid may as well have called the guy a *faggot*. She hit his hot button and he wasn't about to let it slide. He was just getting started and the young girl was in no condition to defend herself.

Alice glanced down at the duffel bag wedged between her feet. "Christ." She didn't really consider herself a Good Samaritan. For Alice, it was always *every man for himself*. Karma would never be kind to her because she was not kind to it. But she picked up the duffel bag anyway, got to her feet, already regretting the decision.

CHAPTER NINE

The l a t e-a f t er no o n c r ow d hunched over two-top tables covered with cheap red vinyl, nursing draft beers and munching on processed chicken fingers, overcooked sliders, and undercooked French fries. Like most low-rent strip clubs, the food wasn't necessarily good, merely edible. Mainly truckers, construction workers, and college students who enjoyed eating their lunch while watching topless girls spin around poles. A few men sat up at the bar, sipping drinks and searching for answers they would never find in the bottom of their glasses.

The Frisky Pony's windows were tinted black, curtains drawn, making it dark enough to pass for night. Like Vegas casinos, daylight's not good for business, so give the clientele the pseudo comforts of night. A smoke machine wasn't necessary—cigarette smoke hovered in the air, thick and gray and oppressive. It was as if smoking was a requirement to enter. Patrons, cocktail waitresses, the bartender. Everybody sucked on cancer sticks.

A techno beat thumped, out of synch with the pulsating lights over center stage. A bleached blond with thicker thighs than the night dancers went through the motions of her routine on the pole, grinding her ass into the metal shaft, her breasts not so much jiggling—barely moving, in fact—due to their freakish implant size.

The left breast happened to be larger, rounder, and firmer. The silicon bag perched too high under pink flesh and it seemed dangerously close to bursting from the result of a hard sneeze. The right one, although still bigger than a cantaloupe, looked like a partially deflated balloon. Matched together, they created the effect of perfect imbalance.

The dancer—Summer was her stage name—moved with little grace or passion. Each gesture, each shake, each smack of her dimpled ass well rehearsed and timed to the music, but her face stood void of expression and emotion. Summer was not in the moment, her mind somewhere else, someplace else, as she arched her back and slid down the pole until completing a painful split. This particular move always hurt her knees, but management required each dancer to perform at least one crotch-exposing split per routine. Summer jammed her index finger into her mouth like she was taking her temperature, then traced her right areola, the size of a silver dollar, and lifted the sagging breast as if in an effort to even up the pair.

The male spectators that gazed up at her, with mouthfuls of processed beef and chicken, weren't prone to harsh judgment against unbalanced breasts. They were tits. They were big. And they were both naked for their viewing pleasure. At the very least, the enormous set of jugs distracted them from Summer's stretch-marked paunch that hung over her red G-string.

The entire scene would be completely depressing and demoralizing for both dancer and spectator without some form of intoxication. Summer drank a few vodka and grapefruits before her routine, and would have a few after it. As for the handful of male observers, beer went down like warm milk.

The front door swung open, giving way to an intense blast of unwanted sunlight, and the drinking, munching, and gawking group of patrons reacted to the light like a coven of vampires. The men held hands in front of their eyes and leaned away from the light as if fearful of bursting into flame and ash. Summer kept dancing, though. Sunlight or no sunlight.

Silhouetted by the blast of natural light stood the outlines of two men, one ridiculously tall and wide, the other small and slight. The view of the two men was like the opening shot of a *Looney Tunes* episode, a father and son cartoon pair. Then the door swung closed behind them, and as the welcome return of darkness settled back in, the rest of the customers resumed shoveling French fries into their mouths and stared back at Summer's less than masterful performance.

The two men remained at the threshold and waited a few moments for their eyes to adjust to the dark, then the one built like a fourteen-year-old paperboy walked straight to the bar with the lumbering gorilla trailing a few paces behind him. The small-framed man crawled up on a barstool, took a pack of Salems from his crisp suede jacket, and lit up. The man's facial features matched his physique, soft and childlike. Pale white skin, rosy at the cheeks from the bitter air outside, and a pair of shocking blue eyes. His delicate lips worked the cigarette, smoke funneling out from his tiny nostrils, and his thin fingers with their perfectly clipped nails strummed on the bar top. His hair, neatly trimmed and combed and parted off to the side, gave him the appearance of a Norman Rockwell character. He looked like he should be off earning a Boy Scout merit badge or sitting at the edge of a pond in Mayberry with a fishing pole in hand instead of perching on a ratty barstool at a strip club. He was a man permanently trapped inside the body of a child—a man-child.

Despite the appearance of youth and innocence, there was something off-putting about the diminutive man. Although well dressed, well groomed, and polite-looking, it was his smile that proved most troubling. It was the smirk of a boy who just did something cruel to the neighborhood cat. Mean and twisted little thoughts dancing around in his head. The man's lips pulled back to reveal a set of perfectly white teeth, mashed together like that of an evil ventriloquist's dummy. In fact, with the large, hulking mass of a man towering behind him, the two men looked like a Vaudeville routine waiting to commence.

The bartender, a hard-living thirty-year-old woman with broad shoulders and jet-black hair buzzed short, wiped away water rings and tossed empty beer bottles into a trash can as she made her way toward the men. A Newport dangled from her lips. Both nostrils pierced with a silver stud. She was used to all types here at the Frisky Pony. And, as she did with most customers, she avoided eye contact as she slung coasters on the bar in front of the two strangers.

"Get you fellas a drink?"

The small man maintained his spooky little grin and answered, barely moving his lips. "That would be fine. A white Russian, please. Ketel One if you have it."

The bartender said that she did and looked up at the giant. "Anything for you?"

"Bud," the big man croaked. The single syllable came out low and baritone. He didn't look her in the eye, just openly stared at the woman's tits.

"Tap or bottle?"

"Bottle," he croaked again, eyes glued to her breasts.

"There's naked tits up onstage, chief."

The bruising hulk kept staring at her tits anyway.

"Whatever," the bartender said.

While they waited on their drinks, the little man spun around on his stool, feet dangling a few feet from the floor, puffed on his Salem, and took in the lopsided dancer's moves in mild amusement. As the song finished and Summer's set concluded, he pulled a crisp twenty-dollar bill from a large roll of bills, folded it neatly in half, and held it over his shoulder toward the giant.

The large man took the bill between thick, sausage-like fingers and lumbered toward the stage to deliver the dancer's tip.

The small man clapped his delicate hands together in polite applause, and in the absence of music, his appreciation got the attention of the other non-applauding customers. They grinned and shook their heads at him, silently mocking the strange little man.

"Nice. Real nice," he called out, his voice nearly as high as a castrato's. Over the years, he had been called many different names due to his diminutive size and odd pitch of voice. Alfalfa. Tiny Tim. Pee-wee Herman. People would laugh, dismiss him as if he were a silly little toy. But appearances could be deceiving.

As the giant returned obediently to his side, the small man stared down at the large man's hands with an expression of disapproval. The hulking mass nodded and grunted, and began to applaud as well, and didn't stop until the small man returned his hands to his lap.

When the bartender delivered their drinks, the woman couldn't help but stare at the undersized man. "You want a private dance with Summer? She'll lose the G-string for the right price."

The man smiled at the offer. "Thank you. But, no. Another time perhaps. I'll let Summer catch her breath."

The bartender shrugged that it was his loss. "Fourteen for the drinks. Unless you want to start a tab."

The small man withdrew his money clip again and pulled out another twenty. "Just the one round, thank you. Keep the change."

As the bartender nodded her thanks and took the twenty, he let his fingers linger on her hand for a moment, his skin icy cold, like he perhaps suffered from a circulation disorder.

"I was hoping that you could possibly help me out with a personal matter."

The bartender withdrew her hand from under his. "Sorry, Charlie. I ain't a dancer."

"And I'm not looking to be danced for." He maintained his toothy grin, slipped a hundred-dollar bill from the money clip and placed it on top of the bar. "My name is Sinclair. I'm an acquaintance of Terry's."

"Sorry to hear it," the bartender replied, her voice cool and flat.

Sinclair kept grinning. "Yes. Not necessarily a charmer, is he?"

"Far from it."

"A bit of a bully, truth be told. Lacks certain social graces. Hard to appreciate a man like that."

"Whatever. Anyways, he ain't been in yet today."

Sinclair nodded. "I'm well aware of that fact." He stabbed his cigarette into an ashtray. "May I ask your name? If I can be so forward."

The bartender stared at him for a second, thinking to herself, *Is this guy for real?* She glanced at the hundred-dollar bill. "Tammy."

"Ah. Tammy. Always loved that particular name. A real sweetness to it. My first crush was a Tammy. Tammy Tucker. Prettiest smile in the third grade. But I'm sure you have no interest in my Tammy Tucker."

"Pretty much, my man," Tammy agreed.

"Candid. I appreciate that." He lit up a fresh cigarette. "Now then, a few more questions for you, then I'll let you go about your business."

"Fire away, chief." Tammy lit up a cigarette as well.

"Wonderful. I appreciate your cooperation. Now then, I am curious about something. Anyone not show up for work today? One of your performers perhaps?"

Tammy smiled at his use of the word *performers*. "No. All the girls are here."

Sinclair took a small sip of his white Russian. "Very tasty."

"Uh-huh," Tammy grunted through a mouthful of smoke.

"One of your cocktail waitresses call in sick possibly?"

Tammy had yet to pick up the hundred-dollar bill. "Why you asking, anyways?" She didn't ask if he was a cop, but that was what she was inferring.

Sinclair sipped his drink again. "Well, I'm afraid Terry has gotten himself tangled up in some unfortunate business that I speculate may involve another one of his employees. I have a pretty strong hunch that is the case."

Tammy glanced up at the giant. His hand gripped the neck of the Budweiser, nearly concealing the entire bottle in his massive mitt. And, still staring at her tits, he tilted the bottle to his lips and emptied half of the liquid down his throat. "Cold," he uttered more to himself than the present company.

"Any information you might be able to provide would be immensely helpful, Tammy. It really would," Sinclair coaxed.

Tammy glanced back down at the hundred-dollar bill—more than she would make in tips all night. "Well, Alice is running late. Nothing unusual there. Bitch is always running late."

Sinclair perked up a little. Kept his glass perched at his lips. "Alice?"

"Yeah. She's kinda new."

"Does Alice have a last name?"

"I'm sure she does. Don't know what it is though. You'd have to ask Terry that."

"Right. Terry. I'll see what I can do on that one."

"Terry's a dick. I hope he gets his ass into some trouble. Serve him right," Tammy said.

"Yes. He's in a bit of a jam. You don't have to worry about that." He wiped some lint off his pristine suede jacket. "I'm assuming Alice is an attractive woman."

"Sure. I guess. Too plain to be a dancer though."

"Is that right? Why so?"

"I don't know. Not slutty enough, I guess. That, and she always looks pissed off at something."

"I see. Interesting. Could you describe her for me?"

"Whattaya mean exactly?"

"What she looks like. A brief description if you don't mind."

Tammy crushed her cigarette into an ashtray. Sighed like she was put out by the question. "Green eyes. Long brown hair. Kinda tall. Athletic. Like she used to play volleyball or basketball. She's still got some freckles on her face. Makes her look like Pippi Longstocking."

"Okay. That's helpful. Anything else?"

"Yeah. Like I said, she always looks pissed off and doesn't smile much."

"Maybe Alice doesn't have much to smile about," Sinclair offered.

Tammy shrugged like it wasn't her problem. "I guess. Bug always seems to be up her ass. Like she's too good for this place."

"Not all of us enjoy our current state of employment, Tammy."

"Yeah. Whatever."

"And do you know where Alice might live?"

"I dunno. Some motel around here, I think. She never invited me over."

"Okay. That's good. Anything else you can think of? Birthmarks? Tattoos? Anything of that nature?"

"I think she used to be a cutter."

"A *cutter*? I'm not familiar with the reference."

"Yeah. A cutter. She's got a few scars on her forearm. Above her wrist." She lit up another cigarette. "Probably won't tell you much, but she's got a slight accent. Sounds like she's from the South. You know? Georgia or Alabama or some place like that. Makes her sound stupid if you ask me."

"Good. Good. That's very helpful. Anything else you can think of?"

"Nope."

Sinclair finished his drink and motioned for the hulk to do the same with his.

"You know, if you're throwing the Benjamins around, Tia will give you a lap dance that will keep that perky little smile on your face. Get one for your big friend here, too."

"Next time. Next time for sure."

Tammy watched him slip his money clip back into his suede jacket pocket. "If Terry shows up, do you want me to give him a message or anything?"

Sinclair hopped down off his stool. "No. That won't be necessary. Terry won't be coming in here anytime soon, I'm afraid."

Another dancer took the stage, but Sinclair slipped through the tables, never looking back, waited for the giant to open the front door for him, then stepped out into the late-afternoon sun.

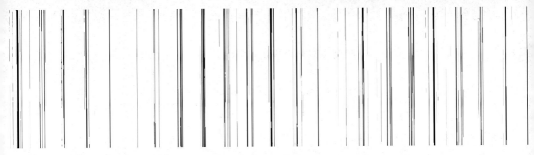

CHAPTER TEN

Buddy, t h e ma n with the ponytail, caught up with the young girl a few cars up, on the platform in between passenger cars where the bathrooms were located and also isolated from gawking eyes. One of the fluorescent lights had burned out in the platform area, casting the two of them in dull shadows. Buddy had the poor kid blocked in front of the exit doors. Both of his skinny arms were spread eagle, touching the two walls on either side of her, and his legs X'd out, completely pinning her in.

The industrial sound of wheels roaring ninety-five miles per hour along the steel tracks hummed below them, and the swaying of the train cars rocked the man and girl back and forth as if in a strange rhythmic, almost sensual dance. The high-pitched whine of metal on metal and the steady *clickety-clack* drowned out everything else. Buddy wore a shit-eating grin, enjoying the young girl's panicked distress.

"Not cool. Not cool at all. You got beer all over me. I was just trying to be hospitable." But Buddy couldn't pronounce *hospitable* correctly. Instead, he said *hospital.*

The girl chewed on a piece of gum so hard that it looked like she might crack her jaw. She clutched at her purse, wanting all this to go away.

"What? Your shit don't stink? Is that it? Too good to drink a beer with me?"

"No," she whispered.

"Well, let me tell you something, honey. I've dealt with uptight bitches like you before. Got my pants all wet. Shit."

"Sorry," she moaned.

"Yeah, you're sorry alright." He stared down at his jeans. "I should make you suck the beer right out of my pants. That's what I should fucking do."

The girl tried to fight them back, but the tears came anyway.

"Save the waterworks, bitch." He reached down and grabbed her by the chin. Forced her head up. Forced her to look right at him. "Bet you're good at sucking. Aren't you?"

Another moan escaped the girl's lips and that made Buddy grin even harder. She clutched her purse tighter and pressed her eyes closed.

"Whatcha got in your little bag, huh?" He reached for the purse, and the girl yanked it back and actually snarled—lips pulled back over her teeth like a rabid dog.

"Whoa. Easy, bitch. Jesus. Don't take my fucking hand off." His eyes stared back down at her bag. "So, now you've *got* to show me what you're hiding. Must be something in there that's pretty damn special."

The girl pressed against the wall, face-first. "Please leave me alone. I didn't do anything to you."

"Not yet you haven't. What's in the purse?"

The girl pressed tighter against the wall. Shook her head. "No."

"Fuck. Have it your way then." He snatched at the purse and tugged hard, but the girl clung onto the straps for dear life.

"Leave her alone."

Buddy glanced over his shoulder—Alice stared right back at him.

"And let go of the purse."

Buddy maintained his grip on the bag. "And who the hell are you?"

"I'm nobody," Alice said.

"Fucking right, you're nobody. Why don't you mind your own damn business and beat it?"

"Sure. After you let-go-of-the-purse."

"Or *what?*"

Alice set her duffel bag on the floor. "Last time. Let-go-of-the-purse."

His eyes went up and down Alice's body, lingering on her breasts for a moment before locking eyes with her. He was grinning again. "She a friend of yours, honey?"

"Nope. Not yours either."

The train zipped around a turn in the tracks and the three of them swayed with the motion.

Buddy kept smiling, liking what he saw in front of him. Even without makeup and looking a little worn around the edges, Alice was still attractive. He finally let go of the girl's purse and held his hands up to illustrate his full cooperation. "Okay. There you go. The purse is all hers. Bitch is too young anyways." He moved closer to Alice, standing over her by more than a foot. "But you're not, are you?" His eyes went up and down her again.

"I'll be honest with you, I'm not having a great day. Been pretty shitty, in fact."

Buddy stroked his ponytail. "Then maybe I'm just what the doctor ordered."

"Fat chance of that. So why don't you do us all a favor and go grab yourself another Budweiser and chill."

He kept stroking his ponytail. "You sure, sweetheart?"

Alice could smell the beer on his breath, and when he smiled down at her, she could see that his teeth were a mess of nicotine brown. "I'll pass."

He faltered a little. His confidence bruised just a bit. But he wasn't about to give up just yet. "You sure look pretty when you're pissed." He reached out to touch Alice's hair.

Alice reacted—her knee shot straight up and pounded him right in the nuts, hard enough to lift his feet off the floor for a second. He grunted and down he went. Dropped and crumpled to the floor in a heap, cupping his throbbing testicles with both hands. He let out a pathetic groan and rolled over onto his back.

Alice stared down at him. "You done, Buddy? You gonna leave everybody alone?"

The man's eyes were leaking water. "Fuck you, you fucking bitch," he managed to gasp. His legs were kicking and slipping all over the floor, then the heel of his construction boots popped her hard in the shins.

"God damn it." Alice glanced over at the young girl. "Open up the bathroom door."

The girl didn't move. Just stared down at the man as he sucked for air.

"Now. Open the damn door," Alice barked.

The girl snapped out of her daze and made a wide berth around Buddy, then opened the bathroom door and stepped back away from both of them.

Alice grabbed Buddy by the arms and hauled him into the bathroom.

"Don't just stand there. Give me your belt," Alice demanded.

The girl kept staring down at the man, her mouth grinding away on her chewing gum.

"Now, damn it."

The girl unbuckled the belt from around her waist and handed it over. Alice ran the tip of the belt through the buckle, making a leather loop, and dropped down onto Buddy's chest. She put the loop around one of his wrists and grabbed for the other when he

swung his free hand toward her head and connected with the side of
her jaw. It was an openhanded slap, but hard enough to make Alice's
head jerk to the right.

She saw him reach for his pant leg, right above the boot. He
grabbed a hold of something. She saw the handle first. Then the
blade. Six inches of polished steel. The knife flashed toward her and
she managed to pull back, the blade missing by less than an inch.
But Buddy wasn't done. He let out a dull grunt and started to swing
the blade again.

Alice didn't have time to think—instead, she brought a clenched
fist down and caught him on the bridge of his nose. The force of it
hard enough to break some cartilage and snap his head back against
the floor. More moaning, and blood flowed from both nostrils.
Alice grabbed his other wrist and cinched the belt tight, pinning his
two hands together.

"Whaddaya doing?" the girl squeaked.

"What does it look like?" Alice dragged him beside the toilet and
wrapped the other end of the belt around the grab bar and tied it
off. She stood, put her boot against the wall, and yanked the leather
belt as tight as it would go.

Buddy groaned, eyes flickering open and closed as blood leaked
down his chin and neck.

Alice was out of breath. Starting to sweat a little. She pushed her
hair behind her ears and stared down at the man for a second before
stepping over him and exiting the bathroom.

The girl backed away from her, half expecting Alice to give her a
slap as well.

"You're welcome," Alice mumbled as she picked up her duffel bag
and slung it over her shoulder.

"You're just gonna leave him there?" the girl squeaked again.

Alice stopped and stared at the young girl. "You got a pen and
piece of paper?"

"What?"

"Something to write with. Something to write on."

The girl rummaged through her purse and finally managed to come up with an ink pen and a scrap of paper.

Alice grabbed both and scribbled something on the piece of paper. She slipped the note in the crack of the bathroom door, and without another word or glance back toward the girl, she returned to the passenger car.

The girl watched Alice disappear, then looked over at the slip of paper: OUT OF ORDER.

* * *

Alice tried to process what just happened. It all went down so fast. She broke a man's nose. *Where the hell did that come from?* Popping a guy in the balls was one thing, but breaking a man's nose?

Jesus.

Sure, she had been in a position to defend herself before. Mostly girl fights. Half a dozen times or so. Slapping faces, scratching necks, pulling hair, even bit a girl on the ankle once.

But before today, she'd only had one altercation with a man. Alice met the guy in a sleazy bar outside of Allentown. He was drinking alone. He claimed he was in town on business—apparently, he produced *adult films*. Alice sat next to him and let the filmmaker buy her a few drinks even though he was wearing a wedding band. She listened to his stories, his successes as a producer, his eye for talent, and matched him drink for drink. Pretty soon she felt his hand on her knee. She removed it, but the man did not lack in self-confidence, and promptly returned his hand on her thigh, creeping its way higher. Alice set her drink down, removed the hand for a second time, and told him she wasn't interested. He grinned, undeterred, and proceeded to offer her a special audition for one of his upcoming films, and Alice proceeded to tell him to fuck off. The filmmaker quickly lost his grin, grabbed her by the wrist, and shook her hard enough to force her off the barstool. She called him a few choice words and never saw the fist coming. He hit her again and she dropped to the floor. Then the bartender stepped in. Not a big guy, but built solid enough to break up fights and take care of the drunks when he had to. The bartender grabbed the filmmaker and twisted his arm behind the guy's back hard enough to bring the man to his tiptoes. He propped the man up in front of Alice and gave her some advice. *Go for the balls or the face. Either one works. And if you're gonna use your hands, curl them into fists. A slap ain't gonna do shit. Now take your shot.* The bartender pushed the man closer to Alice and waited. She didn't think she could do it. Didn't think she could hit someone right in the face. Then the filmmaker smirked at her. Called her a stupid whore. Alice took her shot—she curled her fingers into a tight ball and swung. His head snapped back, and she felt as if she just hit a brick wall. *Again. But harder. You might not always get two shots,* the bartender offered. Alice hit the filmmaker again. Harder. Hard enough to crack his bottom lip open and draw blood. She watched the bartender drag the man out of the bar and toss him onto the sidewalk like a bag of garbage. Then he poured her a drink and slid the glass across the counter. *Not bad. But next time, you're on your own. Make the first one count.*

Alice leaned back into her seat, her hand still throbbing from breaking the man's nose.

She didn't look up as the girl sat down in the seat across the aisle. She felt the girl's eyes on her but wanted—*needed*—separation. It was only a matter of time until someone stumbled upon the guy. Who knew what he would do once he was unstrapped and released from the bathroom. Hopefully, he'd be too embarrassed by the fact that he got his ass kicked by a girl that he outweighed by at least fifty pounds. Hopefully, he'd lick his wounds, nurse his bruised ego with a few beers, and leave her alone. Guys like that would hate for anyone to know what a girl did to him. But if he did blow the whistle and go crying to the police, Alice would be screwed. Questions would be asked, her whereabouts documented, dots connected.

"Thanks," the girl mumbled, barely a whisper.

Alice heard what the girl said, but chose to ignore it. A nasty headache was unfolding inside her skull.

"My name is Delilah," the girl offered.

"Yeah. I heard."

The girl chewed and chewed on her gum, still clutching her purse to her chest like her life depended on it. "You think he'll get out? The guy?"

Alice let her head tilt fall against the headrest and shut her eyes. "Probably."

"What do you think he'll do?"

"Not my problem."

The girl kept working on her gum. "You think I should go tell the conductor or something?"

"Don't care. That's up to you."

The girl rubbed at her knees. "Maybe I should go tell someone."

Alice finally turned her head and stared over at the young girl. "Look, Delilah, I don't really care what you do. I'm done. I probably shouldn't have even gotten involved in the first place, but I did. That pervert will leave you alone for a while, but there's a hundred more from where he came from."

Delilah nodded. She looked dangerously close to tears again.

"You're not going to survive out here on your own. You're not. If I were you, I'd take the next train home and fix whatever needs to be fixed."

They rode in silence for a minute, and Alice thought that they were done.

"I can't," Delilah finally said. "I can't go home."

Alice didn't bother asking why. She turned her attention out the window where the moon poked through a gap in the storm clouds overhead and the snow had been replaced by rain. Fat pellets of water slapped against the window, slow at first, then, with an unrelenting fury, a torrent of rain attacked the glass.

CHAPTER ELEVEN

NOVEMBER 2005

Alice absolutely hated riding alone in the car with her mother. Trapped together in the awful silence. Neither one speaking much. Neither one knowing what to say. Alice could feel her mother's depression hang in the air like a noxious cloud. She could feel it in her bones, crawling all over her skin, filling every inch of the car. But a few weeks after the accident, her mother had insisted on dropping her off and picking her up from school every day, so they were trapped together for an agonizing twenty minutes each way.

And this was the very last thing Alice wanted to do right now—stop at Harris Teeter's grocery shop with her mom. Her hair was still wet and smelled of chlorine from swimming practice, her clothes damp, and she felt cold. She just wanted to go home, take a hot bath, climb into her pajamas, and go straight to bed.

Today was a day worse than most. When her mother picked her up from school, and after Alice got in the car, her mom acted as if she wasn't even there. Her mother just stared forward, both hands clutching the steering wheel like she was afraid to let go, never saying a word to Alice the entire time. Nothing. Not *how was your day?* Not *how are you feeling?* Not *how'd you do in swimming practice?* But her mother's prolonged silences weren't anything unusual lately. She barely spoke to anyone. Alice's dad. Her own friends. Nobody.

Alice reached forward and flicked on the radio just to get some noise in the dead space. The stereo was set to a classic rock station. Some old song played, the singer screaming more than singing, screeching about going down some highway to hell. Alice had heard it before a thousand times. She didn't really care for classic rock—especially heavy metal—but for some reason, this kind of music usually made her mom happy because it was the kind she used to listen to in high school. Her mother would always sing along until she couldn't remember the words, then she would hum or whistle until the chorus returned and she would pick the lyrics back up once again. Alice acted like she hated when her mom sang to the radio, but she actually kinda liked it. It was goofy and embarrassing, but as long as she didn't have any friends in the car, she'd put up with it. Now, she hoped that some music would shake her mom out of her despair.

It didn't. Her mother's expression remained unreadable as she reached forward and clicked off the radio. They pulled into the Harris Teeter parking lot and after her mother parked the car, she cut the engine, removed the keys, and just sat there for a few moments. Stared out the windshield with a dazed expression. Her hair was a mess—greasy and matted knots draped over her eyes.

Alice waited for her mother to do something, but she didn't. She sat behind the wheel of the car like she was waiting for something to happen. Alice couldn't take it anymore.

"Are you going in or what?"

"Hmmm?"

"Are you going in the store? I thought you needed to pick something up."

Her mother nodded, her mind somewhere else. "Yeah." She grabbed her purse from the back seat, swung open the door, then mumbled to Alice, "Come with me." Not really a question or request.

The door slammed shut before Alice could respond. She let out a groan and watched her mother trudge toward the store in the same pink, faded sweat suit she'd been wearing every day for the last couple of weeks. There were stains all over the back of the pants. Yellow stains. Brown stains. From coffee or soup or whatever. She looked homeless.

As Alice reached for the door handle, her sleeve pulled up and she saw the slashes. The scabs on her forearm hadn't yet healed; each of them about an inch long, right above the wrist, that would probably leave scars. She covered the cuts with adhesive pads during swimming practice and always wore long sleeves to school. Coach Houck didn't know. Her teachers didn't know. Not even Rhonda and Shelly knew. But at home, she chose not to conceal them—she wanted them to be seen.

She touched one of the scabs and thought about how her mother never even asked how they happened. The cuts were right there on Alice's arm, plain as day, and either her mother had no idea that her own daughter had cut herself, or she didn't care. Didn't care that Alice might have scars for the rest of her life, scars that would be a constant reminder, like a battle line drawn, marking what life was like before Jason and after his death.

Alice pulled the sleeve down to cover the scabs, then opened the passenger door and followed her mother inside the store.

* * *

She caught up with her mom pushing a cart through the produce aisle, hunched over the handlebar, barely picking her feet up off the floor, her sneaker shoelaces untied and trailing after her. Nothing inside the cart except for her purse.

The store was crowded with late-afternoon shoppers. Everybody rushing around, picking up last-minute items for dinner, lost in their own worlds. Piano music pumped through the speakers, nothing but white noise.

Alice walked beside the cart, neither she nor her mother slowing or stopping to pick up any fruit or vegetables. Alice didn't feel hungry. The thought of food made her queasy. She wondered if she would ever feel hungry again.

Then her mother stopped abruptly in the middle of the aisle and stared at a display of pineapples. She gazed over the selection of pineapples as if searching for the perfect piece of fruit, then she finally picked one up, turned it over in her hands, inspecting the bottom, the top, the sides, all the while taking up the entire aisle.

"Mom. You're blocking people."

If her mother heard Alice, she ignored her. She ran her fingers over the sharp spines on the pineapple's dimpled skin and kept turning it over and over in her hands.

Alice noticed that a few other shoppers were staring at her mother. Awkward stares. Uncomfortable looks. Impatient glances. Alice grabbed the pineapple from her mother and dropped it in the cart. "What else do you need?"

Her mother mumbled something and pointed down the aisle. Alice didn't bother asking her mother to repeat herself. She rolled the cart down one aisle, then up another, her mom trailing after her like a distracted child.

Alice glanced over at her mother and felt a sudden surge of anger toward the woman. She hated how quiet and strange and withdrawn she was acting, even though she knew exactly why. People kept staring at them as they rolled past. Staring at her mother's dirty hair and dirty clothes and zombie-like expression. Other people didn't know what she just lost—they only saw a woman who looked unstable.

Alice didn't want to be seen with her. Didn't want other people to know this woman was her mother. She knew it was wrong to think like that. To care what other people thought, but she couldn't help it. She wanted to grab her mother by the shoulders and shake her and tell her to snap out of it, to stop acting and looking so strange. No one else cared that Jason was dead.

Alice's mother stopped abruptly in the middle of the aisle and clasped her hands to her face. "*Oh, my God...*"

"What? What's the matter now?" Alice couldn't mask her impatience.

Her mother didn't answer. Instead, she pointed a trembling hand toward a woman and her small child, a young boy, maybe four or five years old. They walked hand in hand, chatting amongst themselves, a private moment between mother and son.

Alice's mother continued to clutch at her face, then started to jog down the aisle and kept repeating, *Oh, my God. Oh, my God. Oh, my God.*

Alice watched her mom push past other shoppers, slamming into their carts, bumping into shelves, and knocking cans and boxes all over the floor. "Baby?"

She chased after her mother, grabbed her by the wrist, and yanked her to a stop. "Mom. Stop it. What are you doing?"

Her mother's head snapped toward Alice. Her eyes were wide and crazy and seemed to protrude from their sockets. "Let-me-go." She ripped her arm free from Alice's hand and snapped, "Don't you touch me. Don't you dare touch me." She stared at Alice for a moment like her daughter was something repulsive, something vile, then took off running again and disappeared around the end of the aisle.

Alice felt the eyes of all the other shoppers. People looking at her and whispering to one another. What she wanted to do was turn around and march out of Harris Teeter, and start walking and keep walking until she was far away from this store—away from this humiliation.

But she didn't. Instead, Alice turned down the next aisle and watched with horror as her mother finally caught up with the woman and her small child.

"Jason?" her mother screamed. Her voice, loud and shrill, carried across the store. "Jason? My boy." She grabbed the little boy by the arm and tried to scoop him up in her arms.

"What are you doing?" the boy's mother screeched. "Let him go!" She tried to remove her son, but Alice's mother clung to the small boy, refusing to release him.

"My boy, my boy . . ." Alice's mother stared at the child and ran her hands over his small face, caressing his chubby red cheeks. The little boy's round eyes grew wide, then his face collapsed into terrified snorts and sobs.

The boy's mother finally managed to yank him back to her bosom and cradled her wailing child. "What is the matter with you? You're scaring him. You're scaring him."

Alice's mother reached her arms out toward the little boy once again, her mouth opening and snapping shut, but unable to form any words.

"Leave us alone!" The boy's mother lashed out and slapped Alice's mother across the cheek. The impact made a sharp cracking sound that echoed through the store.

Alice's mother cried out, half in shock, half in pain. She stumbled backwards, collapsing into a shelf. Bottles of ketchup crashed to the floor, glass shattering into dozens of jagged pieces. Red, thick sauce splattered across linoleum like a gunshot wound. Alice's mother tried to stand, but slipped on a ketchup smear and tumbled back into the shelves.

The small boy howled louder, and his mother gripped him tighter, which only caused him to bawl even harder.

Alice stood frozen at the end of the aisle, her heart machine-gunning in her chest. Her cheeks felt hot. Her knees weak below her. She finally forced herself forward and looked toward the woman and her young son. "You don't understand," she whispered, barely audible.

Alice's mother stumbled to her feet and stared at her daughter. Her breath hitched in her chest. Her face blossomed red, her hair standing on end and hanging every which way. "Alice?"

"It's okay, Mom."

"You . . ." She poked her finger toward Alice, then marched over and grabbed her by both shoulders. "You were supposed to be taking care of him. You were supposed to be watching him."

Alice tried to back away. Tried to pull herself from her mother's pinching hands. "Stop it!"

Everything fell dead in the store. Shoppers and employees stared at the two of them.

Alice's mother released her daughter's shoulders and slowly backed away. Pushed past the woman and her child. She shook her head at Alice, then her legs went out from under her, and she collapsed to the floor and buried her face in her hands and cried and screamed and kept repeating the same thing: *No. No. No.*

CHAPTER TWELVE

FEBRUARY 2011

The conductor's garbled voice announced over the PA system the train's pending arrival into Charlotte, right on schedule. The overhead lights flickered brighter in the train car, stirring passengers out of restless slumber. It was almost midnight and the city appeared fairly quiet. Glass towers all lit up but empty of nine-to-five office workers. Traffic lights blinked red, forcing the handful of cars and trucks on the city streets to four-way stops. A few intersections were active with women in short skirts smoking cigarettes, chatting with one another as they waited for their next client. Bouncers stood in front of bars, passively watching drunks stagger in and out. One street with closed-up storefronts had a large collection of the homeless, shopping carts filled with old jackets, bottles and cans, and cardboard shelters leaning askew.

The train shuttered to a stop, and a few passengers gathered their belongings and prepared to disembark. Alice's head leaned up against the glass, her eyes heavy. Tired. Hungover. Muddled. A few more stops, then she would get to Wilmington. From there, she'd take the bus down to Shallotte in the morning. Just a little farther.

Her eyes started to close; sleep so needed. Then she heard a commotion outside on the platform. A raised voice. Other passengers waiting to get off the train all turned and stared out the window. She saw two Charlotte police officers hustle down the platform and move in the direction of the commotion. They moved quickly. Something or *someone* had their attention. Alice craned her head forward to get a better look. An Amtrak conductor was in a heated conversation with an irate passenger. The police officers approached the official and he gestured toward the train. Then Alice spotted the man with the ponytail. He was pacing the platform, swearing at the conductor. Then got into it with the cops.

Alice bolted upright, heart hitching in her chest. She should have known better. Problems don't just go away. They only get worse. Should have just minded her own damn business. What did she really expect? That the guy would never get out of the bathroom? That he wouldn't be pissed and expect some kind of payback? The cops would have questions—about breaking the guy's nose, about tying him up in a bathroom. It wouldn't matter what he had tried to do to the girl. Questions would be asked. Questions Alice didn't want to answer.

Alice felt Delilah's eyes on her again, watching as she grabbed her duffel bag and readied herself to exit the train.

"You getting off here?"

"Yep." Alice saw the disappointment in the young girl's big blue eyes.

"You have family here or something?"

"Nope."

"Oh. You live here?"

Alice took a quick glance out the window. The cops were still pre-occupied with Buddy, trying to calm him down. Alice sighed, reached into the duffel bag, peeled five twenties from a stack. She grabbed the girl by the wrist and shoved the wad of twenties into her palm. "Go home, Delilah."

Alice slung the duffel bag over her shoulder and slipped down the aisle, going in the opposite direction of Buddy and the cops. Hopefully, it would take a little while to sort through his story.

She didn't look back. Just kept her head down and made her way toward the last car. The aisle was clogged with passengers trying to get off the train. Everybody moving too damn slow. She shoved past an old man, and he almost fell into an empty seat. He said something, but Alice kept moving faster. She came to the last car and peeked out the exit. No sign of Buddy or the cops out on the platform. She stepped out of the train and moved quickly toward the station. Not too many people to blend in with. Needed to get out onto the street and disappear into the city.

The cops would talk to the girl. Get her version of the story. But she didn't do anything wrong. Not really. Just young and naïve and a big target to guys like Buddy. Alice knew that Delilah wouldn't go back home. *She* certainly didn't go back home when she should have, and how she was still drawing breath could only be chalked up to sheer dumb luck. And if Delilah didn't get a little of that, she'd end up pregnant or dead—or both.

Not your problem, Alice told herself. *Not your problem.*

CHAPTER THIRTEEN

Sinclair waited for the giant to open the office door to the Comfort Manor and casually hummed a tune. "Camptown Races," a song that he learned growing up, first singing it in music class when he might have been eight or nine years old. The simple melody had always stuck with him, even though he couldn't remember all the lyrics. The tune was his form of mental yoga, de-stressing and calming his mind when the outside world became a bit more unpredictable and chaotic than he preferred. He didn't appear to be in a hurry or particularly anxious about the fact that someone had stolen ninety-one thousand dollars from him—and that the very same person had walked out of Terry's trailer with the cash—and had, for whatever reason, decided to leave the drugs behind. A bit puzzling to Sinclair, but he intended to get it all sorted out soon enough. He nodded his appreciation to the large man—a constant companion—who held the door open for him.

"Thank you, Phillip. You can wait outside, if you please. Stay by the window where I can see you. Shouldn't take me much more than a minute or two."

Phillip grunted that he understood.

Earlier, they had driven past Terry's trailer and discovered it still swarmed with Harrisburg's finest. Everything taped off—the doors, the driveway, the entire perimeter of the lot. Detectives and forensic teams milled about, going over every inch of the trailer with a fine-tooth comb. Physical access to Terry's deplorable tin box of a home would not be possible in the foreseeable future. But for Sinclair, this would not be problematic. One simple phone call would answer his questions about what had been discovered, or more accurately *not discovered*, in the trailer—the advantage of having someone inside the department on a retainer of sorts. Information was a valuable commodity. Maybe not to the extent of his product and the cash it produced, but invaluable nonetheless.

Uncle Henry and Pig were dead. Sinclair was disappointed to lose two of his best men—loyal help was difficult to secure—but he was comforted by the knowledge that they managed to take down two cops in the shoot-out. Terry was dead as well. His drugs scattered about the trailer. But no money. Terry's transgression nowhere to be found.

Sinclair crossed the tiny lobby—not much bigger than a small bedroom—and stepped up to the plexiglass-protected front desk. This was the sixth deplorable motel that he and Phillip had visited in the last few hours. They were all the same: filthy and smelled of rotting fruit. He was eager to step into a hot shower and scrub the stink from his skin. Sinclair took a deep breath. Attempted to push this thought aside. He took solace in the understanding that it was only a matter of time before he approached the front desk he was searching for—that he would find this young woman named Alice. Sinclair was quite confident of that fact.

* * *

Ernie stood behind the front desk licking envelopes. He'd been at it for the last thirty minutes. Paying bills for the Comfort Manor fell to him, a responsibility that he didn't mind—he was considered *management*—but he hated those envelopes that required licking; and there were still two large boxes left, purchased by the previous manager many years ago. Ernie had considered on more than one occasion just tossing the boxes into the dumpster so that he could purchase new envelopes with self-adhesive peel-off strips that didn't taste like a sink full of dirty dishwater. That sure would be nice. He could use Scotch tape and avoid the whole licking process—this thought crossed his mind on a few occasions as well—but in the long run, licking seemed faster than tearing off strips of tape. At least the stamps were the self-adhesive kind.

Ernie noticed the small man enter—or maybe it was a scrawny teenager. All kinds traipsed into the Manor, so he tried not to judge. He licked another envelope, then glanced through the plexiglass toward the petite man.

"Help you?" Ernie asked.

"I certainly hope so."

"Get you a room?"

Sinclair visibly grimaced. "No. That won't be necessary. I'm here to inquire about a certain young lady, early to mid-twenties, that I suspect might be spending her nights here. Alice is her name." Sinclair started to place his manicured fingers on top of the counter, but after a quick glance at the grime-streaked Formica, decided it best to let his hands fall to his sides instead.

Ernie stared at him through the comfort of the plexiglass. Lick, seal. Lick, seal. "A friend of yours?"

Sinclair smiled, revealing his plastic mannequin grin, and shook his head back and forth emphatically. "No. No, she is not."

Ernie had been through this drill a few times over. "Yeah, well, I'm not allowed to . . ."

Sinclair waved away Ernie's words. "I understand all that. I really do. But time is of the essence. Are you the manager?"

Ernie took a drink of water. All the licking made his lips dry. "Assistant manager."

"Is there another manager on duty?"

"No. Just me."

"Then I suppose that you will have to do." Sinclair stepped a little closer to the plexiglass and spoke with a tone of great confidence. "This person. Alice. She has taken something of mine that is of great value, and it's rather imperative that I find her as quickly as possible. If she resides here, short of her actually being in a room here at the Casual Manor, I'm hoping to find something that will give me some sort of an indication of where she might be."

Lick, seal. "*Comfort* Manor," Ernie said. Lick, seal.

"Pardon me?"

"It's Comfort Manor. Not Casual Manor," Ernie corrected.

"My mistake. Comfort Manor." Sinclair withdrew his money clip and held it out in front of him so that Ernie could see the entire wad of cash. He peeled off three one-hundred-dollar bills and spread them out neatly on the Formica countertop, then pointed out the window toward where Phillip was standing. Phillip stood facing the window, close to the glass—close enough that his breath fogged up the pane of glass.

"That is my dear friend Phillip. Quite a large man, as you can plainly see." Sinclair tapped the three bills on the countertop. "This is what I'd like to propose. In exchange for these three one-hundred-dollar bills, I'd like to take a quick peek into Alice's room."

"I didn't say she stayed here," Ernie offered. Lick, seal.

"You didn't have to."

"Look. I got work to do. So." He licked and sealed to illustrate his point.

"I understand. We all have jobs to do. What is your name, please?" Sinclair asked.

"Ernie." Lick, seal.

"Ernie. Short for Ernest, I presume."

Ernie stared at Sinclair like this was the first he had ever heard of such a thing.

"In any regard, my uncle's name was Ernest. He worked as a mechanic and much preferred the company of an automobile to that of an actual human being. Died a few years back as the result of a brain tumor. Wish I could say that I miss him, but I do not." Sinclair tapped the cash again with his index finger. "Now, here's the situation, Ernie. If you choose not to accept my offer and decline to show me Alice's room, I will have Phillip come inside and crush your testicles with his bare hand."

Sinclair maintained his mannequin-like grin.

Ernie stopped licking. Stopped sealing. "Huh?"

"Phillip has crushed testicles before. I have seen it."

Ernie looked past the small man and out toward Phillip. "Look. I don't think . . . You can't get through the plexiglass." But Ernie's voice lacked any trace of conviction.

"True. But Phillip will wait for you to get off work. And if you choose to call the police, Phillip will wait for the police to leave, and then he will crush your testicles. He is a patient man. He will wait for you."

Ernie stared back at Sinclair.

"Three hundred dollars for two minutes of your time, Ernie. You stand to make one hundred and fifty dollars per minute. We will neither touch nor remove anything from Alice's room, I might add. Three hundred dollars. Or shall I go and talk to Phillip?"

Ernie set the envelope he had yet to lick down on the desk. He didn't particularly want to have his testicles crushed. "Give me a second. I'll go grab the key."

* * *

The hotel room was just as Alice had left it—the mattress stripped bare and the dresser drawers yanked open. The shoebox-sized room still smelled of booze and cigarettes. The curtains were drawn and the overhead light didn't work, making the space feel like a cave for a wild animal.

Sinclair held a clean, starched handkerchief over his nose and mouth, glanced around the room, and watched Phillip search for anything of interest. While he waited, Sinclair removed his handkerchief for a moment so that he could light a cigarette, then alternated between puffing and covering his mouth and nose with the crisp white cloth.

Ernie fidgeted in the doorway and kept glancing over his shoulder. He tugged on his Mister Rogers sweater, more out of nervousness and for something to do with his hands. He watched Phillip work the room, thudding around like a caged gorilla. "Alice said that she'd be gone for a few days," he offered. "Going to Allentown is what she said. For a few days."

"Hmmm," Sinclair mused.

Phillip flipped over the mattress.

"Do you really have to do that?" Ernie protested with a less-than-forceful tone.

Phillip proceeded to flip over the box spring.

"Alice said she was going to go see a friend. A friend that was in some kind of trouble. Marriage problems. That's what she said." Ernie pulled on the cuffs of his sweater.

"Hmmm," Sinclair repeated.

Another hotel guest walked by, so Ernie stepped inside the room and partially shut the door behind him in order to block the view. "I don't think you're gonna find anything. Do you? Do you think you'll find something?"

"We shall soon see," Sinclair replied.

"What did she take from you, anyways? Alice. What did she take?"

"My pride, for one." Sinclair sucked on his cigarette like a piece of candy. "Do you think Alice lied to you, Ernie? About Allentown?"

Ernie worked on his collar now. "I don't know. I guess. Maybe. Do you?"

Sinclair sat down on a shabby chair beside the window, his feet dangling an inch off the floor. He held up his cigarette, an ash ready to tumble and fall, and Phillip quickly found an ashtray and held it below the man's burning stick. Sinclair tapped the ash and let out a long, disappointed sigh.

"It's not easy. I tell you, Ernie, it's not easy. Running your own business. Always something. Especially a business such as mine."

Ernie nodded like he understood perfectly.

"Check the bathroom again, Phillip."

Phillip nodded like a good servant and lumbered into the bathroom.

Sinclair glanced around at his surroundings and shuddered. "How much is a room here at the Comfort Manor, Ernie? What do people pay for these kinds of accommodations?"

"Well. Some people just pay by the hour. For. You know. Twenty for that. Fifty for the night."

"Ah. And after the hourly type of visits, are the linens stripped and replaced?"

Ernie nodded. Then shook his head. "Sometimes."

"Fascinating. Truly. Our society, certain aspects of it, completely perplex me. What about you? Do you find it compelling? Or are you merely immune to it by now?"

Ernie shrugged. "I don't know. I guess. Don't really think about it."

"Of course, you don't."

Ernie glanced toward the bathroom. "Are you guys almost done here? I should get back to work."

"In a moment, Ernie. In a moment." Sinclair wiped off some ash that had fallen on his pant leg. "Here's the thing, Ernie. I offer a product that is . . . *sensitive*. I guess that's the best way to describe it. And along with the sensitive nature of my product, I deal with some rather unpredictable people. People that are unstable, desperate, greedy, and quite frankly, morally bankrupt. It comes with the territory, and I signed on the dotted line. I shouldn't complain. I really shouldn't. I make a tremendous amount of money. More in two weeks than you do in over a year, I'm willing to wager."

Ernie looked like he wanted to crawl right out of his Mister Rogers sweater. He remained close to the door, continually glancing over his shoulder. "Okay."

Something shattered in the bathroom. Possibly a glass. Maybe the mirror.

"Your friend just broke something. He's gonna have to pay for that. Somebody will have to pay for it. I don't want to get in trouble," Ernie stated.

Sinclair studied Ernie for a moment. Really scrutinized him. From head to toe. A trace of a smile curved at the edges of his delicate lips. "Tell me something, Ernie. Do you like what you do? And be honest with me. Does this kind of work fulfill you? Does it allow you a sense of accomplishment?"

Ernie glanced toward the bathroom again—Phillip removed the top of the toilet basin and stuck his hand in the water. Ernie stared back at Sinclair, not really sure how to answer that kind of question. "It's all right, I guess. Pays the bills."

"Just *all right*? And is that enough for you, Ernie? Just paying the bills. Barely scraping by. A hand-to-mouth existence. Living in some kind of shabby little studio apartment where the heater probably blows cold and the AC blows hot. Shopping for canned fruit and vegetables at the 99-Cent store. Clothes from Goodwill. That doesn't sound *all right* to me. Directly the opposite, if you were to ask me."

Ernie shrugged—he'd never looked at his life in those kinds of terms. "I should get back to the office now."

Sinclair stabbed his cigarette out in the ashtray. "Should you?"

Ernie nodded that he should.

"Humor me for a moment, Ernie."

Ernie didn't know exactly what he meant by that. "I gotta finish with the bills. I'm responsible for them. You know?"

"Forget the bills, Ernie. For the time being."

Phillip walked back into the room. Shook his head at Sinclair.

"I am seeking any and all information pertaining to Alice. Would you share with me all that you might know?"

"I don't know anything about Alice. Not really. Why would you think that I do?"

"Because, Ernie, when I look at you, I see a man that is curious. I also see a man that has crossed the line into a state of utter loneliness. When you combine those two conditions, it creates the irresistible compulsion to insert yourself into someone else's life that you desperately want to be part of. Do you follow?"

Ernie glanced over his shoulder again. "No. Not really."

"Fine. In the plainest of terms, I'm willing to bet that you eavesdrop and snoop on the affairs of others. I think that you know more about Alice than you're letting on."

Ernie's ears burned bright, but he shook his head. "I think that you should call the police if Alice stole something from you."

"Well, unfortunately, that's something that I can't frankly do at this point in time."

"I'm sorry. But. This doesn't feel right. All these questions about Alice." Ernie edged himself closer to the door. "I think that maybe I should give your three hundred bucks back and call the police."

Phillip lumbered forward, grabbed Ernie by his scrawny arm, and pulled him to the center of the room.

"Disappointing. That is not the type of cooperation that I was hoping to seek from you, Ernie."

Sinclair simply nodded at Phillip, who then closed the door, bolted the lock, and slid the safety chain into place.

CHAPTER FOURTEEN

The walk from the train station to downtown took over thirty minutes. And like every other American city center, certain areas of its downtown proved to be a big, bright neon light that seemed to attract all those desperate, hopeless souls forced to live upon the streets. In Charlotte, that section of town was near the Elmwood Cemetery, off of Eighth Street—close to the Urban Ministry Center, the Men's Shelter of Charlotte, and the main public library—a popular spot for the homeless, junkies, drunks, runaways—all the dregs of society. Most hung out in packs, smoking cigarettes and passing bottles back and forth. There were a few loners. Men in wheelchairs slumped under a heap of blankets. Stragglers that sat on the sidewalk, muttering to themselves and picking at their hair. And for every bail bondsman storefront, there were two liquor stores along with the street dwellers that loitered in front of them.

Alice held the duffel bag tight to her back and stepped into the Graham Street Liquor Mart, no different and no better than any of the other liquor stores other than it appeared to be empty, and she wasn't exactly in the mood to be social.

A bell chimed as she crossed the threshold into a world of bright, obnoxious fluorescent lighting. One of the overhead bulbs flickered and popped, and probably wouldn't get replaced any time soon. The store reeked of pork rinds and stale cigarette smoke, and Alice saw a good reason why. Perched behind a half-inch panel of plexiglass that ran the entire length of the right side of the store sat a massively obese man wearing wire-rim glasses with a cracked lens. He had no chin, just a tire of flesh that ran around his neck. Fat pink sausages for fingers, one hand holding a burning cigarette, the other dipping into a bag of barbecued pork rinds. He wore a stained, threadbare Carolina Panthers T-shirt, more gray than white. Despite all he had going against him, the man's hair was neatly trimmed and carefully combed. Even Alice had to admit that he had a nice head of hair.

She grabbed a bag of potato chips and a few candy bars—the kinds with nuts—and set her items up on the counter. The obese man licked his fingers but didn't bother to look up at her.

"You have any Crown?" Alice asked.

The obese man nodded that he did.

"Can I get a fifth of that?"

The obese man didn't answer. He was focused on ringing up her other items.

"Can I get a fifth of Crown?" Alice asked again.

"I heard you." The obese man sighed, then grunted as he stepped off the wooden stool that somehow managed to support his immense weight and searched the shelves for the Crown whiskey. He waddled down to the last shelf, grabbed a bottle of Crown Royal Black, and by the time he returned to his stool, he was slightly out of breath. He slammed the bottle onto the counter.

"Actually, I'd like a bottle of the Reserve. Treating myself tonight."

The obese man stared at the bottle of Crown Royal Black in his hand. "All we got is the Black."

Alice peered down the whiskey section and spotted a few bottles of Reserve up on the top shelf. "You got a few bottles up there. I'll take one of those."

The obese man followed her gaze and saw the bottles as well. "That's more expensive, that stuff is."

"Yeah, I know. That's okay."

The obese man still had not looked Alice in the eye. "That's up on the top shelf."

Alice just wanted to get her bottle, crack the seal, and have a long drink. A few of them. "Guess that's why they call it *top shelf.*"

The obese man shook his head. "Yeah. I can't reach up there. So."

Alice waited for him to finish his sentence. He didn't. "So?"

"*So*, I can't reach it."

Alice knew that she should just get the bottle of Black, but after the day she had, the things she witnessed, she wanted the Reserve. No, she *deserved* it. "How about I come back there and grab it myself then?"

The obese man finally looked at Alice dead-on, all serious. "You can't come back here." He readjusted his glasses and repeated himself again. "You can't come back here."

"Can't? Or you won't let me?"

"Employees only back here. Store policy."

Alice wondered why she was forced to deal with so many assholes today. "Gotcha. And is it also store policy for you to sit around and smoke cigarettes? Is that store policy, too?"

The obese man's bored expression didn't change. "You got some attitude, lady."

"Yeah, I've heard."

They both stood there a moment. No love lost between them.

"Well? Do you want the bottle of Black or what?"

"No. The bottle of Reserve is what I *want.*"

To demonstrate that the subject was closed to further debate, the obese man took his seat back on the stool and dipped his pudgy fingers back into the bag of pork rinds.

Alice sighed. Ran her fingers through her hair. "Look, man. I'm having a shit day."

"Welcome to the club."

"Right." Alice tried again. Different tactic. "After a bad day, a really bad day where absolutely everything goes wrong, have you ever had your heart set on something? Something that you really want? And it's right there in front of you."

"Every single day."

"Come on. Whatever happened to Southern hospitality?"

The obese man crunched on a handful of pork rinds, then lit up another cigarette. "I don't know. You tell me."

"Fine. I'll take the Black. A pack of Marlboro Reds, too. If you think you can manage that."

The obese man grabbed a pack of Reds.

"Got any matches?"

"Nope. Just ran out."

"I bet you did."

The man smirked—he was the king of the castle. "Got some lighters."

"Sure . . . if you think you can reach them."

The obese man lost his grin, then took his own sweet time ringing up her items and bagging them in a black plastic bag with a hole in the bottom, the entire time smoking his cigarette and munching on pork rinds.

* * *

Delilah pressed against a closed electronics storefront window as she searched the sidewalk that teemed with street people. Mainly men dressed in dirty rags for clothes, hanging out in packs. Everybody seemed to be drunk or tweaking on something. She felt like all eyes were on her. Staring at her. Sensing that she was desperate and alone and in a foreign place, ripe for the picking.

The young girl felt jumpy and was breathing hard, but didn't want it to show. She avoided direct eye contact and kept searching the sidewalk. Delilah had seen the woman from the train go into the liquor store and come out a few minutes later. She kept following her, but when she turned the corner, the woman just disappeared into the night.

Delilah chewed on a wad of gum that had lost all of its flavor and tried to fight back the tears that seemed inevitable. She'd never been this far from home. Never out of the state of Pennsylvania. Never walked alone on the streets this late. Never faced the distinct possibility of sleeping in an alley or park bench. All she had was the money the woman on the train gave her, but how long could a hundred dollars last? She wasn't prepared for all this. Not even remotely. She never thought any of this through. It all happened so damn fast. She found the gun, did what she had to do, and ran out her front door, never looking back, or saying anything to her mama, or even getting the chance to tell Dwayne goodbye. She took off running down the streets, passing stores and fast-food restaurants and bars that she'd known all her life. She didn't stop running until she got to the 30th Street station. All that she knew was that she had to get out of Philly and go somewhere. Anywhere.

Maybe she should head back to the train station. Maybe she could sleep there—it had to be safer than out here on the streets. She glanced to her left, then the right, not sure where she was exactly. She hadn't paid attention to where she was going when she scurried out of the Amtrak station.

She heard a group of men laughing. She stole a quick glance and saw that they were staring right at her, their eyes burning with unkind intentions. When Delilah looked away, they laughed even harder.

"You looking for me?"

Delilah snapped toward the voice—Alice stood a few feet away, holding the duffel bag in one hand, a black plastic bag in the other.

"What do you want exactly?" Alice asked.

Delilah couldn't hold Alice's gaze—she stared down at her feet instead. "I followed you."

"I know. You were pretty obvious."

"I didn't know where else to go," Delilah answered, voice cracking and breaking.

"Kinda figured that, too."

A few tears started to leak down the girl's cheeks.

"Jesus. Don't do that. These guys will eat you alive out here."

Delilah wiped at her face. Tried to catch her breath. "Sorry."

Alice didn't budge. Just stared at the girl for a moment.

"So?" Delilah said.

"So?" Alice answered.

"I'm scared. I don't know what to do."

"Look. God damn it. What do you want from me? I'm not your babysitter, so why don't you just go back to the train station and just leave me alone?"

Delilah nodded but didn't move. "I know. But. You seem smart and I was thinking—"

"I'm not and don't. Just go away. Please. I don't need this crap. I really don't."

"That guy on the train called the cops."

"Good for him."

"They were looking for you."

"Yeah? Looks like you found me instead."

"I didn't tell them anything. The cops," Delilah offered.

"Okay. Am I supposed to owe you something now?"

"No. Just wanted you to know. That I didn't say anything."

"Great. I'm all clear."

Alice set her duffel bag on the sidewalk, took out her pack of cig-arettes, tapped one loose, and fired it up. She let out a cloud of smoke, shook her head for a moment. "This is bullshit." She picked up the duffel bag, readjusted the strap on her shoulder, and started walking. After a few steps, she glanced back at Delilah.

"You coming or what?"

* * *

Delilah walked three paces behind Alice, never uttering a peep. She didn't ask what they were doing or where they were headed, and Alice offered no kind of explanation. Alice chain-smoked, never slowing her stride, while Delilah worked on a wad of gum and did her best to keep up.

Alice finally stopped in front of the Clover Motel. It happened to be the first motel she walked past. She'd look for comfort tomorrow. Tonight, she just wanted to get drunk. Sooner rather than later.

"Wait here," Alice instructed the girl.

"What are we doing?"

"Just wait here." And Alice stepped inside the tiny lobby.

Like the liquor store, the guy in charge sat behind yet another thick panel of plexiglass. *Must be the neighborhood*, Alice thought. But unlike the man at the liquor store, the guy running the front desk looked completely emaciated and sick. HIV-sick maybe. Either that or a meth-head. Alice had seen enough of them to know what they looked like. The guy had dark rings around sunken eyes and a half dozen fresh lesions dotting his shaved head, mainly around his ears. They looked picked at. The worst one, about the size of a dime, oozed with infection. Alice tried not to stare at it. The guy twitched and blinked rapid-fire, and sucked on a menthol cigarette like it was a race to finish it.

Yeah. Meth-head.

"How many hours?" the meth-head asked, but kept his eyes focused on a television that sat on the counter.

"Overnight."

Alice heard someone else cough in the office behind the meth-head. Someone else moving around in the dark. She spotted a waft of white smoke curling in the air behind the meth-head. Someone coughed again, then Alice could smell the distinct odor of something like burning plastic. She didn't think much of it. Didn't really care about anything other than getting a room and pouring a drink.

The meth-head stabbed out his cigarette, then went about lighting up another. "Sixty for the night."

"The sign says forty-nine."

The meth-head shrugged. "Guess they didn't change it yet."

Alice had to laugh. "Of course they didn't."

Meth-head worked on his new cigarette. "Sixty. Cash up front."

"Got a room at the end of the building?"

"Got room 212," meth-head said.

"That at the end of the building?"

Ash dropped from the tip of his cigarette onto his concaved chest, but if the meth-head noticed, he didn't care. "You want the room or not?"

What Alice really wanted to do was to drift away into a dull haze—she was feeling that all-consuming desire to feed the beast. Besides, what was sixty bucks when she had over ninety thousand dollars hanging off her shoulder?

The meth-head's eyes tracked Alice as she reached into her duffel bag and grabbed some cash, and his face twitched.

She slid three twenties through the plexiglass window, noticed that when the meth-head grabbed a key from a box, it was filled with other keys. The place was damn near vacant.

"Checkout is eleven," he stated.

"It's already after midnight. Can you at least give me 'til noon?"

Meth-head shrugged. "Sure. You can pay for the extra hour if you want."

Alice grabbed the key and went outside to where Delilah stood waiting—the girl hadn't budged an inch.

"We staying here? In this place?" the girl asked.

"If you have a better option lined up, please, by all means."

Delilah mumbled *sorry* and watched as Alice walked up the stairs to the second floor. She looked toward the street for a moment as if weighing her options, then ran after Alice to catch up.

When Alice found her room, it was right in the middle of the building. *God damned meth-head.*

CHAPTER FIFTEEN

NOVEMBER 2005

The moon, near full, hung behind a wall of dense, towering clouds that threatened to crack open and deliver more rain. A crisp wind picked up even harder, and Alice could feel the moisture on her face. The rain was coming. Pretty close now.

She had trudged alongside Highway 17 for half the day, just off the road, but far enough away that a passing State Trooper wouldn't spot her in the woods. Twelve hours walking nonstop. The blisters started forming after hour three—in between her big toe on both feet. After a few more hours of treading the uneven ground off of the highway, Alice felt the blisters pop and the warm liquid spread inside her socks. But she kept walking and walking, leaving Wilmington, her parents, her friends, everything but the memories of Jason behind her.

A jag of lightning glowed white for a split second, and Alice counted silently.

One, two, three, four—BOOM. Thunder rumbled up in the sky, and Alice could feel the vibrations in the air. She didn't even get to five. Five seconds equaled one mile. That was what her dad told her. That meant that the storm wasn't even a mile away. More rain, then the November night would get even colder.

She walked down the sidewalk in the small town, every store and shop on Shallotte's Main Street closed and locked up tight. A hardware store, grocery mart, a beauty salon, a secondhand clothing shop, the post office and bank, a few other shops that had gone out of business. She passed by Stan's Pub, a neon Budweiser sign glowing red in the window. She heard some laughter coming from inside. Could smell the cigarette smoke and draft beer. Alice ducked past the front door and kept her feet moving.

No cars or trucks rumbled down the main strip. Most of the homes on Main Street didn't have their porch lights on. It was like everyone up and disappeared.

Alice stopped in front of one of the few restaurants in town. Lucy's Diner—also closed. She stared at the specials board next to the front door and read down the list—softshell crab sandwich, beer-battered fried shrimp, oyster Po' Boy, pulled pork sandwich, lots of dishes covered in gravy. Everything sounded good. Her stomach grumbled and complained, demanding something other than the five or six Snickers bars she'd wolfed down over the last twelve hours.

The clouds overhead got darker, thicker, blacker by the second, and started to spit rain.

Alice shifted her backpack to her other shoulder, stared down both directions of the road, and checked for police cars. Main Street was a ghost town, and Alice doubted that a small town like Shallotte would even have cops.

Thunder boomed again and then it was as if the sky had been sliced open by an invisible box cutter as the rain began to pound down on the sidewalk and road in dime-sized pellets. Alice ducked around the side of Lucy's Diner and searched for a place to escape the downpour. In the back of the restaurant, she stumbled upon a parking lot with a few rusted-out cars, a stack of tires with the treads worn thin, and a bunch of cardboard boxes leaning against a big blue dumpster. Alice tried opening each car, but they were all locked or stuck shut. It kept raining, harder and harder. There was a dark mass of woods at the far end of the parking lot where the trees grew thick and dense. Alice could hear the slow, churning water of the Shallotte River off somewhere in the distance.

With rain pelting at her cheeks and stinging her eyes, Alice sprinted across puddles of water toward the dumpster pressed up against the back brick wall of the diner. She stepped in a patch of bacon grease leaking out from the bottom of the dumpster, and her feet went out from under her and she came down hard. She threw her hands out to stop her fall, but landed face-first, and skidded across the asphalt. As she rolled on the pavement, her backpack tore open, spewing her clothes all over the hard, wet ground.

She tried to stand up, but fell again, this time landing on her back. As the rain pelted down on top of her, she looked at the palms of her hands, chewed up by the asphalt, skin pulled back, tiny pieces of gravel pressing into her flesh. The rain kept pounding harder, the wind howling and snapping at the trees that loomed all around.

Alice scrambled to her hands and knees, stuffed her clothing into her backpack, all of it soaking wet and weighing five times its normal weight. Then she crawled through the puddles and bacon grease and squeezed herself between the dumpster and the back wall of Lucy's Diner.

Rainwater gushed out of a leaking gutter, rolled down the brick like a waterfall, and splattered all around Alice's huddled frame. She pulled tight into a ball, but the water found every inch of her, soaking her clothes and hair, and stinging the torn skin on her palms.

Alice listened to the rain and shrieking wind and thought about her room at home. Her bed and blankets, and how warm and dry and safe it must be. She thought about her parents. What they were doing right at that moment. What they must be feeling after finding the letter she left behind. She had written a half dozen different notes with a half dozen different explanations, but she'd tossed them all away. It didn't matter that she felt guilty and sad, or that she wished she hadn't yelled at Jason and said what she said, or that she knew she should have gone and checked on him sooner. None of that mattered anymore. And it didn't matter where she was running off to, or how she would be able to take care of herself, or if she'd ever come back home again. She tried writing and explaining all those things, but after reading each note, she crumpled up the paper and threw them away. Then, finally, she wrote what had to be said, nothing more. *I'm going away. It's better for everyone.*

Alice stared at the cuts on her palms, watched the rain wash some of the blood away, and she began to cry. She cried from the pain and the cold. She cried from missing her home and parents and her friends, from knowing that she'd never see any of them ever again. She cried because she was scared and alone and didn't know where she was going to go. She cried because everything that she'd become and wanted to be was over—her life died in that dryer that day, too. But most of all, she cried for Jason.

The rain didn't let up. It continued to fall, beating against the pavement and the metal sides of the dumpster, drowning out Alice's chest-pounding sobs. She slid down on her side, curled into a tighter ball, and let it all pour out of her until her body couldn't bear anymore, and finally somehow gave in to sleep.

* * *

Alice's temporary escape from reality was interrupted by the sensation of something tiny, but quick crawling across her legs. A little *poke, poke, poke.* She jerked awake and noticed a thin brown tail disappear under the dumpster.

Before Alice could even let out a scream into the slow falling drizzle, an intense beam of light flashed on her face from the edge of the dumpster.

"Just what the hell are you doing back there, little lady?"

She could tell by the nasal twang that the voice came from an older man, phlegm clicking in his throat.

"Well, don't just sit there gawking at me. Get yourself out of there," the man snapped.

Alice lifted her hand to shield her face so she could get a look at the stranger, but the light stayed right on her, unwavering.

"Don't make me yank you out of there. I'm too damn old for that kind of nonsense."

Alice thought about crawling out the other side of the dumpster, leaving her backpack behind, and running off into the night until she was far away from this town and the stranger holding the flashlight.

"I'm getting pretty damn soaked here. Come on, now."

Alice finally pushed her way out from behind the dumpster, dragging her backpack along with her.

"Well, what do we got here?" The light clicked off and Alice stared up at the stranger. Sixty-five years old, maybe older. Thick around the waist, and most of the hair on the top of his head long gone. He wore a pair of reading glasses with a little silver chain that wrapped around his neck. He stood dressed in an olive-green coverall suit with a white patch over the right breast that said ELTON.

"I'd have to say that you're about the biggest rat I ever did catch." The man grinned at Alice, took off his glasses, revealing a set of light blue eyes that were almost white, and soft red cheeks starting to sag south. "Just what the hell you doing back behind there, kiddo?"

"Nothing."

"Nothing?" He stuffed the flashlight in his back pocket. "Now why would you be doing *nothing* back behind a dumpster this time of night, and in the middle of a rainstorm?"

Alice shrugged.

The man clutched a black plastic box with a hole on one side in his left hand. When he set it down on the ground, something shifted inside the box. "What's your name, kiddo?"

Alice didn't answer his question. She stared past him toward a white pickup truck that idled behind him. On the side of the truck's driver's-side door, black lettering spelled out PARSON'S PEST CONTROL.

"You got a tongue inside that chattering mouth of yours or not?" he asked.

Alice nodded.

"Well?"

"Alice."

"Alice, huh? Tell me something, Alice in Wonderland, you like rats?"

"No."

"Well then, you picked the exact wrong spot to take yourself a nap. Rats like dumpsters to eat in and old tires to nest in."

Alice took an automatic step away from both the dumpster and stack of tires.

The man let out a little chuckle and snorted through a bulbous cartoon nose. "You don't live here in Shallotte, do you, Alice?"

"No."

"Didn't think so. I know damn near everyone here in town, which is kind of unfortunate."

The rain started to fall a little harder again. Picking up speed and dancing down on top of both of them.

"You gonna tell me exactly why a young gal like yourself is hiding back here behind Lucy's?"

Alice shook her head.

"I figured as much." He put his reading glasses back on. "I tell you what, Alice. I'm gonna go collect a few more of these here rat traps. Shouldn't take much more than five or ten minutes. I don't know nothing about runaway teenagers, but if you want to get yourself dry and something to eat other than rat pellets, you go on and climb in the passenger seat of my truck. After I'm done with what's expected of me around here, I'm calling it a night. So, it's up to you. If you're in my truck when I'm done, that's all fine and dandy. If you want to run off into the dark and rain and cold, that's up to you as well. That make any sense?"

Alice nodded.

"Good." He picked up his black box again. "Now if you decide on the latter, I'd keep clear of those woods if I was you. Coyotes tend to roam next to the river at night. Searching for food and whatnot."

With that being said, Elton took the flashlight out of his back pocket, flicked it on, then marched past Alice and disappeared into a wall of mist.

Alice stood under the drizzle for a few moments, watching the spot where Elton had slipped into the darkness. She glanced toward the woods that led to the river, then back over at the old man's truck.

CHAPTER SIXTEEN

The c h a i r h a d been precisely situated in the center of the room and Ernie sank deep into the tattered cushions like he wanted to disappear. His eyes were rimmed red, incessantly glancing toward the door, silently praying that someone, anyone, would come to his rescue. But that wasn't going to happen. The maids were gone for the day, and even if they weren't, they probably wouldn't lift a finger to help him. He was both disliked and ignored by those around him—it's the way it had always been for Ernie.

Phillip stood behind the assistant manager, both his massive paws resting on Ernie's shoulders, keeping him securely in place. Sinclair stood directly in front of Ernie, smoking on yet another cigarette, staring at him, waiting.

"I told you, I don't know anything about Alice," Ernie whispered, his voice hoarse and trembling.

"Yes, you did. Repeatedly. But I think that you do. You merely need assistance—a little nudge—in dislodging pertinent information."

Ernie wiped at his nose and his eyes kept darting toward the motel door. "Why are you doing this? It's not right. What you're doing is scaring me."

"Not quite, Ernie. What you're experiencing is anxiety. Like William Barrett once said, 'Anxiety is not fear, being afraid of this or that definite object, but the uncanny feeling of being afraid of nothing at all. It is precisely nothingness that makes itself present and felt as the object of our dread.'"

Ernie stared at Sinclair, his face blank and unresponsive.

"I take it that you do not know who William Barrett is?"

Ernie shook his head, his eyes watering up.

Sinclair sighed, woefully resigned. "Does no one visit the library anymore?" He inhaled deeply on his Salem. "You are here, Ernie, as it appears to be the only means to extricate the information you have about Alice."

"But I don't know nothing."

"Don't know *anything*," Sinclair corrected. "Your grammar is appalling."

"Sorry, but I don't know anything."

"You have stated that repeatedly, and if that truly is the case, then I will apologize to you with all due sincerity after our conversation and send you on your way."

Sinclair drew on his cigarette and blew out a plume of smoke. "So, then, think deep and hard. This is your moment to shine. To impress me, rather than to disappoint. What else can you tell me about our friend Alice?"

When Ernie squirmed and tried to stand up, Phillip applied pressure on his shoulders and neck. He settled back into the chair, albeit reluctantly. "Like what?"

"Tell me what you know about her, Ernie. Little things. Start with that, and we'll see where we go from there."

"Well. She's pretty. Not like a model or anything, but she's pretty."

"Okay. Keep going."

"Kinda keeps to herself, but seems nice enough. Doesn't talk much."

"Right. That's vague. Not helpful," Sinclair said.

"I guess I just don't know much about Alice. Not really. I'm sorry."

"Don't be sorry, Ernie. It shows weakness."

"Sorry. I really am. I just want to go. Can I go?"

"How long have you known Alice?"

"Five or six months, I guess."

"Uh-huh. And did you ever have relations with Alice?"

"Relations? What do you mean?"

"You know what I mean, Ernie."

"No. Nothing like that. We talked. That's about it."

"Okay. Just friendly encounters then?"

"I guess."

"And do you like her, Ernie? Are you keen on Alice?"

Ernie fidgeted in the chair. His face reddened a bit.

"You are. You like this girl."

Ernie shrugged. "Well. Like I said, she's nice. But I don't think she likes me. Not in that kind of way."

"You never know, Ernie. Women are a funny bunch."

"I guess." But Ernie didn't seem altogether convinced.

"What else can you tell me? Did Alice talk about friends, where she comes from, things of that nature?"

"She didn't exactly talk a lot. You know? Just kinda came and went. Paid cash for the room every day. Worked at the Frisky Pony."

"Surely she must have told you something that might provide some manner of insight about who she is," Sinclair coaxed.

Ernie gave this some thought, trying to replay their conversations over in his mind. "I think she said she used to live in South Carolina. Or maybe it was North Carolina. One of the Carolinas. I always get them mixed up."

"Okay. That's something. A start, if you will. Do you recall where in the Carolinas perhaps? A city name?"

"I think it was near a beach because I think I remember her telling me she hates the sand. Kinda funny, huh? Living near the beach and hating the sand."

"Yes. Very funny," Sinclair said without a hint of a smile. "Did Alice ever bring friends back to the motel? A boyfriend maybe?"

"No. Never. Not that I saw anyways."

Sinclair took another hard pull on his cigarette. "My patience is growing precariously thin, Ernie. It truly is. I suggest you tell me something of value, or circumstances could really go south on us from here."

Ernie could feel Phillip increase the pressure on his neck and shoulders. "She said she was going to see a friend in Allentown for a few days. Remember? That's what she told me. Maybe you should look there."

Sinclair shook his head. "No. That was a lie."

"How do you know that?"

"Because I do business with liars every single day."

Ernie looked down at his hands and wanted desperately to chew on his fingernails. "What are you going to do to Alice when you find her? After you get your money back?"

"You needn't concern yourself with that matter, Ernie. All you need to know is that Alice will be better off after she returns my property."

"Okay. But, like, will she be in trouble or go to jail?"

"I think that perhaps we are done here." Sinclair glanced toward Phillip. Gave the big man a slight tilt of his head.

Ernie's eyes suddenly widened and he licked at his lips. "Oh, yeah. Something else. Alice was driving her friend's truck. I remember that now."

Sinclair pressed his hands together, as if in a moment of prayer. "Oh? Tell me about this truck, Ernie."

"It was a big black truck. A pickup. The kind with big tires."

"A Chevy perhaps? With tinted windows?"

"Yeah. I'm pretty sure. She said it was a friend's."

Sinclair smiled. Extinguished his cigarette.

"Can I go now? Are we finished?"

"Yes, Ernie. We are finished with you."

Ernie smiled as well. A sense of relief falling over him. He didn't see Phillip withdraw the black plastic bag from his back pocket. "Does that mean I get to keep the three hundred dollars?"

"Of course, Ernie. A deal is a deal," Sinclair whispered.

Phillip pulled the plastic bag over Ernie's head and cinched it tight. Ernie issued a muffled, startled yelp. Tried to stand but was forced back into the chair. The big man gripped the plastic bag tight around Ernie's throat and held him down with brutal hands as the motel clerk fought and kicked and thrashed in the chair.

Sinclair watched for a moment before lighting another cigarette, then stepped into the bathroom to relieve himself.

CHAPTER SEVENTEEN

The bottle of Crown—Black, not Reserve—that perched within easy reach on the nightstand remained a little over half-full. Alice had hoped that catching a good buzz would allow her to forget about the situation she had gotten herself into.

It hadn't. Not one damn bit. She *was* drunk—that much had happened—but she couldn't block out a thing, the events of the day playing over and over again in her head.

The sound of the shower's lousy water pressure came spitting out from the bathroom—Delilah had been in there for a half hour.

Good. She can stay in there all night for all I care.

Alice poured herself another drink.

Sleep wouldn't come. Too many scenarios kept spinning in her mind, even with the television blaring a *Judge Judy* rerun. Each scenario got her to one of two places—getting caught and going to prison, or winding up dead at the hands of whoever would be looking for their money. Somebody would be looking for that kind of cash. She would be traced back to the Frisky Pony and they would hunt her down.

This is so stupid. What the hell am I thinking?

She wasn't. At least not much. She poured another inch of Crown into her glass.

No one knows my last name.

That much was true. Alice never, ever used her last name. She worked for tips and a shit hourly rate that paid under the table at the Frisky Pony—no questions asked. She always used cash when paying for motels or skid row apartments in towns that she never stayed in for long. No credit cards. Never had one. Didn't even have a driver's license—she left home before reaching that particular milestone. But Alice knew how to drive. Not officially through the DMV. No, Alice had learned how to drive with a girl named Candy, back when she lived in Pittsburgh for a few months and cleaned apartments for a maid service. There was something about Candy, only twenty-four and already with three kids and pregnant with the fourth, that Alice liked, even though the woman was reckless and more than a little promiscuous. Candy would do anything for money. If a male client propositioned cash in exchange for a hand job or blow job, Candy accepted whatever offer came her way. And being pregnant didn't stop her either. Alice would keep cleaning the apartment as Candy went into the bedroom and serviced the men with her specialty—a two-fisted hand job.

Alice never said anything about the sex, and also knew that Candy would usually steal something from each apartment they cleaned: cash, earrings, necklaces, anything she could sell for extra money.

Despite how demeaning the job proved to be, it was actually a good time in Alice's life, hanging out with Candy. The mother to three was the closest thing Alice had to a friend since she ran away from home. That's what she *thought*, anyway. Alice learned otherwise one spring morning when she got called into the boss man's office. The boss man, an older man in his sixties from Armenia, with a thick accent and thicker lips, informed Alice that he knew what she had done, and that he wouldn't press charges if she just returned what she had stolen. Alice didn't know what the hell he was talking about and told him just that. The boss man sighed, said that Candy told him everything, and that if Alice wouldn't return the stolen items, then he would keep her pay for the last two weeks.

The boss man wouldn't accept Alice's contention that it was Candy who stole whatever was stolen. He said that Candy was honest and would never steal a thing. The boss man also happened to be a recipient of Candy's hand job special.

So, that was it for Pittsburgh. If anything, she walked away having learned two things: how to drive a car and not to fool herself into thinking she could make a real friend.

Alice drained her glass, still wishing she was drinking Crown Reserve, and finally let her eyes flutter closed. She listened as Judge Judy chastised the plaintiff for wanting to keep an engagement ring she clearly didn't honor in light of the fact she admitted to sleeping with the defendant's best friends—as in *plural*.

Judge Judy's voice started to drift away. Sleep so close.

Then the shower squeaked off and Delilah stepped out of the bathroom wrapped up in a towel. The girl stood beside the bed and stared down at Alice and waited until Alice opened her eyes.

"What?"

"So, I was wondering. Can we talk?"

* * *

Just when Alice thought Delilah to be a complete wallflower—a seen-but-not-heard kind of girl—she proved her dead wrong. The big-eyed kid started yapping up a storm the second she had stepped out of the bathroom.

Alice half-listened to bits and pieces of the girl's story. Born and raised in southwest Philly. Never met her father. Two younger brothers—both white—from two other fathers she never met either.

Bang, bang, bang. By the time her mother turned twenty, the woman had three kids. Delilah's youngest brother, Dwayne, had Down's syndrome and was forced to wear a bicycle helmet to protect his head. Still wore diapers at the age of eleven. "It's one thing," Delilah claimed, "to change a baby's diaper, but a twelve-year-old? Phew."

Her other brother, JJ, was only fourteen, but already running with a gang. Wearing the colors and inked up to demonstrate his loyalty. JJ dropped out of school and hung out at the basketball courts all day. He had already come home a few times with a busted lip, smashed nose, and black eyes. He told Delilah that his name wasn't JJ anymore. *Call me T-Bone*, he informed her.

Delilah tried to help out the best she could around the home, taking care of Dwayne, but she had wanted to finish school and get her degree. She knew that a diploma would be her only way out. Graduating would be the one thing that might save her from ending up just like her mother. And she would have, if it hadn't been for Leon, her mama's newest boyfriend. Leon was nothing but white trash, just like her mama. He didn't have a job. Said he couldn't work because of an alleged back injury he suffered years ago, but he sure could drink—*that* he could do.

Leon insisted on being served hand and foot by Delilah and her mama, but her mama was too messed up most of the time to even crawl out of bed in the morning. They collected some money from the State due to Dwayne's condition. That and the welfare. Leon had forced Delilah to quit school last fall so that she could stay home and take care of Dwayne full-time. Delilah stood up to him for the first time. Told him that he wasn't her father and that she was staying in school, and that proclamation resulted in a fat lip and a chipped front tooth, which she showed to Alice to illustrate her point. The girl never smiled, so it was the first time Alice had seen Delilah's teeth.

Alice listened to the same old story, the same old song and dance, and kept drinking her Crown, the whiskey going down like water. She started to finally doze off again when Delilah poked her on the shoulder.

"Someone's at the door."

Alice squinted over at the girl. Delilah sat perched on the other twin bed, and the girl pointed toward the door. She put one hand on her purse and still chewed the hell out of her gum.

"Someone's at the door," she repeated.

"Screw 'em." Alice's head was mush. She hadn't eaten anything substantial in God knows how long. Mainly a liquid diet for the last twenty-four hours.

"Shouldn't you go check?" Delilah snapped and chewed.

"You go check. Sleeping."

"Think it's the cops?" Delilah whispered.

Alice swung her legs off the bed. "Why would it be the cops? Thought you said you didn't say anything to them."

"I didn't."

"So why would it be the cops?"

Delilah didn't respond.

"The cops looking for you?"

"No," the girl answered with little conviction.

"Bullshit—" The word caught in Alice's throat as the dead bolt clicked open, and the door creaked forward.

"Someone's got a key to the room," Delilah moaned.

A man stepped inside. Maybe thirty years old, but he looked completely wrecked. He stood at an average height, but due to being so damn skinny, he seemed smaller. His ratty T-shirt hung off his frame like a sheet on a clothesline. Unwashed, matted hair clung to the sides of his head, which was dotted with half a dozen lesions. His eyes bulged from their sockets as he stared from Delilah to Alice. His body jerked and twitched, all strung out on something.

"Wrong room, asshole," Alice snapped.

The man took another step into the room. He held a key in one hand; the other hand hidden behind his back, clutching at something. "Where's it at?"

"Where's *what* at?" Alice said.

The man continued to search the room, eyes snapping opened and closed. He licked at dry lips, and when he swallowed, he winced as if in pain. "Your bag. Where you hiding your bag?"

Alice should have known better, but she was drunk and pissed off, a one-two combo that never helped her think straight. She reached to grab the junkie by his scrawny arm, when the man's hidden hand shot forward and something hard cracked her on the side of the head. Her vision blurred to streaks of white, and she dropped to the floor. A high-pitched squeal sliced through the haze in her head and a trickle of warm blood leaked down her neck.

Alice tried to get back to her feet, but she went right back down on her ass instead, and she could hear Delilah screaming nonsense through the ringing in her ears.

"Shut the fuck up," the junkie growled.

Alice peered up as the scrawny addict slammed the door closed behind him. In his right hand, he clutched a two-foot section of metal pipe. The piece of piping was rusted and corroded at each end, and he gripped it so tightly that all his scabby knuckles were bone-white.

He pointed the makeshift weapon at Delilah's face. "Sit down." His eyes twitched even faster.

Delilah complied. Backed up and dropped onto Alice's bed.

"I know you got money in that bag. Now where the fuck is it?"

Alice touched her ear, and then stared at the red stains on her fingertips. The squealing inside her head ratcheted up a few notches to an unbearable pitch. She tried to get to her feet again, but the junkie rammed his boot into her side. She felt a spark of pain flare from one of her ribs, and she rolled up into a ball, her face planted into the carpet that stank of cigarette smoke.

The junkie paced around the room, eyes wild, lips pulled back over rotting teeth. "I know you got money in that bag. We saw it. *We saw it.*"

Delilah jammed one hand over her mouth, trying to hold back the scream that wanted to erupt.

Alice tried to say something, but could barely catch her breath.

"Tell me where the fucking bag is!" The junkie grabbed the bottle of Crown off the nightstand and hurled it against the wall, glass shattering and falling like shards of rain.

He swung the piece of metal back toward Delilah, who couldn't hold back any longer, and started up with a desperate, high-pitched cry. "I'll fucking use this on you. Shut up and lay your ass down."

The girl tried to stifle her whimpering the best she could and curled up into a tight ball on top of the bed.

The junkie started to rip through the room—yanked open dresser drawers, flipped over the nightstand, checked the closet and under the beds, then he ducked into the bathroom. He kept mumbling to himself—half the words unintelligible, the other half obscene. Alice finally managed to haul herself back up to the sitting position and touched both sides of her head gingerly. When she breathed in, she could feel a sharp stab ripple up her side from the damaged rib. It felt like she had a six-inch steak knife sticking into her back.

Alice watched as the junkie stumbled out of the bathroom, toting the duffel bag. He kept the section of pipe clutched in his hand, dropped the bag on the other bed, and eased down the zipper. His snarl loosened, then slowly eased into a grin. "Shit." He kept licking at his lips.

Alice's head throbbed and her side shrieked out in pain, the entire room moving underneath her. She thought that she might vomit or pass out. Maybe both.

Delilah started up with the crying again. Little cat-like mews.

"Would you just shut the fuck up?"

Delilah slapped a hand over her mouth and bit down hard.

Alice brought her fingers to her face. Wiped at the blood. Everything spinning all around her. "*Please . . .*" She reached out for the duffel bag, but the junkie yanked it away from her and the man screamed like a trapped animal.

"This shit is mine now."

Alice lunged forward, grabbed the strap with one hand, and tried to tug the duffel bag from his grasp.

"Let it go, bitch."

But Alice wouldn't let go. Too much had happened. She wasn't about to let go.

The junkie screamed again. Tried to dislodge the strap of the bag out of her hands and shake Alice loose, but ended up dragging her across the floor instead. "Let it go!"

Alice clung to the duffel bag strap and heard Delilah screaming at her to *Let it go, let it go, let it go.*

"Goddammit," the junkie hissed. He dropped down on Alice's chest, pinning her arms under bony knees.

Alice could see how dilated his pupils were—like two black holes. He had managed to bite his tongue and a trickle of blood leaked off his chin and dotted at her cheek. He shoved the piece of cold steel against Alice's throat and pressed down hard.

Alice fought him, but even though the junkie was rail thin, he still outweighed her by twenty-five pounds, and his callused hands were stronger than they looked. The harder she bucked against him, the harder he pressed the pipe against her throat, slowly, methodically crushing her larynx. Alice sucked for air. Her eyes bulged and her vision grew fuzzy—everything starting to go dim and fade away.

Alice heard a dull *POP,* and her first muddled thought was that the junkie had snapped her neck. Then she heard the junkie moan.

Felt the pipe loosen from against her throat and the weight on top of her dissipate.

Her head lolled to the side, cheek sinking into the filthy carpet, and she watched the junkie crumple beside her, blood pumping from where his left ear used to be. His boot heels thudded against the floor, wild at first, then they jerked to a stop as he lost consciousness. His body still twitched, breath ragged, but he clutched at the pipe in his right hand, refusing to let go.

Alice sat up, gasped for air. Her vision dim and speckled with dots of light. She gazed down at the junkie and watched as blood spat from the open wound on the side of his head. He kept moaning, his eyes snapping open and shut, but not really seeing anything.

The sound of mewing got Alice's attention. She looked up at Delilah. The young girl stood in the center of the bed, holding her opened purse in one hand, a pistol in the other.

The junkie issued a gargling sound from deep inside his throat, like water tumbling over rocks in a stream, and that was the last thing Alice heard before the darkness sucked her in.

CHAPTER EIGHTEEN

Certain sounds always made Alice think of Jason—running bath water, toaster coils heating up his Pop-Tarts first thing in the morning, the squeak of magic markers against paper. Sounds anchored her memories, especially the bad ones, and she knew she'd probably never escape that reality. This particular sound, the one to her right, she knew without even having to look up. Most people probably wouldn't even notice it. Nothing but white noise. Tiny pockets of air breaking the surface of water. Jason used to watch his goldfish for hours on end, the fish darting from one end of the tank to the other, occasionally bobbing to the surface in search for food, then to the bottom, sucking up colored stone pellets, then spitting them right back out. The fish never stopped moving, back and forth; their entire world contained behind four walls of glass.

She finally looked over at Elton's fish tank, much larger and more elaborate than Jason's. The filtration system pumped a steady flow of oxygen into the water, and that was the only sound that disturbed the otherwise complete silence in the house.

Alice perched on the edge of Elton's overstuffed floral-print sofa, and gazed around at the rest of the man's living room. It sure didn't look like the kind of place that a sixty-five-year-old exterminator would live in. Thick, lush curtains perfectly matched the upholstery on the sofa; a piano commanded the corner of the room next to a bay window with a panoramic view of the river; hundreds of hard-bound books lined wood shelves; vases with freshly picked flowers were placed here and there. Everything was neat and clean and precisely situated.

When they entered the house, Elton had boasted to Alice that he built the single-story, red-brick home from the foundation up. Framing the walls, running the electrical and plumbing, installing the floors, painting every surface, and even laying the roof tiles by himself. The house was situated right next to the Shallotte River, with the living room opening up to a wraparound wooden porch that had been constructed over the edge of the water.

Alice peered out the bay window. The rain had finally tapered off, but was now replaced by a dense fog, thick as paste, that rolled in off the glassy surface of the slow-moving river.

Wet hair clung to her face and neck, dripping onto the shiny hardwood floor, meticulously mopped and waxed. The water created a half dozen little puddles that beaded against the wood.

A cup of herbal tea steamed atop a coaster in front of her. And next to that, a marble chessboard stood as the centerpiece on the glass coffee table.

Elton entered the room carrying a stack of neatly folded laundry: a large bath towel and washcloth, a blue T-shirt, and a pair of men's pajama bottoms. He set the pajamas on the sofa beside her, then handed her the towel. "Need to dry that hair of yours before you go and catch yourself a cold."

"Thanks."

"And you best take off them clothes so that I can run them through the wash and dry." He glanced down at her backpack, which sat in a puddle of water. "Might as well give me that stuff in there, too. You're a wet mess."

"Thanks."

"Hell. You don't have to keep thanking me. I just don't want you to go and muck up my floor."

"Sorry."

Elton waved the apology away. "Just pulling your leg, kiddo."

Alice noticed that Elton appeared so different inside his own house. He had changed out of his green overalls, and now wore a pressed pair of khakis and a starched Hawaiian shirt, even though it was almost midnight. His hair was perfectly combed, and Alice wondered if he had shaved, too. It was almost as if he was planning on going out for a night on the town.

Alice dried off her hair and kept glancing around the room. "You live here alone?"

"I do now."

"Were you married?"

"Something like that."

"Are you divorced?"

Elton chuckled. Shook his head. "Why don't I show you to the bathroom and let you change into something dry. Then I'll rustle up something for us to eat, and we'll get better acquainted. Sound like a plan?"

This entire situation should have been so uncomfortable and awkward—getting into a stranger's truck out in the middle of nowhere, going to the house of an old man that she didn't even know, putting on his pajamas, but the way Elton looked down at Alice, with his pressed pants pulled up too high over his round belly, and the expression in those bluish-white eyes, Alice felt more comfortable and at ease than she had in a very long time.

But even though there was something about the old man that Alice felt worthy of trust, she couldn't shake the realization that she didn't even last twelve hours without needing someone's help. After only a half-day of deciding to run away from home, she found herself cold, wet, hungry, and already completely helpless.

It was as if Elton could read Alice's mind. "You want me to call your folks?"

"No."

"You sure?"

"Yeah. Positive."

"Okay. But look here, kiddo. I ain't sure why exactly you ran away from home, but I imagine that you had your reasons. This here is a safe place for you for the night. Maybe a good night's sleep will help put things in perspective. In the morning, maybe your situation won't seem all that bad."

"Maybe."

"I'm sure your folks are worried sick about you."

"I know."

"One call to them to let them know you're alive ain't the worst idea in the world."

Alice stared at the stack of folded pajamas. Her mouth opened to say something, but the words wouldn't come.

"You know, the easiest way to open a clamshell is to boil it, but I ain't fixing to plop you in a pot of boiling water just yet. You'll talk when you're good and ready, I guess."

She smiled back at Elton and grabbed the folded pajamas off the couch. "Thanks, Mister Parsons."

"You can just refer to me as Elton. I ain't no kind of mister."

"Okay."

"Alright, then. Let's get you cleaned up, kiddo."

Alice followed him down a long hallway where dozens of framed photos hung from hooks on both walls. Elton was in most of them. Many of the photos were taken when he was a younger man with more hair on the top of his head. Pictures taken at the beach, riding on a horse, holding a string of fish, a few snapped on the porch outside. And also, in a majority of the photos, Elton posed with another man who had a full red beard and wore thick-framed spectacles, and the man's wide grin was nothing less than contagious. Elton and the red-bearded man posed cheek to cheek in some of the pictures, arms around each other in many more. In the last picture on the wall, Elton and the red-bearded man wore dark suits and fancy ties, their hair all slicked back, and they both seemed so joyful, so thrilled to be pressed together. Alice lingered a little, staring at the image of Elton, a moment frozen in time, looking blissful and content alongside the red-bearded man.

"All right. You can use this washroom. If you'd like, take a bath or shower. Whichever you'd prefer. Water takes a minute to get hot, so give it some time before hopping in."

"Okay."

"I'll make us a couple of omelets, unless you object."

"No. That sounds good."

"You like bell pepper and onions?"

"Sure." She didn't sound so sure.

Elton gave her a bemused grin. "You hate 'em both, don't you?"

Alice flushed a little. Covered it with a smile. "Not my favorites, I guess."

"There. The truth is out. Cheese omelet then?"

"Yes. Definitely."

He held the bathroom door open for her. "There's some shampoo under the sink there. Old man shampoo that makes you smell like a sailor, but that's all I got."

"That's fine."

"Okay. I'll see you in the kitchen when you don't smell like a rat's nest." He turned and ambled down the hallway.

"Thank you, Elton."

He held his hand over his head without turning around. "I should thank *you*. I could use the damn company."

Alice closed the bathroom door, locked it, then caught her reflection in the mirror. She looked horrible. Hair wet and stringy. Dark rings under both her eyes. Skin broken out from all the stress and lack of sleep and utter sadness. She forced her eyes away from the mirror and stared down at the shirt and pajama bottoms that Elton gave her. She unfolded the blue T-shirt. It was way too big and not the kind of shirt she would normally wear in a million years. On the back of the shirt, there was a graphic of a cartoon rat with a red circle and line through it. Below that, it said PARSON'S PEST CONTROL - SHALLOTTE, NC.

The T-shirt felt soft and dry, and smelled nice and clean. And Alice actually liked the picture of the cartoon rat. She set the shirt on the counter, then started to run the bathwater until it got good and hot.

CHAPTER NINETEEN

Terry's Chevy pickup truck hogged a couple of parking spaces, straddling the line between two spots, and one of them happened to be for handicapped patrons. Someone had left a nasty note on the windshield, but the entire vehicle stood covered with a few inches of soft snow and the note would never be read by the owner of the truck—Terry being dead and all.

Sinclair had his hands stuffed in his jacket pockets and watched Phillip slide a slim jim in through the passenger-side window. A blanket of heavy snow kept falling all around them, slow and easy, partially obscuring the Amtrak station in the background.

"How'd you know she would come here, anyways?" Phillip asked while he jiggled the thin piece of steel a few times.

Sinclair smirked like he was thinking dirty thoughts. "Well, driving a stolen truck isn't very smart. It was either here or the airport, but it would be a little difficult to sneak what Alice stole from me onto an airplane."

The big ox wore heavy gloves and kept wiggling the slim jim inside the door panel until *click*, the lock popped open.

Sinclair waited patiently as the large man slipped inside the cab and began to root around, opening the glove compartment, checking under the seats. Sinclair hummed to himself, the picture of calm. Big, white plumes of breath streamed out of his nostrils and dissipated into the gray morning air.

Phillip stepped out of the truck and shook his head at Sinclair. He locked the door, slammed it closed, and waited for Sinclair to tell him what to do next.

Sinclair stared at the big man for a moment. "You searched the entire truck?"

Phillip nodded. "Nothing."

"I trust you looked everywhere?"

Again, Phillip nodded his thick neck. "Nothing."

"Hmmm. I wonder," Sinclair mused. He stepped forward and peered into the bed of the truck. "Phillip."

Phillip lumbered forward and stepped beside Sinclair. Stared down into the bed of the truck as well. "Snow."

"Yes, Phillip. Snow. What else? What might be *under* the snow?"

Phillip buried his fist into the white powder and pulled out a pillowcase full of dirty sheets and dropped it to the pavement. He shook out all the linens and kicked them with his boot for good measure. "Dirty laundry."

"Indeed. Keep searching," Sinclair said.

Phillip reached into the snow one last time and yanked out a red suitcase from the bed of the truck, crusted with frozen chunks of ice. The big man peered down at Sinclair like he wasn't sure what to do.

"Well? Open it," Sinclair said.

Phillip squatted down and unzipped the red suitcase. He pulled out all the clothes, tossed them over his shoulder one by one, picked through some toiletries—a tube of toothpaste, a toothbrush, tampons, a hairbrush. He checked the side pockets, ripped out the lining, and even shook the suitcase upside down for good measure. He stared up at Sinclair. "Nothing."

Sinclair sighed. "One must be more thorough, Phillip." He leaned down and picked up one of Alice's shirts off the pavement. A blue one. Looked like a man's T-shirt. Well-worn. Tiny holes around the collar.

"Just an old shirt," Phillip said.

Sinclair smiled. Lips pulled back over his tiny teeth. "I beg to differ." He turned the T-shirt around. The print on the back, faded and worn, but still very legible. *Parson's Pest Control – Shallotte, NC.*

Phillip read the back of the T-shirt a few times. "So?"

"*So,* Phillip, it could very well be a link to our friend, Alice. A distinct possibility." Sinclair grabbed another shirt and spread it across the ice, then knelt down on top of the material so that his pants wouldn't get wet from the snow. He poked amongst the clothing with an extended index finger, half-curious, half-repulsed to be doing so.

"Whatcha lookin' for?" Phillip asked.

"More, Phillip. More." He kept digging through the articles of clothing, then reached into the back pocket of a pair of blue jeans. He withdrew a tattered piece of paper, carefully folded a few times. "Ah." Sinclair held the piece of paper in front of him and slowly uncreased and opened the flier. He stared at the note, smiled, then carefully refolded it and slipped it into his breast pocket.

"Anything?" Phillip queried.

Sinclair stood back up and inspected his knees to see if his trousers had gotten soiled or wet. They had not. "Gather everything. Do it now, please."

Phillip knelt down and began to stuff everything back into the suitcase.

Flurries of snow began to tumble harder from the gray sky above. The wind picked up and blew across the parking lot. Sinclair watched Phillip scrabble around on the ground, then took out his pack of Salems. He cupped his hand against the wind, and it took a few flicks of his lighter, but finally, he managed to light up his cigarette.

CHAPTER TWENTY

"How much money is in your bag, anyway?" Delilah asked.

"Why are you carrying a pistol in yours?" Alice asked right back.

Both girls sat pressed together at the back of the bus even though only a half dozen other passengers rode on board. The sky outside swirled a mix of cotton candy pink and Carolina blue, the sun still easing its way above the skyline. On a normal day, it would be the kind of sky to be appreciated and grateful to be a part of. But for Alice and Delilah, the sky happened to be the furthest thing from their minds.

Since Alice didn't answer the first question, Delilah moved onto the next one. "Why Wilmington?"

"Wilmington's just a pit stop. Going to a small town just south of it. Shallotte."

"Shallotte? And what's there?"

"You really want to stay here in Charlotte?" Alice snapped, growing weary of the girl's constant questions. Her side felt like she was lying on shattered glass, the bruised rib sparking hot every time she breathed. She tried to hold it in, but a little moan escaped from between her lips.

"You okay?" Delilah asked.

"What do you think? I might have a broken rib, my ear hurts like hell, and my neck will be black and blue in a few hours. So, no, I'm not okay."

"Sorry."

"Me, too."

"Should you go to the hospital?"

Alice stared at the girl. "Sure. Right after I go to the police station and report that junkie for assault."

Delilah chewed on a piece of gum for a minute. "Anything I can do?"

"Got any vodka? Motrin?"

"No."

"Then, no. There's nothing you can do."

Delilah glanced out the window as the bus rumbled down Tryon Street through light early morning traffic. Delivery trucks, city buses filled with morning commuters, a handful of cabs.

They rode in silence for a few minutes, each replaying the showdown with the junkie in their minds.

"He was going to kill you. You know that, right?" Delilah finally said.

"You want to say that any louder?" But no one else heard the girl's statement. The rest of the passengers sat in the front of the bus, most dozing off or lost in their own set of worries.

"You think he's gonna die?"

"I don't know. Maybe. Do you really care?"

"I had to do it. You know? I didn't have any choice. I didn't."

Alice didn't say anything. Didn't offer any comforting words to make the girl feel better or relieve her conscience.

Delilah's distinctive mewing started up again, threatening to get louder and gaining a lot of unwanted attention.

Alice rubbed hard at her throbbing temples, the Crown not even close to being out of her system. "Look. You did what you had to do,

I guess." That was as close to a thank-you as Alice could offer in her current condition.

Delilah nodded and the mewing grew softer.

"It's not easy pulling the trigger on someone. I'm thinking that you've used the pistol before," Alice stated.

More mewing.

"Your mom's boyfriend? Leon?"

And more mewing. A little louder.

"Okay." Alice stopped there. She didn't want to tell the girl that she was screwed. "The junkie's probably gonna be okay. They're like cockroaches."

"You think—" Delilah choked and struggled for air—"You think someone heard the gunshot?"

"Yeah. I think someone heard the gunshot."

The girl moaned. "The cops?"

"Take a breath and listen to me. The motel clerk is a junkie, too, and he's the one that gave the guy our room key. He's not going to say anything. And it's not like the sound of gunfire is anything new in that area. We've got a few hours. Maybe more."

Alice felt Delilah's hand reach for hers. The young girl squeezed it hard, and Alice let it linger for a moment before pulling away and resumed massaging her throbbing temples.

"You know somebody in Shallotte?" Delilah asked.

"Yeah, I know somebody."

"Are they gonna be able to help us out?"

"Us?" Alice asked a little too sharply.

The girl's face collapsed and the annoying mewing cranked back up.

"Look. I've got my own problems."

Delilah nodded. The girl sure had *that* mannerism down to a science. "I know. But the thing with the guy . . . in the room . . . if he lives, he knows what we look like."

"When we get to Shallotte, we'll figure something out."

Delilah stared out the window as the bus took an on-ramp for the 74 South.

"Your mom is going to be looking for you, you know," Alice said.

Delilah's body tensed up at the mention of her mother. "I doubt it."

Alice stared at her and waited for the young girl to look her back in the eye. "And what's that supposed to mean?"

"She was out of it when it happened. With Leon."

"Leon. What exactly happened with Leon?"

Delilah tried to answer the question, but the words just wouldn't come.

"What did you do to Leon?"

"I did what I had to."

"Can we stop with the riddles? Is Leon dead?"

"He had it coming," the girl whispered.

"Jesus."

"Nobody saw me. Not my mama. Nobody."

"So? Who's she going to think did it? Your little brother? The youngest one?" Alice didn't have to say the one with Down's syndrome.

"Leon had it coming," Delilah spat out.

"You already said that. And it's not the point. The cops will be looking for you. Probably already are. Doesn't matter what the asshole did to you."

"And nobody's looking for you?"

"People are looking."

"Who are they?"

"I don't know. I guess if they catch up with me, I'll find out."

Delilah stared at Alice's neck. The bruising had started. Light crimson with five slightly darker marks left by the junkie's fingers. "You ever kill anybody?"

"No, Delilah, I've never killed anybody. And how about we stop with the twenty questions? Better off for the both of us."

"Okay." The girl gazed out the window at the passing traffic. "I'm hungry."

"I gave you a hundred bucks. You can buy yourself something at the next stop."

"Okay."

Alice closed her eyes and let her head fall back. She tried to take small, easy breaths, but it still felt like her side was on fire. "And you should lose the gun. Sooner rather than later."

Delilah didn't nod this time. She just clutched her purse tighter and kept gazing out the window.

CHAPTER TWENTY-ONE

Sinclair waited patiently for his turn in line at the ticket counter. In front of him, an elderly couple paid for their train tickets with a handful of crumpled five-dollar bills and stacks of quarters. As the old man counted out the money on the counter, his wife double-checked his math quite carefully. The process proved to be long and agonizing, but Sinclair neither rolled his eyes nor exhaled loudly to demonstrate his impatience. He simply waited and clutched Alice's blue T-shirt in both hands.

Phillip lingered over next to the vending machines where he had been instructed to remain. The big man stared forward, eyes focused on nothing in particular, hands dangling restlessly at his sides as if eager to use them on something.

Sinclair continued to wait, and when the elderly couple finally passed over their wad of bills and stack of coins in exchange for their tickets, he smiled at them both. "Safe travels."

The elderly woman returned his smile. The elderly man did not.

He stepped forward and greeted the ticket clerk with the same frozen grin. "Good morning, my dear."

The ticket clerk couldn't help but grin back at him. "Good morning to you." The woman was completely gray and had a soft face on which she applied too much rouge upon loose cheeks. Her lips were fire engine red, painted and repainted perfectly. She may have been sixty, but she looked much older. "Can I help you?"

"I sure hope so. I've been having a very rough day. Very rough, indeed. But I must say, that smile of yours is helping matters tremendously."

The ticket clerk blushed, causing her cheeks to blossom redder, and glanced away for a second. "Well, thank you, sweetheart. And what can I do for you?"

Sinclair glanced at her name tag: Dolores. "My, my. Dolores. That is a delightful name. Such an old-fashioned ring to it."

Dolores settled into her seat, eating up the compliments like grapes.

"My sixth-grade music teacher's name was Dolores. Sweetest woman. Of course, we called her Miss LaFrance at the time. Students certainly didn't refer to their teachers by their first names back then."

"It was my grandmother's name. Passed it down to me."

"Perfect fit for you. It truly is." Sinclair took a moment to look down at his shoes. He lowered his shoulders to exhibit utter despondency, then peered back toward Dolores with doleful eyes. "I have a situation that I hope you can help me with, Dolores. I'm at quite a loss."

Dolores perked up. "Oh?"

"Yes. Well, to get the ball rolling, I was wondering if you work this desk every day."

Dolores nodded. "Monday through Friday. From eight until four."

"Good. So, you worked here yesterday?"

"Yes. Of course."

"And, if I can be so forward, do you have any children?"

Dolores edged closer to the tiny man. "Two boys and a girl. All grown now, of course. Why do you ask?"

"Because I am hoping for some empathy. I, unfortunately, do not have children, but my brother does. A daughter. Or at least he did. Alice is her name. And Alice is in some trouble."

"Oh, my."

Sinclair leaned in closer and spoke softly as if in great confidence. "My niece has gotten herself into drugs. The serious kind. She is an addict and she has chosen to run away from her problems."

Dolores just shook her head.

"And to complicate the matter, Alice has a little baby girl that she left behind. A six-month-old angel with the bluest eyes you'll ever see."

"That's awful. Drugs and all that nonsense."

"Yes. Drugs are the devil's candy." He paused a moment before continuing. "Alice needs help. And she belongs at home with her baby."

"Yes, yes."

"And this is where you come in, Dolores. We need to find her before she hurts herself or does something even worse. I need you to help me find her."

Dolores clutched at her bosom. "What can I do?"

"I believe she came here yesterday afternoon. I believe she took the train or the bus somewhere."

"So many people come through here every day. So many."

"I know. But I think perhaps she was headed toward a place called Shallotte, North Carolina, but I can't be sure. And until I know exactly where she's headed, I'm facing a needle in a haystack."

"Yesterday?"

"Yes. Probably in the late afternoon."

"And you're sure she came through here?"

"Yes. Of that, I am quite positive."

"What about the police? Can't they help you find her?"

Sinclair shook his head solemnly. "Alice is an adult. A drug addict running from her problems is not placed high on their priority list."

"I see." Dolores glanced at her computer screen for a moment. "What does your niece look like?"

"Tall. Athletic. Brown hair. Freckles. A slight Southern accent." Sinclair retrieved the folded piece of paper from his breast pocket. He unfolded it and slid the slip of paper across the counter. "Perhaps this will help."

Dolores looked down at the paper—a photo of a fourteen-year-old Alice under the caption RUNAWAY. HAVE YOU SEEN ME? There was a phone number listed as well.

"Taken a few years ago. Just a child here," Sinclair stated with an echo of melancholy.

"I remember her. I do. She looks older now, of course. A little bit rough around the edges. Seemed to be in a hurry."

"That would be poor Alice."

"We don't register customers' names, but I can check the manifest for destinations from yesterday."

"That would be so helpful, Dolores. So helpful."

Dolores grabbed a pair of reading glasses from the counter and began to peck at her keyboard. "Just give me a second here."

"Take your time, Dolores. I can wait."

"What was the name of the town again?"

"Shallotte, North Carolina."

She kept typing and scrolling. Eyes searching the screen. "Well, Amtrak doesn't stop at Shallotte. Nearest town is Wilmington."

"Okay. Perhaps Wilmington."

Dolores stopped and tapped her fingernail against the screen. "Well. Here's something. We had seven passengers leave here yesterday on Amtrak that was headed to Wilmington. And only one of those tickets was for a one-way fare to Wilmington. Maybe that's your niece."

Sinclair smiled. Reached across the counter and clutched Dolores' arm. "You are a lifesaver, Dolores. I don't know how to thank you."

Dolores removed her glasses and squeezed his hand in return. "You go get that girl and bring her home to her baby."

"Will do, Dolores. Will do." He returned the flier to his breast pocket. "There's certainly a place reserved for you in heaven."

CHAPTER TWENTY-TWO

WHAT IF ELTON doesn't even live there anymore?

The question had been kicking around inside Alice's head for the last hundred miles. Elton could have moved, could be dead, or maybe he wouldn't want anything to do with her due to the circumstances behind her abrupt departure from his home. After all the old man had done for Alice, after showering her with nothing but kindness and understanding, she disappeared without even saying goodbye. No thank-you. No note. No nothing. She simply walked out of his life as fast as she had walked into it.

Chances were good he'd given up the exterminator business and was enjoying retirement. Not everybody was like Alice, spinning their wheels, going nowhere, making the same mistakes over and over, and having absolutely nothing to show for her life.

I've got ninety-one thousand dollars to show for it, she tried to convince herself.

Even if Elton was still there, what could he really do for her? Let her sleep in his extra room, take her fishing with him, and *oh, yeah,* help her hide the money she had stolen?

No. She wasn't expecting miracles. She was only hoping that Elton would tell her that everything would be all right. Make her feel safe yet once again. Maybe just listen to her and not pry or make her feel guilty about what she'd become. But the plain and ugly truth was that Alice felt as if she had no other options—not a single one—and she didn't really know where else to turn or who else to trust.

So, Elton it was. Her one and only hope. In all reality, it was probably just another lousy idea that fit in nicely with all her other lousy ideas that left her running from problems and situations that she and only she created. But *this* problem, *this* situation, happened to be worse than anything that she had ever gotten herself mixed up in before. This one happened to be massive. And to make matters even worse, she found herself tangled up with Delilah, who shot a guy's ear clean off his head. Maybe the junkie bled to death, but maybe not. If he survived, he'd be talking to the police about exactly who did it.

The best thing to do—the *sensible* thing to do—would be to cut her losses, ditch Delilah, and let the girl face her own lousy music. The girl may have been abused by her mother's boyfriend, but that wasn't Alice's problem. The fact that Delilah shot him, too, *that* was Alice's problem if she chose to let the girl stick around. The cops would be looking for the kid. Full name, full description, the city she fled from. Only a matter of time before the authorities caught up with her. And when that happened, Alice would go right down with her sinking ship.

Alice glanced over at Delilah and the girl stared right back at her.

"You're gonna ditch me, aren't you?" Delilah stated more than asked.

Alice turned her attention back toward the front of the bus and watched two college frat guys pass a bottle in a brown bag back and forth. "No."

"Because I wouldn't blame you if you did. I really wouldn't. Probably the smart thing for you to do."

Alice kept watching the frat guys drink from the bottle, laughing without a care in the world. She wanted to leap up, snatch the bottle from their hands, and tilt it back until it ran empty. She wanted to feel that familiar burn inside her stomach, then the comforting glow from within her head, and wait for the effects to pull her into a numbing cocoon, safe from reality.

"Yeah. You're right about that. It would be the smart thing for me to do," Alice said.

"So why don't you?"

Alice finally returned the girl's gaze. "Because I guess I'm not very smart."

Delilah smiled. Actually smiled. The first time Alice had seen the girl express any form of joy, and the smile completely transformed her. She didn't look like someone who shot two men and was on the run. She simply looked like a kid, a young girl whose biggest problem was that she had a crush on a boy that didn't have a crush on her in return.

"Well, I wouldn't say anything if you did ditch me. I mean, I wouldn't tell anything about you to the police or anything if I got caught."

Alice couldn't help but smile back at the girl.

"What?" Delilah asked. "I wouldn't tell the police about you. Really. You've been . . . I don't know. Nice, I guess. You're the only person that has been nice to me in a long time."

"Me? Nice? You've got real problems if you think I'm *nice*."

Delilah's face flushed red a little.

"Another thing. You might want to consider not being so honest with people. That's the first lesson I'll teach you. Give that one to you for free."

Delilah nodded. "Don't be honest. Got it. Anything else?"

"Yeah. Stay away from drugs and assholes."

"In that order?" Delilah asked with a smirk.

Alice played along. "Yeah. In that order."

Delilah looked down at her lap, fingering the strap of her purse. "How old were you when you ran away?"

"Who says I ran away?"

Delilah didn't buy it. "Uh-huh. So why did you?"

"Sorry. I'm not going there. I'm a closed book on certain topics, and I'd like to keep it that way."

"Why?"

Alice didn't answer and started to put the wall back up, brick by brick. Things were getting a little too personal. A little too intimate.

"You got any brothers or sisters?" Delilah tried again.

"Look. Let's not confuse the situation we're in together as friendship. Okay? I don't have friends, and I'm not looking to make one."

"Sorry. I was just curious. Wanted to get to know you a little better is all."

"Yeah? Well, that's not what I want."

"Sorry."

"You already said that. Makes you sound weak."

Delilah opened her mouth. Started to say sorry again. Instead, she just pressed her lips back together.

Alice stood up, grabbed her duffel bag, and moved a few rows toward the front of the bus. She crouched down in the seat and closed her eyes. She needed sleep. She tried to block out the pain—inside her throbbing head, the aching rib, her burning ear and throat—but she couldn't. Her body was wrecked. And not only her body, but her mental state as well.

And as she had wished for a thousand times before, Alice wished that she died that day instead of Jason.

* * *

It was a fifteen-minute layover in Goldsboro, a place where passengers were permitted to step off the bus, stretch their legs, and buy some crappy vending machine food—chips, cookies, candy bars, bags of pork rinds, and other high-salt, high-sugar snacks. Alice fed quarters into the machine and selected two Snickers bars, craving the chocolate and figuring that the peanuts would provide her with some much-needed protein. When she bent down to retrieve the candy bars, she moved too quickly and a flare of staggering pain rippled throughout her side, causing her to twist and clutch at the bruised rib. She could feel the heat pulsate from under her shirt. It hurt like hell. She decided to take a peek. Check out the damage. She lifted her shirt and immediately regretted the decision. Her whole side was dark red, and it wouldn't be long before it turned an ugly purple. She traced a finger over the bruised area and couldn't help but moan—even the slightest touch aggravated the rib. Sharp stabs of broken glass churned inside her.

She stood slow and easy, praying that she wouldn't move the wrong way. She needed something for the pain. Motrin. Tylenol. Either one would do. Probably should even wrap her sides with something. An Ace bandage. Something. Anything. She would need to find a drugstore for any of that kind of stuff.

The bus driver, a short, stocky Asian man, had instructed the passengers that fifteen minutes was the allotted time before the bus would shut its doors and pull out of the station. Not a minute longer. The driver wore white cotton gloves that were stained black on the fingertips, and his shirt buttons threatened to pop from their threads over a pronounced belly. A visor that read *Greyhound* perched right above his prescription sunglasses, and he had a toothpick tucked behind his ear. The bus driver had given those passengers who opted to disembark disapproving glances, knowing that each of them threatened to put him behind schedule.

Alice ate the Snickers bars, one right after the other, all the while searching the street for a drugstore. Didn't see one, but she did spot a liquor shop across the street from the station. And just like any other liquor shop in Harrisburg, or Philadelphia, or Charlotte, or wherever, the token dregs of society hung out in front, smoking the last of their cigarettes, begging for change from customers coming and going. Those that managed to scrape together enough spare change promptly marched inside, made their liquid purchase, and drank from bag-covered cans in the parking lot, numbing themselves for a while until they repeated the vicious cycle all over again.

Alice wanted her own brown bag, preferably hard liquor. She had even crossed the street once to enter the liquor store, but stopped herself. She wanted to be clearheaded for a while. *Needed* to be clearheaded. She had to start making some sensible decisions. If she hadn't been drunk, she wouldn't have gone home with Terry. If she hadn't been drunk, there was a good chance she would never have taken the money in the first place. The list could go on and on.

Stay the course. Just get yourself to Shallotte.

The two frat boys made their way back toward the bus, both wearing their baseball caps backwards and sporting Sigma Phi Epsilon shirts. The taller, better-looking one who probably did pretty well with college women, gave Alice a sweet smile, dimples and all. "Hey," he said.

Alice locked eyes with him for a moment. He was cute, with his dirty blond hair and deep-blue eyes under thick eyelashes. Faded Levi's and an intentionally snug shirt showed off a well-toned body. Alice might have been this guy's girlfriend if she hadn't let Jason die. She could be in college now, switching majors and pledging sororities and planning for spring break, instead of running with a duffel bag full of stolen money.

Alice didn't say *hey* back. Didn't smile. Instead, she returned her gaze toward the liquor store.

The rest of the passengers had already loaded back on the bus. She was the last. Fifteen minutes all used up. Right on cue, the Greyhound's engine rumbled back to life and the entire bus rattled. Alice gave the liquor store one last glance, then climbed on board the bus as well.

The bus driver shook his head at her. "You're pushing it."

Alice shrugged. "It's not every day you get to see Goldsboro."

"Funny," the bus driver replied and cranked the hydraulic doors closed behind her. "Not so funny for your friend though."

Alice stared at the rear of the bus—the last seat empty. She walked back to Delilah's spot, but the girl was gone. Her jacket, her purse, everything.

The bus rolled backwards and Alice grabbed at a seat to catch herself from falling. Her rib barked at the sudden movement, and she dug her fingernails into the vinyl seats.

"Fuck." She said it louder than she meant to—confirmed by an elderly woman's sour, disapproving look.

The elderly woman started to say something, to give Alice some kind of condemnation, but noticed the bruises on Alice's throat and the bloody scab on her ear. A quick flash of discomfort, then a hint of fear swept over the woman's face. Her mouth snapped shut and she stared toward the front of the bus instead.

Alice glanced out the windows, searching the parking lot for Delilah, but the girl was nowhere to be seen.

"Hold up. Give her a second," Alice called up to the driver.

He stared back at her in the long mirror above his neatly combed hair. "No can do. Fifteen minutes." He cranked the steering wheel to the left and shifted the bus into drive.

"Jesus Christ. Don't be such an ass," Alice spat.

Now all necks craned toward Alice, the frat boys smirking at the confrontation.

"Take a seat, please," the driver instructed.

Instead, Alice marched up the aisle and stared down at the pear-shaped driver. "Give her another minute. She's just a kid."

"Not my problem. Take a seat."

"Look . . . she's a runaway. Give her a break."

The driver tapped the brakes and forced the bus back into park. He rotated in his seat and poked a gloved finger toward Alice. "Well, maybe she ran away again. And again, not my problem. So, either take a seat or get off the bus."

"You're being an asshole."

The driver's face went a dark shade of red and he licked at his lips. "You got a mouth, young lady."

"Tell me something I don't know."

The driver opened his mouth to say something else, but Alice beat him to the punch.

"Just open the damn door."

CHAPTER TWENTY-THREE

NOVEMBER 2005

Elton perched on a green-and-white, foldable aluminum lawn chair at the edge of the deck, a fishing rod in one hand, a mug of coffee in the other. The sun barely peeked over the horizon on the other side of the river, the day just getting its start. A slow, steady breeze swept along the surface of the water, rustled the branches of sweetgum trees, and tugged on the few remaining brown leaves that had yet to tumble loose. A few of them finally untethered, swirled and danced in the wind before settling on the face of the water and floating like miniature boats. Other than the song of the river rippling over rocks and fallen trees, the countryside was quiet and peaceful.

Alice walked out on the deck, still dressed in Elton's pajamas, her hair going every which way. She plopped down on a chair next to him and gazed out over the river.

"Morning, kiddo," Elton offered.

"Morning."

Elton stared out over the river for a moment, sipped his coffee, and reflected upon the view. "Beautiful out here, isn't it? I'll tell you, even though I've sat in this same spot nearly every morning for over thirty years, I never tire of watching this old river roll on past. Never."

Alice craned her neck, looking in both directions of the river. "No one else lives out here?"

"Just me and the birds." Elton took another sip from his mug of coffee. "You sleep well enough?"

"Yeah. Pretty tired, I guess."

"I imagine yesterday was a long day for you."

Alice said that it was.

"Could've slept in."

"Not really."

"An early riser like me?"

Alice shrugged. "Used to waking up for school."

"Ah. Right. School. You'll be missing it today, I'm guessing."

"Looks that way."

He snapped the fishing rod back and played with the line. "What grade you in anyways?"

"Tenth."

"Tenth grade. I hated tenth grade. And eleventh and twelfth, for that matter."

"Why's that?"

He set his mug of coffee on the deck and proceeded to reel in his line a little bit at a time. "For starters, I got picked on something terrible in school."

"Really? Why?"

"Guess because I was different than everybody else."

"You don't seem different."

Elton chuckled softly. "Tell that to the bullies of the world."

She watched him reel the line in the rest of the way, then with a snap of his wrist, he recast, sending the sinker a quarter way across the river.

"You catch anything yet?"

"Nope. Usually don't. Not much of a fisherman, sorry to say."

"Why do you do it then?"

"Guess I like the challenge."

They sat in the early morning silence for a few moments, both watching the river water pull on past. A hard gust of wind rustled through the trees, causing the branches to sway back and forth, and a pack of crows swooped by, settled in a clump of longleaf pine across the water, then set about cawing and cawing.

"Aren't you going to call the cops? Tell them that I'm here?" Alice asked, but she didn't look toward Elton, keeping her gaze on the flock of crows instead.

He shrugged. Took another sip of his coffee. "I don't know. Guess I could. You steal something or commit some other kind of felony?"

"No."

"Okay. Guess I don't have to call the authorities about anything then."

Alice finally peered over at the old man. "Aren't you curious? About where I ran away from? Why I ran away?"

"Sure. I got all sorts of questions kicking around in my thick skull, but I figure that you'll tell me when you're good and ready. We all have our ways and reasons for doing what we do, and there's nothing I can do or say to force you to pony up some answers. Kinda like trying to pull a tomato vine from the ground when it's still ripe. It can be done, but it takes a helluva lot of sweat and elbow grease. I find that it's best to let the plant be. Pull it out when it's dead."

Alice smiled. "Great. So, I'm kinda like a tomato plant, and you're waiting for me to die?"

Elton thought about this for a moment. "Yeah. Maybe that wasn't the best analogy in the world."

"You don't have any kids, do you?"

"Is it that obvious?"

"Kinda. Parents don't usually like to wait for answers and explanations."

"Good to know. If I ever decide to have kids one day."

Alice watched him reel in his line, then recast once again. She inspected his profile, his soft chin and bulbous nose, his balding head, the way he kept wetting his lips—he looked like a cartoon character. She thought that Elton was probably around her grandfather's age, maybe a few years younger, but there was something just a little different about the man.

"Who's that man in all your pictures? Your brother?"

Elton refrained from smiling the best he could. Shook his head a few times. "In some ways he was like a brother, but he was much more than that. Ben was my very best friend."

Alice looked away. A little uncomfortable as she slowly realized what Elton was implying. "Oh."

Elton laughed. Patted her knee.

"He looks nice."

"He was. Tamed the hellfire out of me."

"He's gone?"

"Yep. Well before his time."

Something across the river spooked the crows and they all took flight in unison. They screeched and flapped right over the heads of the both of them.

"Did Ben like to fish?" Alice asked.

"He did. Taught me the joy of fishing. Also taught me that it wasn't necessarily what you caught or how many you reeled in. It was really about being in the moment, alone with your thoughts, enjoying the time you were in. You and the river. Nothing else mattering. Took me a good, long while before I got it, but when I did, I understood what Ben meant."

Alice stared over at the empty pail, noticeably absent of a single fish. "Was he a better fisherman than you?"

Elton glanced down at his empty pail as well. "Hell. That and just about everything else."

"What happened to him?"

He patted her again. "For someone that doesn't really take a shine to answering questions, you sure ask a lot of them."

"It's called deflection."

"Ah. Deflection. You're pretty damn good at it."

"It's a coping mechanism."

"Too many fancy words. I'm not even gonna ask."

She played with the seam of her pajamas. "You miss him?"

"You miss your folks, or whoever you left behind?"

Alice nodded without thinking about it. "Yeah."

"Well, at least you got the choice if you want to see them again."

She grinned over at the old man—she knew what he was trying to do. "So that's why you fish?"

He gave her a wink. "So that's why I fish."

A solid gust of wind swept up off the river and tugged at Alice's hair, sending it to and fro. Elton turned his attention up to the sky and noticed that the clouds were growing darker and inching their way closer.

"Looks like round two's headed this way. Pack it up here pretty shortly."

They both watched the clouds churn and fold in amongst themselves for a minute or so, then a flash of lightning cracked the sky, and few seconds after that, a low boom shook their seats.

"Is it okay if I stay here? For a few days. Until I can figure some stuff out?" Alice asked.

Elton kept his eyes cast toward the sky. Thought about it for a moment. "Well, if I said no, would you take off running again into the wild blue yonder?"

"I wouldn't have much of a choice."

"Figured as much." Elton wet his lips. Fingered his fishing line. "A few days then. I sure wish you'd call your folks though, but I'm guessing you won't." He set his empty coffee mug down on the deck.

"Get you another cup?" Alice asked.

"That'd be fine."

Alice stood and grabbed his mug. "I don't know how exactly to thank you."

"I do. If you're gonna stay on here with me for a while, you gotta earn your keep. After you fetch me a cup of coffee, go on and get yourself dressed. We've got work to do. Your clothes are washed and folded on the sofa in the living room."

"I have to help you kill rats?"

"In my profession, we prefer to say *exterminate*."

"Do they end up dead?"

"That they do."

Alice smiled, then held out his coffee mug. "Cream and sugar?"

"Yep. Three scoops of sugar. And a big splash of cream."

"Three scoops?"

"Three *big* scoops. Don't be stingy."

"That's not good for you, you know."

"Either is tampering with a man's cup of coffee."

Alice watched him reel back in his fishing line, then went into the kitchen to fetch the old man a fresh mug of coffee.

CHAPTER TWENTY-FOUR

The only reason that Delilah had gotten off the bus in the first place was because she wanted to get rid of the stupid gun. Throw it away and never see it again. It was bad luck. She probably should have tossed it sooner, but she had been too scared, too frantic, too confused to think straight.

After she got off the bus, she considered stashing the gun in a trash can in the women's public bathroom, but that seemed like an obvious place for it to be discovered. A janitor would probably find it and turn it over to the police with her fingerprints all over the gun. So she walked out of the bus terminal and kept searching for a place to ditch it.

The gun belonged to Leon. He liked guns. He had a bunch of them. One in his truck, one under the bed, another in his toolbox. She hadn't known he kept one in the front closet. She had been looking for a pack of cigarettes in one of his jacket pockets yesterday morning but found the 9-millimeter pistol instead. Leon was sprawled out on the couch, all messed up. He'd been drinking rum the entire night, passed out for a few hours, then started up again right after sunrise. He was all drunk and nasty, and when he leered at her, Delilah knew what he had in mind. He had raped her a few times before. The first time, six months ago. Snuck into her bedroom late one night, put his hand over her mouth, and whispered that he would kill her if she screamed. He ripped her panties right off and forced himself inside. She'd never experienced pain like that before. It was her first time. But she stayed quiet. She knew he would do as he said he would do. He'd kill her. Especially when he was all messed up.

He didn't touch her for a few weeks after that. Wouldn't even look at her. Delilah thought that maybe he didn't remember what he did. Then it happened again when she was in the shower. He yanked her out of the tub, bent her over the toilet, and took her, grunting like some kind of wild animal. Delilah got back in the shower that was still running after he finished, curled up into a ball, and cried until her mama banged on the door, yelling at her to get her ass out of there and cook something for breakfast.

It happened more often after that. A half-dozen times at least. And somehow, Leon always caught her by surprise. The last time, she knew that her mama was in the next room, drunk but not drunk enough to be oblivious. Her mama sat right at the kitchen table smoking her Newports, drinking her wine, and listening to her oldest baby get raped by the man she couldn't satisfy anymore.

So, as soon as Delilah found the pistol, she knew she was going to use it on Leon.

An alley ran along the backside of the Greyhound station, and it had three dumpsters filled with cardboard boxes and bags of trash from a Chinese restaurant and a pizza place. Delilah opened a black trash bag filled with chicken fat, moldy noodles, and dozens of cigarette butts, and stuck the gun into the bag. She tried to let it go. Tried to let it fall from her hand, but she couldn't. The 9-millimeter pistol wouldn't drop out of her hand yet. Still part of her. Its use perhaps not yet complete.

She stood there for another few moments, hand still shoved in the pile of trash. Then she made her decision. Stuffed the gun back into her purse and moved in the opposite direction of the bus station. Down the alleyway and onto a street that ran through downtown Goldsboro.

Delilah knew the bus driver said fifteen minutes, and he looked like the kind of guy that took pride in being punctual. The bus would be gone by now. Probably better off that way.

Alice didn't want her around anymore. She made that pretty clear. And why should she? Why should she take on someone else's problem?

Delilah started thinking about poor little Dwayne. Who would take care of him now? Not her mama, that much was for sure. If Dwayne got taken in by the State and placed in a decent foster home, he'd be better off. Three meals a day. A real bed to sleep in. Medicine if he got sick.

She walked by a sprawling park. More grass than she had ever seen, with baseball fields, swings and slides, and a box of sand for kids to dig and run around in. A group of girls played soccer. They looked like they were twelve or thirteen, all wearing nice uniforms with matching sneakers. Their hair pulled back into perfect little ponytails. Golden hair. Delilah had never seen so many white kids.

Along the sideline of the soccer field, parents sat in lawn chairs with coolers at their feet, drinking sodas and snacking on home-made sandwiches. Moms and dads talked and laughed under the midday sun. Little brothers and sisters ran around, screaming, playing tag and rolling around in the fresh-cut grass.

Everybody seemed so damn happy. So damn normal. Delilah had never played a team sport. She always had to come home after school to help take care of Dwayne. She couldn't remember her mama ever taking her and her brothers to a park, either.

Delilah sat down on the soft green grass in the park and watched the white girls kicking the ball around, making it look so easy. She

didn't understand all the rules of soccer, but knew you were supposed to try and kick the ball into the net. Seemed kind of boring to
her, really. But watching all the soccer girls running around made
her sad that all these kids got to go home every night to a real house,
with real parents that worked jobs, and that cared enough to come
out to a park and watch them play a stupid game of soccer. She
would never be able to finish school now. Never be able to make
something of herself and be everything her mama wasn't.

"What the hell?"

Delilah looked up and saw Alice standing over her. She looked all
pissed off, and sweaty around the face. Her neck looked terrible, all
red and swollen.

Alice glared down at her and dropped her duffel bag onto the
ground. "Bus is gone, thank you very much. We're stuck here."

Delilah simply nodded, then turned her attention back toward
the field and continued to watch the girls play soccer for another
minute. "I'd like to learn how to play one day. Bet I'd be pretty good
at it."

CHAPTER TWENTY-FIVE

Sinclair stared over at Phillip—the big man squeezed in behind the wheel of the Grand Marquis looking as if a crowbar would be required to extract him. The top of Phillip's head grazed the roof of the car, his knees pressed up under the steering wheel with no space to spare, his left shoulder smashed against the tinted window. If they were to have a head-on collision and the airbags deployed, there would be little room for them to inflate.

Then, he glanced down at Phillip's feet, so easily in command of the gas and brake pedals, and his massive hands gripping the wheel with ease. Driving a motor vehicle was nothing more than a tedious task that most adults performed on a daily basis. After the age of sixteen, normal people sat behind the wheel of an automobile for hours on end, driving to and from work, embarking on family vacations, going wherever and whenever they saw fit to do so. Driving a vehicle was as automatic as taking a shower in the morning—simply something that needed to be done. But Sinclair had never sat behind the wheel of an automobile with the exception of a motorized cart—a ride for small children—at Knoebels Amusement Resort in Elysburg, Pennsylvania. Sure, cars could easily be retrofitted with pedal extensions and modified seats installed that would allow someone *short of stature* the ability to operate an automobile safely. Expense wasn't an issue. Not at all. The real cost came in the form of humiliation. He felt as if he would resemble the ten-year-old child he had been when he drove the motorized car at Knoebels Amusement Resort.

After the age of thirteen or fourteen, Sinclair came to accept his condition—nothing could be done about his circumstance at that point. Too late for that. Despite the playground taunts he endured for many years as a child, it only made him stronger and more determined. Whereas the other children around him grew bigger and taller every month, Sinclair focused on his mounting intelligence. As his classmates sprouted, blossoming into *normal* heights, Sinclair nurtured his mind, consuming books and information as if they were water and air.

The derivation for his stunted stature was an endocrine disorder, a rare disease in children that results in little or no growth hormone if not treated proactively. His pituitary gland did not produce the necessary hormone that would have enabled him to grow at an average rate. At the age of twelve years old, he merely stopped growing. His parents waited for nature to take its course—assumed that he would catch up to other children—but a growth spurt never happened. They waited too long. Perhaps if his parents had taken him in for treatment, doctors would have been able to stimulate the growth hormone or prescribe replacement therapy. But, for whatever reason, they did not.

His parents were psychologists—both at the top of their field and well respected by their peers. They didn't seem like the type of people who would want to start a family in the first place, since children would interfere with their professional pursuits. But they had conceived him, late in life, in their forties. He was an only child, and Sinclair always assumed that his birth was a mistake.

When the doctors informed them that their son had stopped growing, his parents took this information in stride. If anything, both his mother and father were fascinated by their son's limited size. Their education, their profession, their passion, was the study of the human mind. His parents were far more interested in analyzing the brain than the machinations of the body. They seemed to accept, even embrace, their son's physical limitations, focusing instead on his intellectual potential, which they believed would be greater than average due to his bodily deficits. They treated him like a human case study, pushing him to challenge himself, forcing him to compensate for his growth retardation, and all the while observing him like a guinea pig. He was not allowed to participate in frivolous activities like organized team sports or general roughhousing or playing outdoors. They rarely let him watch television. Silly board games that did not promote intellectual growth were prohibited. Instead, discussions of substance became a daily activity. His parents were relentless. Demanding. Their son had the benefit of their psychological skills and influence, and they knew he was destined for greatness. Sinclair hated them for what they did and didn't do.

He knew that if his parents were still living today, they would be mortified by the occupation he chose. They would wonder how their only son—educated in an Ivy League school and groomed to accomplish anything—could turn his back on becoming someone important and a valuable member of society. A doctor. A scientist. Maybe even a politician. But Sinclair knew that even if he dedicated himself to work in one of those fields, he would never be truly respected or accepted. He would be marginalized due to his size and it would be the very first thing his peers would see and judge—a small man. Additionally, all those professions lacked one specific thing that he had come to crave—danger. Sinclair embraced and thrived on living in the element of danger. It was what fed his soul. His parents would never understand that. Most people could not.

He glanced out the window, watching the blur of trees whip past on both sides of the I-95. Phillip guided the Grand Marquis along the freeway, maintaining a speed of seventy miles per hour.

"Rather remote, are we not?" Sinclair observed.

"Uh-huh," Phillip answered.

Sinclair pointed to an approaching exit sign. "This should do fine. Pull off here, please."

Phillip activated the blinker, and after taking the next off-ramp, they drove east for some time, delving deeper and deeper into the rolling countryside. Occasionally, they passed a random farmhouse or trailer set right off the road.

Sinclair lit a cigarette and kept his eyes cast out the windshield. "Always been a curiosity to me." He pointed to yet another trailer set up on cinderblocks just thirty feet off the country road. "If one chooses to live out here, in the absolute middle of nowhere, why would you want to live right next to the road? I would think if I decided to reside away from the city, far from the hustle and bustle, and I had all this countryside to live in, that I would build a home with a view of my surroundings. When I look out the window, I would want to see birds and trees and the mountainside. Instead, people like that decide to live in a tin box, mere feet from the road, with a view that leaves much to be desired. Why do you think that they would do that, Phillip?"

The big man shrugged.

"I'm sure you must have some thoughts on the matter. Humor me."

Phillip stared into the rearview mirror, scrutinizing the shrinking trailer behind them before they turned a corner and were surrounded on both sides by nothing more than trees and high-standing kudzu. "Dunno. Maybe they like it. To live close to the road."

"So you think it's a matter of choice? Is that it?"

Again, the big man shrugged, but then followed up with a thought. "Maybe they don't care about a view. Or maybe it's all they can afford and they don't have any other choice. Some people don't have choices. They get what they get."

Sinclair stared over at Phillip, quietly amused by the big man's observations. Generally, his sentences were restricted to two or three one-syllable words. "I guess I never considered putting it into those kinds of terms." He gestured out the window with his cigarette. "What about you? Would you live out here? In the middle of nowhere?"

"Too quiet."

Sinclair smiled at how quickly Phillip reverted back to his sparse usage of words. "I would think for that very reason it would suit you. Being quiet and reflective in nature."

"No."

"You like city life?"

"Yeah."

"Why?"

"Dunno." Phillip adjusted himself in his seat. Rubbed at his square jaw for a moment. "Cuz I like the noise, I guess. Distracts me."

"Distracts you? From what?"

The car approached an old dirt road that wound its way up the side of a hill shrouded by thick foliage. Phillip motioned toward the dirt path. "Up there?"

Sinclair flicked his cigarette out the window. "Fine."

Phillip checked the rearview mirror before pumping the brakes and turning onto the road. The Grand Marquis bumped over the heavily rutted surface, causing both men to jostle upon their leather seats.

They drove for another mile in silence, the road getting more and more rough and unforgiving.

Sinclair tapped on his window with his index finger. "This should be far enough, I would think."

Phillip slowed the car and pulled it off to the side of the road. He kept the engine running and extracted himself from his seat with great effort, then leaned down and popped open the trunk. "I'll take care of it."

Sinclair unclipped his seat belt and opened his door as well. "I think I'll join you. Like to stretch my legs for a moment."

As both men walked to the rear of the car, Sinclair took a deep breath of the country air. "Well. To the business at hand."

Phillip swung open the trunk, reached inside, and grabbed Ernie's corpse from within the well. The black plastic bag was still securely wrapped around his head, his body already starting to become rigid.

Sinclair watched as Phillip effortlessly slung Ernie's body over his shoulder like a baseball bat, and scrutinized the dead man's sweater, khakis, then finally stared at the worn soles on his shoes. "I never quite understand why people don't put a little more thought into how they dress. Appearances are crucial. First impressions and all."

Sinclair lit a cigarette and motioned toward the woods. "A hundred yards or so. See if you can find a ravine of some kind. And perhaps you should cut a vein. Let the predators take it from there." He puffed on his cigarette. "And try and hurry. I'm getting rather hungry."

Phillip adjusted Ernie's corpse on his shoulder like a lumberjack carrying an axe, then stepped into the woods.

CHAPTER TWENTY-SIX

"Ain't t o o s a fe , two pretty young ladies like yourselves, hitching a ride with a complete stranger."

Alice and Delilah had met the truck driver in The Golden Chicken Diner back in Goldsboro. The man had polished off a stack of flapjacks, a side order of thick-cut bacon, and a sizable bowl of grits smothered in butter and maple syrup, without blinking an eye. He kept a cigarette going during his entire lunch and must have consumed about a quart of black coffee, and never once got up to relieve himself. He talked to anybody that would listen, and even to those who wouldn't. Waitresses, customers, busboys, deliverymen, whomever. The man was short and burly, shirt open at the neck revealing a thick blanket of black chest hair. A well-worn green cap with no insignia of any kind tilted back on a square-shaped head, his hair neatly trimmed.

Dale was his name, a name that he offered to anyone. He did most of the talking. Talked about the rainstorm heading their way, how good the thick-cut bacon was at The Golden Chicken, about some damn funny show with some kind of alien puppet that lives with a family. One of them syndication shows—couldn't remember the name of it. The truck driver discussed the upcoming election and how neither candidate was worth a goddamn. He drove a semi-trailer truck, loaded with pet food—dog food, cat food, rabbit food, fish food, you name it—and was making his way down to Lumberton.

So, Lumberton would have to do for now—the only current option on the table for Alice and Delilah. Either that, or sticking out their thumbs and risk being picked up by a State Trooper. Alice thought that, once they got to Lumberton, they could figure out how they would then get down to Shallotte. Probably better off this way. The trucker would be able to identify them, and if it ever came to that, it would be better that their trail ended in Lumberton. From there, they could try the whole bus thing again, being able to blend in with a crowd of other passengers.

Dale the truck driver was way too social to be driving a truck for a living, sitting in a cab all alone for miles on end. He eagerly accepted the request to carry two passengers for a spell and seemed downright tickled to be hosting the girls for a few hundred miles.

The cab of the truck smelled of old socks, salted potato chips, and the pine tree air freshener that dangled from his rearview mirror. He ground the truck into fourth gear and the semi labored up onto the 95 South on-ramp. He lit up yet another Camel Light and tossed the match out the window.

"We appreciate this. We missed our bus and the next one doesn't come through for a few hours," Alice offered up. She didn't really know if that was true, but she felt the need to have some kind of story.

Dale waved away the explanation. "Never ridden in one of them Greyhounds before, and hope that I never do. Don't really like the notion of other folks driving my big backside around. Let me tell you, I make for one poor back-seat driver." He let out a snort and kept chuckling to himself for a few seconds.

Alice nodded like he was preaching to the choir.

"Most folks on the road shouldn't be behind the wheel of a moving vehicle, if you ask me. Yakking on their cellular telephones, doing that texting business, not paying any kind of attention to the road. Hell. Traffic fatalities are the number one killer in America. Did you know that? Forget murders and cancer and all that other stuff. Anyone thinks that they can drive. But that's just a load of BS. Shoot, most folks should not be driving if you ask me." He chuckled to himself again. It appeared to be a pattern in the man's speech: make a completely obvious statement, then chuckle like it was the funniest damn thing on earth.

Alice slouched in the passenger seat, bearing the brunt of most of the senseless chatter. Behind her, Delilah perched on the edge of the unmade cot in the back of the cab, clearly afraid to come into contact with the soiled sheets where the trucker slept.

"Well, I'll be honest with you two little ladies. I normally don't give rides to strangers and hitchhikers and whatnot. Most of them folks don't have all their eggs in the carton. Bunch of crazies out there. Shoot, I made the mistake of giving a ride to a few nutjobs in my day, and half the time I didn't know if they were going to shoot me or crow like a rooster. I tell you what, there are all kinds out there."

Dale gave Alice a little wink. A piece of ash dropped off the tip of his cigarette and settled between his legs, but he paid it no mind.

"But I don't think I'll get much trouble from the two of you, now will I? You're not going to shoot me or crow like a rooster, are you?" Again, with a long, prolonged chuckle.

Alice shook her head. "No. We might bore you to death though."

The trucker exploded with laughter, his hard, low-hanging belly bouncing up and down. "Hell, I won't bore you to death, but I might talk your damn ear off. That much is true. My old lady says I talk too much, and she's probably right about that fact. I even talk to myself. Right out loud. I'll ask myself a question and answer myself right back. And if that isn't a sure sign of losing your marbles, I don't know what the hell is."

The trucker sucked on his cigarette, checked to see how much he had left to smoke, then stuck it back in the corner of his mouth.

"Mind if I have one of those?" Alice motioned toward the trucker's pack of smokes.

"Hell, no. Help yourself. Got a few cartons of them in the back there. One good thing about driving in the South, the cigarettes won't cost you an arm and a leg. Next to a good cup of coffee, they're a trucker's best friend."

Alice lit up, savoring the blast of nicotine. She let her head fall back against the seat and hoped for a lull of silence.

But Dale the trucker thought otherwise. "So what takes you ladies to Lumberton, anyways? Winter break?"

Alice hesitated before responding. "A funeral. Friend of ours passed away." She hoped that a lie like that would shut the trucker up for a while.

It didn't.

"Ah, hell. Sorry to hear that. Something unexpected? If you don't mind me asking."

Alice felt a little light-headed from the cigarette. "Car accident."

The trucker shook his head like he expected something like that. "Damn shame. Never think it's gonna happen to someone you know. But, God knows, I've seen my share of car accidents. They happen in a split second. *BAM*. Nothing worse than the sound of breaking glass and the crunch of metal on metal. Horrible way to go."

"Yeah. Thanks." Alice stabbed out her cigarette in the ashtray that was stuffed with old filters—a morgue for cigarettes. "I'm going to close my eyes if you don't mind. Been a rough couple of days."

"Please. By all means. You girls get some shut-eye. I promise to try and keep my big trap shut for a while. Might sing to myself a little, but other than that, I'll be as quiet as a church mouse."

Alice closed her eyes. She had no intention of falling asleep, just needed a break from his chatter for a while. But the hum of eighteen wheels strumming along the pavement quickly coaxed her in. She heard the trucker strike another match, smelled the sulfur and wave of cigarette smoke, and let herself fold together and slip into the blackness that was determined to swallow her whole.

* * *

The sound of the truck engine cutting off finally stirred her from sleep. Not that she would complain about waking up. The dream was another bad one—about Jason again. In the dryer like he always was, his little body banging against the drum, making that awful sound. *KA-THUMP. KA-THUMP. KA-THUMP.* Alice's eyes snapped open, forgetting where she was until she looked over at the truck driver, smiling his gap-toothed grin.

"Gonna go gas her up. Won't take but a minute or so." Dale let out a little chuckle and shook his head. "Some kind of dream you were having. Talking out loud, flapping your hands. The whole nine yards."

Alice rubbed at the sleep in her eyes and noticed that Delilah had finally given in to her repulsion of the trucker's bed. She laid curled up in a ball on the well-worn mattress, dead to the world.

"Get you a soda pop or something?" Dale opened up his door and slid out of the cab, and when he landed on the pavement, only his square head poked above the seat.

"No. I don't want to make you stop every ten miles because I have to pee," Alice said.

"Heck to that. I'll fetch you both an orange soda." The trucker tilted his cap back further on his head and waddled off toward the gas station.

Alice checked on Delilah again. The girl didn't stir a bit. Asleep, she appeared even younger and more innocent than a girl of fifteen. Just a kid and already in way too much trouble. Alice knew that she would have been better off leaving the girl back in Goldsboro, staying on the bus and driving away, but for some reason, she couldn't, and her gut told her that had been a mistake.

Coffee swished in her bladder and she decided to go search for a bathroom. Another two hours or so until they got to Lumberton, and if she was going to have to listen to the trucker yammering on about his wife or baseball or the price of milk, she preferred to do it on an empty bladder.

She found the restroom tucked around the side of the filling station and it was as filthy as you'd expect a roadside gas station bathroom to be. Graffiti covered the walls, sketches of women with giant vaginas and even larger breasts. Male genitalia another favored subject, all super-sized as well.

The mirror over the sink was yellow with age, half of it rusted over from a leak in the ceiling above it. Her distorted reflection stared back at her—she looked like hell. Her face puffy from all the alcohol, lack of sleep, and complete and utter stress she brought upon herself. Her neck had turned a darker shade of scarlet. The scab on her ear had broken open and leaked fresh blood. She barely recognized the murky reflection that stared back at her. This was no way to live. Always running. And not just the last thirty-some hours.

She splashed cold water on her face and neck, but it didn't help either her appearance or state of mind.

Screw it.

She swung the bathroom door open and swallowed in some fresh air. The sun felt warm on her face, and she wished she had the ability to enjoy it. She headed back toward the semi and noticed the truck driver on the other side of the gas station, pressed up inside a glass phone booth, jabbering into the pay phone. The square-headed man spoke into the receiver with a sense of urgency, waving his free hand in the air in a big sweeping motion. He appeared to be telling quite a tale. Definitely seemed anxious. His lips moved a mile a minute, and he kept glancing back over at his waiting rig.

Alice held back and watched him for a minute. Wild gestures. Marching in place. Then his hand pointed toward his truck. Dale nodded and listened for a moment, then hung up the phone. The trucker stared at the receiver and rubbed at his face with both hands. He took a deep breath, then waddled in the direction of his rig. He didn't notice Alice. Too caught up in his thoughts.

Alice glanced back at the gas station office and saw a television set above the counter. It looked like a news program of some kind. Someone being interviewed. Someone wearing a cop uniform. In the top corner of the television screen there was a photograph of a young woman. Alice was too far away to see it clearly, but she could tell that the photograph was of someone African American. She didn't need to see any more.

When she hoisted herself back into the cab, the truck driver greeted her with twitching eyes, and his big, easy grin had slid right off his face.

"There you are. Thought maybe I lost you," Dale said, and tried to chuckle a little. But his voice sounded different. No humor in his laugh.

Delilah sat up, wide awake now, perched on the edge of the sleeping mattress and chewing on a fresh stick of gum.

"Had to use the little girl's room," Alice said and watched the man fiddle with his keys.

"Oh. Good. Good."

"You already gassed up?" Alice asked.

Dale stared over at her like she asked him if he beat his wife. "What?"

"Thought we were stopping for gas?"

The truck driver kept glancing over his shoulder toward Delilah. "Right. Yeah. Well. Having a little engine trouble, I'm afraid."

"That right? Engine trouble? Want me to take a look?" Alice asked.

He stared at her again, attempted to chuckle, but failed miserably. "No, no. That won't be necessary. The mechanic there is gonna come take a gander. Might be a few minutes though." He kept glancing at Delilah. "A few minutes, it might be. So. So, we'll all just have to sit tight."

Alice saw that the man had started to perspire badly. Streams of sweat rolled down his neck. She nodded and helped herself to another one of his cigarettes. "Okay."

After Alice lit up, the trucker snatched at the pack and fired one up as well.

"You forget our orange sodas?" Alice asked.

"What?"

"Orange sodas. Thought you were going to grab a few sodas."

"Oh. Forgot all about that. I can go get them right now if you like," the man stammered.

Alice sucked on her cigarette. "No. That's okay."

"You sure? Just take me a second." The truck driver talked fast. Fidgeted in his seat.

"I'm sure. Thanks."

It was quiet for a few moments. Dale played with his keys and wouldn't look at either girl.

"Delilah, my phone is in your purse. Can you hand me your bag?" Alice looked to the young girl and waited.

Delilah stared at her purse—ever-present on her lap—and tilted her head like a dog hearing a strange, new sound. "Your phone?"

Alice reached her hand back toward the girl. "Yeah. My phone. In your purse." Alice didn't wait for Delilah—she snatched the purse and set it in her lap. "Guess I could use the pay phone." She stared over at the truck driver. "There's a pay phone, right? Thought I saw you using one."

Dale sucked hard on his cigarette. "No . . . I . . . What?"

"The pay phone. Beside the gas station. I saw you talking."

"No. No." Nervous laughter. "Not me."

"Really? Huh. Guess you have a twin."

The trucker clutched at the steering wheel hard. Ten white knuckles.

"Who were you talking to?"

"No one." Then Dale reached for the door handle, heard the *click,* and looked back at the pistol pressed toward his belly.

"Is the back locked?" Alice asked, both hands gripped around the gun.

The truck driver didn't answer. Just kept staring down the barrel of the pistol, his hands held out in front of him.

"The back of your truck. Is it locked?"

Dale nodded that it was. The cigarette burned gray from the corner of his mouth, stinging at his eyes, but he kept his hands right where they were.

"Okay. Here's what's going to happen. We're going to go to the back of the truck. You're going to unlock the doors and climb inside. I'm betting you're too out of shape to try and outrun me, so don't even think about it. Do you understand me?"

Delilah's wide eyes matched those of the truck driver.

Alice nudged the pistol into his ribs. "Do you understand?"

He nodded that he did.

"Delilah," Alice said.

The young girl remained transfixed by the sight of her own gun in Alice's hands.

"Delilah. Stay with me here. Grab my duffel bag while I escort our friend here to the back of his truck."

"What's going on?" Delilah whispered to Alice as if the trucker couldn't hear her.

"You've made the news. Now grab my bag and follow me. Okay?"

Delilah kept staring. Kept chewing. But managed a nod anyway.

Alice nudged the pistol into the man's soft belly a little harder and waited for him to climb out of the truck. When the trucker lifted his hands higher out of sheer reflex, Alice whispered, "Hands at your sides. Let's not be obvious."

Dale dropped his hands, smoke still working at his eyes, and opened his door nice and easy, just as Alice instructed.

Alice hugged the side of the truck—the side facing away from the front of the gas station—kept the pistol low at her waist and followed the man to the back of the rig. The rear of the truck stood in clear view of the gas station, and Alice's eyes skirted toward the front doors, saw the television playing, and the attendant smoking at the counter, looking up at the screen.

Dale fumbled with his keys for a moment—there had to be at least twenty different keys on the ring.

"What did they say on the news? About the girl?"

The man glanced up, his face as white as a bleached sheet, and swallowed hard. "That she's gone missing."

"And that's it? That's what's got you all worked up?"

He stared down at his handful of keys. "They want to talk to her. Said that she killed a man in Philadelphia. Shot him. And they're looking for her."

Alice nodded. "Okay. Get the door unlocked."

His hands trembled, and he nearly dropped the set of keys. Then he tried again. Found the slot, and the lock finally unsnapped with a sharp *click*.

"She really kill that man?" the truck driver braved.

Alice reached over and removed the spent cigarette from the corner of his mouth. Flicked it to the ground. "You really want to know the answer to that question?"

Dale the trucker did not.

"Go ahead and open the door."

The trucker grunted as he hoisted up the rolling door.

"Climb inside."

His short little legs somehow got him up and inside the trailer.

"Thanks for the ride, Dale. Sorry you got involved. Police on their way?"

He nodded that they were.

"Pull the door down."

The door clapped down with a bang. Alice slid the handle back into place, then secured the lock. She dropped the keys into a water grate and heard a metallic *plunk* a few feet down.

Delilah still squatted on the edge of the sleeping mattress inside the cab of the truck—the girl hadn't budged an inch.

Alice poked her head inside. "We gotta go."

The young girl took a break from her chewing for a second. "Why?"

"Because of you. That's why. Now, grab my bag."

Delilah didn't move. "No. Why *run*? It's too late. Cops are looking for me."

"Right. You knew that was bound to happen eventually. So you can either stay here and get caught, or come with me."

"I'm tired of running," the young girl said.

"You're just getting started, Delilah. You're just getting started."

The girl stared down at her hands.

"Fine. Whatever." Alice was done with her. The next move, up to her. Time to move on. She grabbed her duffel bag and hopped back out of the truck.

Delilah resumed snapping on her gum. Watched Alice walk across the parking lot, then quickly climbed out of the truck and trailed after her like a six-week-old puppy.

Alice made a beeline toward a middle-aged man wearing matching camouflage pants and a shirt as he recapped the gas tank on his station wagon. A ten-foot boat, banged and nicked up, tied to the top of the car. A few fishing poles jutted over the edge of the aluminum fishing boat.

"Excuse me, sir, but I was wondering if we could hitch a ride with you?"

The fisherman had a plug of chew stuffed into his cheek and his nose was peeling a layer of skin from a nasty sunburn. He stared at Alice. Then at Delilah. Then back to Alice. "Hitch a ride?"

"Yeah. If you don't mind. We were riding in that truck over there, but it's having some engine problems."

The fisherman stuck his finger in his ear. Scratched at what was itching him. "Don't mind, I guess. Just going up the road a mile or so, though."

"Perfect. So are we."

The fisherman scratched at the other ear. Motioned for them to go ahead and climb in the back seat.

When Alice opened the door, she could smell dead fish. A mile or so would probably be all that she could handle.

CHAPTER TWENTY-SEVEN

The parking lot at the North Carolina/Virginia state line Welcome Center stood packed with cars, minivans, pickup trucks, and a separate area for eighteen-wheelers, all lined up in nice and even rows. Motorists stretched their legs, families ate snacks at picnic tables set away from the restrooms, and dog owners let their four-legged friends off leashes to roam, sniff, and answer the call of nature.

Sinclair strode across the grass, Phillip at his heels, and made his way to a public telephone that appeared as though it hadn't been used for quite some time. The silver box surrounding the phone was covered in dust and grime, and tagged with indecipherable graffiti in various colors. Sinclair waited for Phillip to pick up the receiver and watched as the big man withdrew two packets of hand sanitizer towelettes from his pocket and proceeded to wipe down the mouth and earpiece carefully.

"Dirty," Phillip said.

"Indeed. I shudder to think who has pressed their lips to this device," Sinclair agreed.

Phillip kept wiping down the phone, waiting for the signal from Sinclair that it was clean enough.

"Do you have the change?"

Phillip grunted that he did.

"And a pen?"

Another grunt, and he handed Sinclair an ink pen.

"After you dial the number, I would like a Mountain Dew and some cookies from the vending machine. Nothing with raisins, please. I shouldn't be more than a minute."

Phillip glanced down at a slip of paper, dialed the number, fed the slot with some quarters, waited for the connection, then handed Sinclair the telephone.

Sinclair counted each ring silently and produced a faux smile as someone finally picked up. "Good afternoon. My name is Mark Weatherford. May I ask whom I am speaking to?"

A man's voice issued a dull response.

"It's nice to make your acquaintance, Robert, and I realize that you have no idea who I am, and this may come out of the blue, so I will cut straight to the point—"

The man cut Sinclair off; his voice curt and dismissive.

"No, Robert, I can assure you that I am not a telemarketer. Please, do not hang up, and listen to me for a moment. Time is of the essence. Tell me, do you happen to have a daughter by the name of Alice?"

There was a moment's lull, dead silence on the other end of the line, then the man answered, his voice going up an octave as he stammered into the phone.

"Yes, yes. Alice is alive, but"—Sinclair listened to the man's desperate flurry of questions for another moment or two—"I understand. I really do. I'm sure you have a thousand questions, but suffice it to say that I am a friend of Alice's and I only want to help."

Again, Alice's father fired off a barrage of frantic inquiries.

"Yes, I have seen her recently, but, unfortunately, she's gotten herself into a bit of trouble."

More questions. More pleading.

"I know this must be difficult for you."

In the background, Sinclair heard a female's voice plead and crack, and Alice's father shushed the woman to be quiet.

"Listen to me for a moment, Robert. I am on a public pay phone and I am running out of quarters. I can promise you that Alice is safe—for the moment—but the trouble that she finds herself in is rather serious. I think it would be best if we met in person."

An automated operator's voice came onto the line, requesting more change.

"Robert, we're running out of time here. So, please let me know where to find you so that I can answer all your questions face-to-face."

Sinclair listened into the earpiece for another few seconds, and jotted down an address on the back of the flier. "Thank you, Robert. I shall be seeing you very shortly, and trust me, we will sort through all of this. You have my word on that."

As he returned the phone to its cradle, he watched Phillip approach, clutching a can of Cheerwine and a package of chocolate chip cookies.

"I specifically asked for Mountain Dew."

"Sold out." The big man extended the can of Cheerwine toward Sinclair.

"Then I guess this will have to do."

CHAPTER TWENTY-EIGHT

The fisherman in the station wagon hadn't uttered a peep during the five-minute drive over pothole-riddled roads. His belly pressed up against the steering wheel, and the man cleaned his fingernails with a pocketknife as he drove. The car rattled and squeaked as a few black flies buzzed here and there, landing momentarily before taking flight once again.

Alice knew Delilah was staring at her with those big, almond eyes, but she chose to ignore the girl. The car rounded a turn in the road and they slid across the vinyl back seat that was both sticky and reeked of something rotten.

The station wagon rumbled past a bullet-ridden stop sign, never slowing, cruised beside a barn that stood charred and black, ready to fall down at a moment's notice. They drove for another minute, then the fisherman pulled the creaking station wagon to an abrupt halt in front of a little shack with a hand-painted sign that hung over the front door, the writing barely legible. Looked like a child had scrawled the letters—*Larry's Market*.

"Far as you go," the fisherman said, then spat a mouthful of brown tobacco juice out the window.

Alice and Delilah didn't argue. They piled out of the car and sucked in the fresh country air. The station wagon jerked to a start before Alice could even close the door, kicking up a brown cloud of dust and rumbling down the single lane dirt road shrouded by live oak and cypress trees hanging heavy with Spanish moss.

The sound of the station wagon faded into the afternoon air, replaced by the call of crickets and cicadas, constant and loud. They were in the middle of the sticks. No other houses. No other cars. Just the song of insects that seemed to get shriller and shriller with each passing second.

Delilah stared at all the trees and kudzu, then pressed up close to Alice and whispered as if they were in church, "What do we do now?"

Alice looked over toward Larry's Market, nothing more than a clapboard shack not much bigger than a kid's tree house, with paint missing in fist-sized chunks on the warped pieces from wood that curled up at the edges. Sections of termite-ridden wood planks had fallen off long ago and lay buried in the dirt. A tin roof rattled in the wind. Most of it rusted and covered with dark green moss.

"Go talk to Larry, I guess." Alice walked up the front steps to Larry's porch, sidestepping a gaping hole in the rotten wood the size of a pancake. Something brown scurried in the darkness below the porch floorboards. She forced her eyes away from the hole in the wood and stepped onto a small porch. Crap everywhere. Empty cans of baked beans used for ashtrays. Bags of generic cat food. Stacks of old newspapers black with mildew piled up beside a wicker rocking chair. When Alice opened the screen door, it shrieked like a fox caught in a trap.

The front room was cast in darkness, not much sunlight able to peek through the layers of filth on the small windows. One window had been taped over with cardboard, aged and swollen by years of rain. Two buck heads were mounted onto the back wall, their antlers tangled up with cobwebs that ensnared a collection of dead flies.

A stuffed raccoon, a few stuffed piglets, and a bird that looked like it might have been a turkey once stood frozen in mid-motion along the front wall next to the door.

Larry's Market offered little more than generic sodas, boiled peanuts, and homemade beef jerky displayed in a rusted-out wheelbarrow. But the salty curing of the beef jerky couldn't put a dent in the stench of cat piss that permeated the air.

Alice spotted the oxygen tank in the corner of the room before she saw who it was attached to.

"Help ya?" a phlegmy voice hissed from the shadows.

Delilah let out a low moan and clutched at Alice's arm. She bolted for the front door, but Alice grabbed the girl by the wrist and held her still, then ventured a little closer to the voice in the corner of the room.

"Hello."

An old man, who appeared more dead than alive, perched atop an overturned pickle barrel, sitting perfectly still as if he had been subjected to taxidermy as well. The old man wore blue jean overalls on top of a threadbare shirt that might have been red a decade ago. A twenty-pound cat that looked as ancient as the old man curled up on his lap, and the oxygen tube snaked over the tomcat and wound its way up into the old man's nose, poking its way through the patches of nose hair that sprouted out of his nostrils like tiny shrubs.

"Bags of the boiled nuts is a buck fifty," the old man wheezed, each word and breath sounding like an effort.

"Are you Larry?" Alice asked.

The hiss that squeezed out of his lungs didn't exactly answer her question but it was all that he offered.

"We're looking for a ride," Alice said.

"Ride? What kind of ride?" Larry grunted.

"We need to get to Shallotte. We're kinda stuck. Do you know anybody around here that might be willing to give us a ride down there?"

Larry stared at her with jaundiced eyes, took a pouch of tobacco and rolling papers from the center pocket in his overalls and twisted up a perfect cigarette without even looking down. "A ride to Shallotte? All the way down there near Myrtle Beach?"

"Yeah. We're willing to pay someone for their time, of course."

An old woman, bent as a twisted stick, shuffled into the front room and gnawed on something inside her toothless mouth. Alice nodded at her, and the old woman kept chewing and stared at Delilah like she wasn't sure what to make of the girl.

"Whatcha going to Shallotte for?" Larry spat out.

Alice forced a little smile and glanced over at the old woman who hadn't taken her eyes off Delilah. "Got some friends down there and we missed our bus."

"This here's a market. Selling pop and nuts and such," Larry wheezed.

"Right. I understand. Just thought you might know someone. We'd be willing to pay them three hundred dollars."

"Cash money?" the old man asked before seizing up with a coughing fit.

Alice waited him out for a minute. "Yeah. Cash. Up front, of course."

Larry spat something brown into a coffee tin at his feet, then smoked on his hand-rolled cigarette some more. He let out a cloud of gray and joined the old woman in chewing on something. "Three hundred's a lot for a ride, ain't it?"

"I guess it is. But it's important that we get there. Kind of a hurry. So, if there's anyone that you might know that lives around here with a car."

"Eli Brown's got him a car."

"Okay. Great."

"Broke down, though. Hasn't been running for a few months or so. Transmission is shot, I would guess."

"Okay. Anybody else live around here?"

"The Shoemakers live down the road a ways. 'Bout a quarter mile."

"And they have a car?"

"Naw. Bill's got him that multiple sclerosis."

"Guess we're out of luck," Alice said.

Larry grunted and chewed. He took another look at Delilah. "Got me a truck."

Alice nodded. "A truck would be fine. As long as it gets us there."

"Drives fine enough. A Ford. Not any of that foreign shit."

"Perfect. We'd really appreciate it."

Larry turned to the old lady and shouted at her like she hadn't been standing there the entire time. "Going for a drive. Gone for a couple of hours. Fry up that chicken for when I get back."

The old woman tilted her head and kept chewing.

"The truck will be needing some gas. Ain't got enough to get there and back," Larry said.

Alice nodded. "Of course. We'll pay for that, too."

"All right, then. Let me fetch the keys." Larry blew his nose hard into a handkerchief and stuffed it back into his pocket. "Grab yourself a bag of the boiled if you want." He grunted to his feet and the tomcat dropped to all fours. He shuffled closer to Alice and jabbed his thumb toward Delilah. "That one there rides in the back of the truck though."

* * *

The oxygen tank rode between Alice and Larry, wedged in between the two bucket seats along with a few empty cans of generic beer.

The cat once again curled up on Larry's warm lap, like they were connected at the hip. The nub of a burnt-down cigarette nestled in the corner of the old man's lips, and he still chewed on something.

Alice glanced over at the speedometer—the old Ford farm truck puttered along at forty miles per hour on the I-95 South. Traffic zipped past them, semis and cars, horns blaring, middle fingers extended, but Larry paid them no mind.

"Where are we exactly?" Alice asked.

The old man gave her a sideways look. "Whatcha mean?"

"Been hitchhiking for a while. Not even sure where we are."

Larry grunted. "Just outside Hope Mills."

"Not much out here, is there?"

"Guess that depends on what you're looking for," Larry said.

"And how far are we from Shallotte?"

Larry dug at his ear for a second. "Don't know. Ninety, maybe a hundred miles or so."

Alice did the quick math in her head. At the rate and speed Larry was driving, it would take them over two hours to get there.

Tires hummed, horns blew. The tomcat stood up in Larry's lap. Circled a few times, then settled back in the same exact spot.

Alice shifted in her seat. Moved the wrong way and her rib clicked. She bit her lip and repressed a moan. She took a few shallow breaths, careful not to move the wrong way.

"Mind if I roll one of your cigarettes?" Alice asked, hoping that a cigarette might help distract her from the pain.

"Naw. Help yourself." He grabbed his pouch of tobacco and rolling papers out of his overalls and handed them over to Alice.

"Thanks. Haven't rolled my own cigarette in a long time," Alice said.

Larry nodded. "Only way to smoke 'em if you ask me."

Alice took a pinch of tobacco leaves and sprinkled them onto a rolling paper.

"You friends with that colored?" Larry jabbed his dirty thumb-nail toward the bed of the truck where Delilah pressed up to the back of the cab. The young girl sat amidst assorted junk—an old bicycle with no tires, a beat-up floral-patterned armchair, and greasy-bottomed cardboard boxes loaded up with car parts, toasters, and jars of assorted nails and screws.

Alice licked the edge of the rolling paper and twisted up a pretty decent cigarette. "Don't know if I'd call us friends exactly. Just met her, but she's a good kid."

"Steer clear of them, myself. Better off that way."

"Kids?" But Alice knew what he meant.

"Naw. Colored folk. Their kind's different from white folks. Oil and vinegar."

Alice didn't know why she baited him, but she did anyway. "How so?"

Larry snorted a laugh like that was the dumbest question ever posed. "I'll tell you how. Not working jobs. Stealin' stuff, drinkin' and whatnot."

Alice found a pack of matches on the dashboard and lit up. "I don't know, Larry. I know plenty of white people that do the same or worse."

Larry just shook his head. "Not like them. You just ain't been around long enough to see it. You'll see. You best watch out and not turn your back on 'em."

Alice's cigarette burned at her lungs. Raw, unfiltered tobacco. Alice didn't want to cough. That would just about kill her rib. "Well, I don't think we'll have any kind of problem with her. Like I said, she's just a kid."

Larry pinched the cigarette nub between his fingers and tossed it out the window. "Don't matter how old they are."

Alice forced her eyes out the window, staring out at the vegetation that hugged the freeway—cypress, goldenrod, and longleaf pine. It was quiet for a minute and she preferred the old man's long runs of silence.

"Pass me that bag of boiled nuts, will ya? Ain't had my supper yet."

Alice passed him a lunch bag–size brown paper sack, the bottom of it black and soft from peanut oil. Larry grunted a thank-you and proceeded to stuff a handful into his mouth, shell and all.

The hand-rolled cigarette went straight to Alice's head, giving her a mellow little buzz. She let her neck tilt back and she watched the North Carolina landscape roll on past her. Her eyes were getting heavy again. She stabbed the cigarette into the ashtray and thought about trying to get some sleep.

Right before she let her eyes slip closed, up ahead, about a hundred yards or so, Alice spotted a North Carolina State Trooper parked in the grassy median that separated each side of the I-95. The black and silver vehicle sparkled in the sunlight, freshly washed. She reached behind her, tapped on the glass, and Delilah gazed through the back window. Alice motioned toward the State Trooper, then waved her hand for the girl to duck on down.

Delilah's eyes went wider than usual, then she scooted down flat on the bed of the truck.

As the old Ford puttered toward the State Patrol car, Larry began to tap on the brakes, slowing down and crossing lanes toward the median. Alice shot a look at the speedometer and the truck dipped below fifteen miles per hour.

"What's the matter?" Alice asked, attempting to keep a mounting panic in check.

"Got some business to attend to. Won't take but a minute or so."

"Well, we really need to get to Shallotte as soon as possible."

Larry nodded. "Getcha there soon enough." The truck bumped along as it rode atop the gravel berm and jerked to a stop right in front of the State Patrol cruiser. Larry tooted the horn. Once. Twice.

Alice peered back through the window and could see Delilah pressed down tight to the bed of the truck. When she looked back up, the State Trooper hauled himself out of his vehicle, hiked up polyester trousers over a low-hanging belly, and strolled over toward the truck. The man's face was tomato red from the sun, his left cheek bulging fat with a plug of chew. A few dribbles of brown juice dotted his double chin.

Larry unrolled his window partway with a few grunts and groans, then had to use both hands to get it the rest of the way down. "Say, boy, I got some business to discuss with you."

The State Trooper tucked his thumbs under his belt. Chewed and spat and didn't look at all pleased that he had been forced to climb out of his vehicle. "That right?"

Larry spat right back. "Yup."

The State Trooper's right hand went to the stock of his service pistol. "I'm listening, old-timer."

Larry looked over toward Alice for a moment, shook his head, then directed his attention back on the Trooper. "If I didn't know any better, I'd say you've been gettin' your boiled nuts from some-place else, Mackie."

Mackie spit some more brown, then leaned in through the window. He had hairy arms. Big thick forearms. From the elbows down, he looked like a caveman except for a Timex strapped on his right wrist. "Naw. You should know better than that, Larry. You got the best in the county. Everybody knows that."

"Well, then, where the hell you been at?"

"Ah, hell. Up against the kidney stones again and the doctor says to me to steer clear of peanuts for a while. All nuts, for that matter. Walnuts, pecans, almonds. All of 'em. Christ almighty."

Larry rubbed at the stubble on his chin. "That right? Them kidney stones, huh?"

Mackie nodded. "Yeah. Hell."

"Had the stones myself years back. Hurt like a son-of-a-bitch, let me tell you. Felt like I was pinching out wooden nickels."

Mackie spit again. "Shoot. Durn things bring tears to my eyes and leave me on the floor next to the toilet. Rather wrestle me a wild boar than piss out one of them stones again."

Larry started with a laugh that resulted in a painful hacking fit.

Mackie let the old man cough his way through it, smiled over at Alice, eyes falling on her breasts for a second. "And just who's your pretty lady friend here? You trade in Sally for a younger model?"

Larry chuckled and hacked some more. "Naw. Just giving her a little lift is all."

Mackie kept smiling, taking another look-see at Alice's breasts. "Young lady, you sure you wanna be ridin' with this here fella? He's about as shady as they come."

Alice smiled back at the trooper, leaned forward a little, giving the man a glimpse that would keep his eyes away from the back of the truck. "Larry's been nothing but a true gentleman. A real sweetheart."

Mackie guffawed and slapped the roof of the truck. "Shoot. Bet that is the first and *last* time Larry here will ever be called the likes of that."

Larry nodded his head that that was true. "I'll take what I can get. That much is for sure."

"Oh, boy." Mackie wiped at his eyes. "The wife good? Old Sally giving you any fits?"

Larry chewed on his boiled nuts and nodded. "Mean as a three-legged dog with fleas and ticks. I swear she's gonna up and kill me one of these days."

"Sounds about right," Mackie agreed.

"And how's your folk? Your youngest boy must be growing like a weed."

"Yeah. He's nearly up to my chin now. Gonna be a tall one, that one is. Helluva football player. Left tackle. He's gonna be good, alright."

"I hear that. The boy gonna go off to Community?" Larry twisted up another cigarette and had to strike two matches before getting it lit.

"Hell. If I can afford it." Mackie cleared out his nose into a handkerchief, folded it over, then wiped his neck with the same piece of material. "We'll see. Gotta graduate first."

They were quiet for a moment. Larry smoked and Mackie swatted at a fly that kept going after his ear.

"Any interesting stories to tell me, Mackie? Or are you just having yourself a little taste in that squad car of yours and passing the time?"

"Naw. Been pretty quiet to tell you the truth. Did stop a fella earlier this morning that blew out his right front tire, riding that old rim, sparks going every which way. Doing about fifty. Dumb son-of-a-bitch."

"Ha. Probably a Yankee," Larry said.

Mackie nodded. "He was."

Larry rubbed at his face some more. "Say. Whatcha know about the traffic on the 95 anyways? Heading down to Shallotte."

Mackie gave him a sideways look. "Shallotte? What the hell you driving down to Shallotte for, Larry?"

Larry shrugged. Motioned over toward Alice. "Taking these two young'uns down there. Needed a ride and such."

Mackie glanced back over to Alice. "Younguns? I only see but the one."

"The other one is in the back there. Ain't no room up here. Not for her, anyways."

Mackie started to take a look in the back of the truck when the radio from his cruiser squawked. "Christ. What the hell they want with me now?" Mackie leaned back off the truck, hiked up his pants again, and started for his cruiser.

Alice leaned over even further, pushing her breasts out even further as well. "Officer?"

Mackie looked back into the truck, eyes falling on Alice's prizes. "Ma'am?"

The radio squawked again and Alice displayed a nice, sweet smile. "Will you be sure to tell Sally that if Larry doesn't come back home tonight, that her husband is in good hands?"

The radio continued to jabber away behind them, but Mackie couldn't hear a thing. His face went slack for a moment, staring at Alice's big, green eyes, then the man broke out into a toothy chuckle. He gave the roof of the truck another good pounding.

"You're darn tooting he's in good hands. Shoot. That's rich. Rich, I tell ya."

The radio went quiet and Alice leaned back into the seat.

"Well. I reckon we'd be best moving on, and let you get back to your business. Hello to your missus," Larry offered.

Mackie hiked up his pants once again—the damn things wouldn't stay up. "All right then. You folks take care now." He tapped the roof of the truck one final time.

"And you take care of those kidney stones, Officer." Alice smiled and gave him a wink.

"You bet I will. You bet I will," he said and winked right back.

As Larry pulled the old Ford back out onto the highway, Alice took a deep breath, wishing she had a bottle to drink from, but reached over for a handful of boiled peanuts instead.

CHAPTER TWENTY-NINE

DECEMBER 2005

The first thing Alice noticed was that Mr. Roberts didn't nod to her when she entered his store. She grabbed a basket at the front of the small grocery mart, walked past the cashiers counter, glanced over at Mr. Roberts, and he looked away without nodding.

A little odd, Alice thought.

Apart from Food Lion, Roberts was the only grocery store in Shallotte, more of a mom and pop place that carried the basics, everything overpriced. They stocked white bread and milk and sodas, coffee and beer, canned foods, cigarettes, candy, chips, and cheap magazines.

Alice had gotten to know her way around the store the last few weeks. She'd become Elton's official errand girl, pedaling down to the store every other day on an old Schwinn bicycle that he kept in his garage. *Earning your keep*, was what he called it. She picked up the usual items he favored: black licorice, pretzel sticks, and a few bottles of root beer.

Mr. Roberts perched on a stool behind the counter like he always did. He wore the same white apron he always wore and listened to the radio, set on some sports talk station that emitted mostly static.

Alice had been in here a dozen times and never saw the man smile, never heard him speak a word, but in his own peculiar way, he seemed friendly enough. After a while, she thought that maybe he was mute. She always meant to ask Elton, but she never did. It slowly became a quiet challenge to her, to see if she could ever get the man to speak. She'd say *hello* and *thank you* and *how are you* and *see you later*, but nothing elicited a verbal response. She came to think of him as the *nodder*. He would look up from the counter when she entered the store, nod, then would proceed to watch her move around his shop more out of boredom than actually keeping an eye on her. And every time Alice looked his way, he would nod, expressionless. Then, when she got to the counter to pay for her groceries, he would point to the cash register display to indicate how much she owed, and nod again. And finally, after she paid and he bagged up her items, he would give her one final nod goodbye. He was a human bobblehead.

But not today. Not a single nod. And he was watching her. Watching her every move. But when she glanced in his direction, he quickly averted his eyes and fiddled with the radio dial.

Alice carried her basket to the counter and set out her items. "Morning."

Mr. Roberts kept his chin to his chest, focused on ringing up her handful of groceries. His radio squawked behind him, a rundown of some college football scores. He cleared his throat without bothering to look at her. "You living up there at Elton's place, ain't you?"

Alice almost flinched at the sound of the man's voice. Low and gravelly, and it didn't seem to match his appearance. "Yes, sir. You know Elton?"

"I know *of* him." The man still wouldn't look her in the eye.

"I thought everybody knew everybody here in town."

"I know of him, I said. Sure ain't no friend of his though."

Alice wasn't sure if the man was joking, but judging by his tensed jaw and mouth pulled straight in a line, he was as serious as hell. "Maybe if you got to know him. He's real sweet."

Mr. Roberts jammed her groceries in a brown paper sack, then slid it across the counter toward Alice. "A man like Elton oughtn't be letting someone like you live under his roof. Ain't right. Ain't right at all."

Alice smiled uncomfortably. "I'm sorry."

Mr. Roberts finally leveled his eyes on hers, shook his head. "A man like that could get in all sorts of trouble, doing what's he doing."

Her face went flush. "I really don't understand what you mean. What's he doing wrong?"

"You ain't fooling no one. People are on to you." He glanced toward the front of his market, then stared back at her. "Ten eighty for your items."

Alice handed him a twenty. Waited for her change.

"You best take your business elsewhere from here on out. You can tell that to Elton."

"I'm sorry. But I really don't know what you mean."

"I've said enough. You go on, now. Like you out of my store."

Alice felt a sudden rush of anger, confusion, and embarrassment, all muddled together in the pit of her stomach. She'd only known Elton for a few shorts weeks, but she already felt protective of him, not appreciating someone like Mr. Roberts speaking badly of the old man. She wanted to say something to the shop owner. Wanted to tell him that he had no right to talk about people like that. Instead, she bit her tongue, plucked up her bag of groceries, and hustled out of the store without glancing back.

* * *

A community bulletin board hung on the wall outside of Roberts, right beside the newspaper vending machines. Notices for garage sales, kittens for adoption, upcoming bake sales, and fliers for community events. Many of the fliers were faded from the sun or crinkled up and brown from the rain, but in the center of the bulletin board, a brand-new eight-and-a-half-by-eleven piece of card stock stood out like a big, sore thumb. The piece of paper was bright orange so that it would get your attention. And it did. Right in the middle of the orange piece of paper was a picture of Alice. A smiling photo of her taken on her fourteenth birthday. A happier time— before Jason's accident. She had a wide smile, stared right toward the camera, looking so carefree and happy, unaware that her baby brother would be dead in a few months.

Under the photo, in big block letters, it announced: RUNAWAY. HAVE YOU SEEN ME? There was a phone number as well to encourage anyone with information to call about the smiling girl's whereabouts.

Alice nearly dropped the bag of groceries at the sight of her photo. She hadn't noticed the flier before. Must have walked right past it. She backed away from the bulletin board, almost tripped over her bicycle, but kept staring at her picture. A strange thing to look at a photo of yourself posted on a bulletin board. Alice could barely remember what it was like to be that girl anymore. She shuffled back toward the street, and felt as if she were floating, her feet lifting off the ground and hovering in the air like a dandelion shoot.

She noticed that Mr. Roberts was staring out through the shop window. Looking straight at her. She marched forward and snatched the piece of paper off the board and started to crumple it between her hands, but stopped herself. She stared down at the ball of paper, then slowly uncreased the wrinkled flier, folded it in half, and stuck it in her back pocket. She stood rooted on the sidewalk for a minute, clutching the grocery bag to her chest like a stuffed animal, unsure of which way to go. She could feel Mr. Roberts' judgmental eyes burning a hole right through her, so she started to move down Main

Street, slow at first, but then she stopped when she noticed a few more fliers stapled to light poles and taped to store windows. She counted six, then seven fliers, but it seemed like they were everywhere. The photos of her younger self fluttered in the breeze, watching her, as if they were waiting for her to come back home.

CHAPTER THIRTY

FEBRUARY 2011

"I'm so t e r r ibl y sorry to have to meet you under these circumstances," Sinclair said dolefully. He stood alone on the red brick porch—Phillip nowhere to be seen as he had been instructed to park down the street, tucked safely out of sight—and clasped his hands in front of him in a deferential manner. "And I apologize that I had to be so abrupt on the telephone earlier, but unfortunately the agency I work for doesn't have the financial means of providing cell phones and whatnot."

Alice's parents huddled side by side in the foyer of their home, both looking beaten down and exhausted. They were in their mid-forties now, but appeared to be approaching sixty. Hair mostly gray. Deep wrinkles creased the flesh around their cheeks and eyes. Alice's father had a double chin, his face puffy and doughy from alcohol. Alice's mother's hair stood dry and frizzy on her head. Her plain blue dress hung loosely from her frail frame. But it was her eyes that were the most pathetic. Dark circles under a vacant gaze as if she had been lobotomized.

"I should introduce myself properly," Sinclair said. "I'm Mark. If you would allow me to come into your home for a moment, I'll explain everything about myself, and the situation that your daughter finds herself in."

Alice's father shook Sinclair's extended hand—a glimpse of mild surprise crossed his face at how soft the small man's palm was— then he invited the stranger into their home.

* * *

Mr. and Mrs. O'Farrell, Robert and Kathy, perched on the edge of their couch, leaning forward and clinging onto every word Sinclair so eloquently spoke. They pressed closely together as if attached at the hip, both appearing so fragile, so brittle, that they might shatter into a thousand tiny pieces at any moment. Behind them, a long bookcase ran the length of the wall, lined with various framed photographs of Alice—as an infant sprawled out on a blanket in the grass, dressed as a pumpkin for Halloween, sitting on Santa Claus' lap, school class pictures, swimming on the high school team—and there were just as many pictures of Jason, growing like a weed, until the photos stopped abruptly at the age of four.

Sinclair deliberately alternated direct eye contact with both of Alice's parents, maintaining a pleasant smile that somehow offered comfort without a sense of pity. He noticed the slight tremor in Robert's hands as the man sipped from what appeared to be a cocktail.

"What sort of agency do you work with, Mark?" Robert asked, tongue thick in his mouth.

"We are a nonprofit group that specializes in working with troubled young women. Safe Choices, based out of the Philadelphia area. We primarily work with young women that are runaways. Girls that find themselves in situations that they are ill-equipped to deal with on their own. We strive to educate and attempt to reform bad patterns with the girls that have ended up living on the streets."

Alice's mother covered her mouth at the mention of those four words—*living on the streets.* Her lips began to quiver silently and she tugged at the hem of her dress as she tried her best to keep a flood of emotions in check.

"I know. I understand. It's difficult to hear it in such plain terms when discussing your own child. But I can assure you that they are safe under our care. We put a roof over their heads, provide balanced meals, and of course, most importantly of all, we give them counseling."

Alice's mother kept playing with the hem of her dress, fingers tearing at the material with a growing sense of dread. "When did you see Alice last?" Her voice barely a whisper.

"A few days ago."

"I mean, what happened? Why did she leave your facility? Why did she run away?"

Sinclair crossed his legs and leaned forward, pressing his face closer to theirs. He took a moment to consider what he wanted to say. "When Alice was found by our agency, she was living on the streets. An addict. Hooked on heroin. Doing whatever she could do to survive and maintain her fix."

Alice's father set his drink down on the coffee table, then picked it right back up.

"Since joining us, Alice eventually got clean and sober. For a little over a year now. Twelve months is quite an accomplishment. She made real progress. We were all quite proud of her."

"So, why did she leave?" Alice's father asked.

"Well, let me backtrack for a moment. To give you a better perspective of our situation." He paused, pressed his hands together. "When we found your daughter, Alice had a criminal record. Two different arrests and convictions that included petty theft, public intoxication, assault and battery. After we convinced Alice to accept our help, she worked the steps, slowly made her amends, and devoted herself to sobriety. She was truly on the road to recovery." Sinclair finally, deliberately, pulled his eyes away from theirs. He cast his gaze down toward his hands that were folded in his laps. "But, as often happens in a very high percentage of addicts, something triggered a relapse. Maybe something from her past. A moment of weakness. Possibly she came into contact with someone that she associated with in her previous life. Whatever the cause, she began using again."

Alice's mother stood. Clenched and unclenched her fists that dangled at her side.

"After Alice ran away from our facility, I thought maybe she would come home. I thought maybe this would be the safe haven where she chose to return."

They shook their heads, but it was Alice's father who finally spoke up. "Alice hasn't been home in over five years." He sipped his drink. Drank until the glass was empty. "There was an accident at home. Her younger brother. She took it badly. Felt responsible. We haven't seen her since she left. We searched for her. The police. Private agencies. Everything. But, we don't know where she went . . . or if she is even . . . you know."

Alice's mother paced the room for a moment, chewed at her lips. "We have to call the police. She's alive. She's out there, Robert. She's still out there."

Sinclair nodded. Uncrossed his legs. "Yes, but I'm sorry to say that matters are a bit more complicated. Like I mentioned, Alice has two convictions against her."

"So? What does that have anything to do with going to the police and finding our daughter?" Alice's mother snapped at the stranger. She glared at Sinclair, then at her husband, waiting for him to speak up, waiting for him to support her unconditionally. "Robert? Say something."

Alice's father cleared his throat, but all he could do was stare into his glass.

"If I may," Sinclair coaxed. When Alice's father didn't object, he continued on. "A few days ago, Alice broke into our administrative office and stole some money. Not a lot, but for a nonprofit like ourselves, it was a substantial amount. After she took the money, Alice fled Philadelphia. She left the city, and based on the information we have gathered, we strongly believe that she was either coming home, or possibly, to a town called Shallotte."

Alice's mother sat back down and continued to tug at the hem of her dress. "Shallotte? What's in Shallotte?" Whatever strength and defiance she had a moment ago quickly dissolved into doubt and despair.

"I don't know, to be quite frank. I really don't. But we think she might be headed there." He stood and held his arms out before him, as if making an offering. "Could we bring in the police on this matter? Certainly. Should we go to the police? Probably. But my dilemma is this. If the police are involved in this matter, Alice would face charges and most likely earn her third strike." He began to pace the room, waving his arms as he spoke. "I am fond of your daughter. Very fond of Alice. I believe she is *this* close to a full recovery and turning down the correct path. I was hoping, possibly foolishly, to avoid involving the authorities and to resolve this matter another way."

"How?" Alice's father whispered.

Sinclair reached out and ran his finger along the top of the bookcase as if checking for dust. "How? By finding her as quickly as we can. By having her return the stolen money before she crosses the line. Before it's too late. And, more importantly, by finally bringing Alice home where she belongs. Back to family."

Alice's mother clutched at her husband's hand. From Robert's reaction, it was both unexpected and excessive. "Do you really think you can find her?"

"Yes. Yes, I do."

"Tell us what we can do," she urged.

Sinclair turned and glanced at all the photos of Alice. He smiled, his small teeth exposed, as he picked up a photo of Alice with a small boy riding on her back. "Alice's brother?"

They both nodded. What little light was left in their eyes faded away like a wisp of dust.

"Jason. Jason was his name," Alice's mother whispered.

"Ah," Sinclair replied. "What a sweet-looking boy." He studied their faces. Observed the devastation that ravaged them from the inside out. "You can help Alice before it's too late. You really can."

They stared at the strange man in their living room, unsure of what exactly he meant.

"When I find her, and I will, I promise you that, I will need you to come at a moment's notice."

"Of course," Alice's mother pleaded.

"Good." Sinclair tapped the photo of Alice and Jason with his index finger. "May I borrow this? Sometimes memories of what used to be good in someone's life can help encourage that individual to finally accept help and go back to the person that they're meant to be."

Alice's mother finally broke down and cried, unashamed to do so in the presence of a stranger. Her husband placed his hand on her back and patted her like soothing a fussy infant.

"I will keep this safe. I promise," Sinclair whispered over the woman's disturbing sobs. "And I'll find your daughter. You have my word on that."

CHAPTER THIRTY-ONE

The small town remained pretty much how Alice had left it six years ago, a place frozen in time. As Larry guided his truck down Shallotte's Main Street, Alice watched through the window, recognizing stores and shops that she used to frequent when this was her home for a few brief weeks. Roberts Grocery was still there. As was Lucy's Diner and Stan's Pub. A Burger King had opened up on Main Street. A new coffee shop, but not much else.

It all seemed familiar yet foreign at the same time. She felt like an outsider, an unwanted guest traveling in a distant land. She had never really been part of this community and she probably would never be. Alice didn't know what she expected to find here. There would be no definitive answers or solutions waiting to be revealed. What she *hoped* to recover was the feeling of being safe once again. She wanted to watch Elton fish, ride in his truck, and help him set rat traps, make him coffee, and not think about everything else—Jason, her parents, her lack of purpose, her drinking problem, and now, a bag full of stolen money. As she sat in Larry's old Ford truck—in a moment of reflection—she silently regretted that she had taken the money in the first place.

The truck passed the last of the commercial buildings at the outskirts of town, and the road narrowed as a section of dense woods pressed in on both sides of them. Sweetgum, river birch, and slippery elm all seemed to compete with one another, standing tall and reaching toward the road. The truck began to wind this way and that way, and the turns got sharper and sharper, and Larry coughed and cussed, and slowed the Ford to a crawl, barely traveling ten miles per hour.

"We getting close yet? Just where the hell we goin' anyways?"

Alice stared out the window, trying to recognize the turnoff to Elton's house. "It's been a while, but I think we're almost there."

"Gonna be gettin' dark soon, and I don't like driving all over creation when the sun gets to settin'."

"Left here," Alice said and pointed toward a dirt road on the left-hand side.

Larry thumped on the brakes and the cat went flying down at his feet, and in the process, knocked the oxygen tubes straight out of his nose. "Goddamnit, Lilly. Watch yourself now."

Lilly clawed around down at his feet, and Larry braked harder, jerking the truck forward and causing all the junk in the back to slide forward. Delilah banged up against the glass and Alice could hear her mutter. Lilly finally managed to right herself, then hopped back onto the seat and right into Alice's lap.

"Don't think so, kitty," Alice said. She promptly lifted the twenty-pound tomcat and deposited it back upon Larry's lap. "It's down here about a mile. Next to the river."

"About a mile?"

"Yes."

"Next to the river?"

"Yes." Alice couldn't wait to be done with both Larry and Lilly.

"Damn wild goose chase." Larry wound the oxygen tube around his neck and stuffed it back into his nostrils, all the while smoking a crooked cigarette.

The cab of the truck darkened as the trees that hung over the dirt road swallowed them up. The path got rougher, deeper ruts and potholes, and blackberry bushes clawed and scratched at the sides of the truck.

"Damn wild goose chase is what this is," Larry spat out again.

They cut around another turn and the trees finally opened up to a clearing, and there it stood: Elton's single-story brick house with newly painted white trim around the windows and doors. A few birdfeeders hung from the low-hanging limbs of sweet birch trees. The well-manicured lawn, mowed in neat rows with nary a weed in sight. Rosebushes had been planted along the sidewalk that ran up to the front door. Resting up on the front porch railing, a dozen fishing rods stood at attention.

Larry stopped the truck and motioned toward the house. "This here the one?"

Alice stared at the place that was like a home to her for a few moments in time. "Yeah. That's it."

Delilah poked her head up, her hair wind-whipped and standing on end, with bits of leaves and chunks of paper sticking out of it.

Alice reached into her duffel bag and counted off five twenties and handed them over to Larry. "Thanks, Larry. An extra hundred for you."

Larry accepted the cash and slipped it into the center pocket of his overalls like he expected nothing less. "All right, then."

Alice climbed out of the truck, stretched stiff legs, and noticed Larry doing the same. "Really appreciate you driving us down here."

"Uh-huh." Larry reached back into the truck and grabbed a hold of his oxygen tank. "Like to have me a beer before I head on back." The old man spit onto the sidewalk and shuffled up the walkway toward the house.

"There's a market down in town, Larry. Passed it on the way here," Alice said.

Larry kept shuffling. "I'm sure there is. But I ain't paying no two dollars for a can of beer."

Alice slung the duffel bag over her shoulder and winced—she kept forgetting about her bruised rib. She took a quick breath, then quickly caught up with the old man.

"I'll tell you what, Larry. I'll give you some extra cash for a few beers. My treat. I don't even know if my friend is home."

Larry sidestepped his way up the porch steps and stopped to catch his breath. "I ain't in no hurry. Got to relieve myself anyways." The old man plopped down on a wicker chair and held the oxygen tank on his lap while he searched for his pouch of tobacco.

"Well, well, well. Howdy, kiddo."

Alice looked up toward the front door and there was Elton, wearing a pair of khakis and a powder-blue button-up shirt. His face looked thinner than she remembered. He still wore a pair of glasses, but the lenses were much thicker and they magnified the creases that swarmed around his eyes. He hunched over a bit and leaned against a hand-carved wooden cane. Alice could smell a pot of coffee brewing from inside the house, and for the first time in far too long, she felt like she was finally home.

CHAPTER THIRTY-TWO

The river churned brown with tiny whitecaps the size of summer melons, breaking under the glow of red from the setting sun that dipped quickly to the west. A slew of recent rains had widened the river considerably—the waterline pushing much higher up on the banks than usual. The sounds of a woodpecker going after stubborn bark echoed through the damp air with a rapid *tap, tap, tap*.

Alice perched next to Elton out on the deck in the same set of green-and-white folding chairs that they sat in so many years ago. The wood-slat decking appeared newly sanded and stained, the color of soft cherry. Behind them, the glass sliding doors were pulled closed, and inside the house, Delilah sprawled on the couch, flicking through the channels on the television and making herself completely at home.

Elton sipped from a mug of coffee. Alice had yet to touch hers. They sat in silence, slowly adjusting to one another's company once again, and taking their time in doing so. They listened to the river push past, the constant rush and gurgle with its easy, soothing water song. Everything in front of them perfect—the setting sun, a handful of soft clouds, and a slight breeze that wasn't chilly enough to warrant sweaters.

Elton finally broke the lull of comfortable silence. "That Larry fella sure was a character. Where'd you dig him up from?"

"You should have seen his wife."

Elton snorted out a laugh. "Well, he comes from a different time, a different way of life, and it takes all types, I suppose."

"Thought he'd never leave."

Elton shrugged. "Shoot, bringing the likes of you two young gals down here was probably the most excitement that old-timer's seen in years."

Alice nodded and another prolonged period of silence passed between them.

"River looks higher than I remember," Alice finally offered.

"Yeah. She is. Been raining here pretty much nonstop for the last few weeks. And from what I hear, more is on the way. That's what the local weatherman says anyway, but that doesn't usually mean diddly-squat."

They watched as a red-shouldered hawk seemed to appear out of nowhere, swooping down low, skimming the surface of the river, wheeling and calling, searching for crayfish in the water. *Kee-ah, kee-ah.* The hawk's wingspan must have measured three feet across, the tips of its feathers nearly grazing the waves, then the bird made an abrupt turn, soaring up and settling into a thick tangle of white pines.

"That there is Daisy. She's been nesting in that set of pines for the last four seasons now."

"You named her Daisy?"

Elton gave a knowing shrug. "Yeah. Not the most creative of names. I guess not. But she keeps me company."

They both watched the red-shouldered hawk flap and snap her wings, making adjustments to her nest.

"You still fishing?" Alice asked.

"I pretend to."

Elton played with his cane for a moment. Tapped the tip between his feet a few times. "So, kiddo. All this small talk aside, how you doing exactly?"

"Fine," Alice answered quickly. "How about you? You still killing rats?"

"Naw. Gave that up two years past. I had my fill of crawling on my hands and knees in basements and attics and whatnot. Figured I should enjoy my *golden years* before I was too old to know any better." He blew on his mug of coffee. "I see you're still good at that art of deflection."

Alice just nodded.

"The coping mechanism thingy, right?"

"Yeah."

"Guess you haven't changed much."

Alice laughed, but there wasn't a hint of humor in her voice. "No. I have. More than you know."

"Well, change can be a good thing, right?"

"For some. Not so much in my case, though."

"I see. Well, kiddo, you're here for a reason, I guess. Brought a friend along with you this time, too."

They both glanced over their shoulders toward Delilah. The girl was lying on her stomach on the floor now—shoes off, sipping on a bottle of RC Cola, her face three feet away from the television screen.

"Your friend seems like a sweet kid. Just a young'un," Elton said.

"She is. Not really a friend, though. Just somebody I met along the way."

"Along the way to where?"

Alice stared back at the river. "I don't know exactly." She ran her fingers through her hair and noticed how filthy and tangled it was. "I'm in some trouble, Elton."

"That right? A little bit, or a lotta bit?"

"It's not good."

"Okay. We'll see about that. What have you gotten yourself into this time?"

Alice's first instinct was to lie to the old man. Make up something harmless, or at least a different version of reality. Tell him that she was passing through and thought she would drop in and say hello. Or tell him that she was pregnant and needed a place to stay for a few weeks. Something. Anything other than the truth.

But then she started speaking, and all the ugly facts and details came spilling out. She told him about everything—Terry, the money and drugs, the shoot-out, the run-in with the junkie in Charlotte, locking the truck driver in his trailer. Everything. Too much.

And the entire time, Elton just listened. Drank his coffee and didn't interrupt once. No judgment in his eyes as he watched Alice unburden her soul and squeeze out shameful confessions.

Alice didn't take a pause. Ran right through the story from beginning to end, until her throat went dry. She sipped at her coffee and wondered if Elton noticed the tremor in her hand.

"I'm tired of running, Elton. For over five years, that's all it seems I've been doing. Running from one place to the next. Always hoping and praying that the next town will be different. That the next job will be better. But they never are." Her voice sounded strained, on the verge of breaking. "I want real friends. A decent place to live in that's mine, and not some crappy hotel room or the back of someone's car. I'm tired of looking over my shoulder. Tired of being unstable. Tired of distrusting everyone that I meet. I'm just tired of everything."

She looked over at him and waited to see what the old man would say.

Elton took a deep breath. Shook his head. "All this breaks my heart, kiddo. It truly does. You deserve something better in life than all of that mess."

"I don't know about that."

"You might not know it, but you do."

"I want to believe that. I do." Alice wiped a wisp of hair from off her face. "I don't even know why I came here really. To you. The last thing you need is another headache." She gazed out across the river. "I'm sorry, Elton."

"Shoot. Don't be sorry. And the last thing that you are is a headache." He twirled his cane between his palms. "To be honest, I'm tickled that you came back. And it means a helluva lot to me that you thought of me. That you needed my help."

"Again."

"Well, we all need some help every now and then." He took a moment to clean his glasses with a white handkerchief. Once satisfied, he neatly folded and returned the cloth to his back pocket. "And all that money. You were hoping that it could change things?"

She laughed. "Pretty pathetic, huh?"

"Nothing wrong with money."

"Then you think I should keep it?"

"Do you think you should keep it? Is that what will fix things for you?"

Alice didn't answer.

Elton reached over and patted her knee. Gave it a little squeeze. "This is a safe place for you, Alice. Always will be. Do you understand what I'm saying?"

Alice said that she did.

"Now, would you care to hear my two cents on this whole matter?"

She smiled at him. A genuine smile this time. "I'm afraid to say yes, but go ahead. Give me your two cents."

"Fine. But before I do, I need to make a confession."

"You finally want to have kids?"

Elton grinned and replied without missing a beat. "Yep. A little boy or little girl. Either one would do just fine." He let out a soft chuckle and tapped his cane on the deck to accentuate the point.

Then he set his coffee mug down and stared out over the same river he'd been staring at for thirty-some years. "I'll tell you this, kiddo. Something has been eating at me for a long time. I regret not doing more for you last time you were here. I've thought about it almost every single day since you left. You were nothing but a lost little sheep, and I didn't do a damn thing to give you guidance. I didn't try to get in that head of yours and help make sense of your whole situation."

"That's not true, Elton."

He held his hand up. "Hold on a second. I listened to you, now you listen to me. I know what I did and didn't do. The truth of the matter was that I enjoyed having you here. Liked waking up in the morning and having someone to talk to. And I guess I didn't want to rock the boat and have you slip away. I wanted the company and I put my needs and wants ahead of yours." He pressed the cane's wooden handle to his lips for a second. "I've thought about it a million times. Should I have called the police? Should I have at least tried to get a hold of your folks? Should I have sat you down and tried to talk some sense into your head?"

He looked straight at Alice. "Hell, yes. I should have done all those things, but I didn't. It was selfish and wrong and I've never stopped being sorry about all that."

Alice reached over and squeezed his thick hand—his fingers twisted and knotted with arthritis. "You *did* do the right thing. I needed a safe place where I wasn't being judged. I needed some stability. I needed to know when I woke up in the morning that the sight of me wasn't causing someone complete heartbreak."

Elton squeezed her hand back. "But then you up and left here. Like a puff of damn smoke."

"I had to."

"Why? Because your folks were looking for you? Because they were closer to finding you?"

Alice took a sip of her coffee. Her hands rattling even worse. "No. Because when they found me, found me living here with you, you'd get in trouble. Not me. You."

Elton chewed on that for a few seconds. "Hell, kiddo, I ain't afraid of what folks think of me."

"I was. Still am." She sipped more coffee, but needed something stronger—something to stabilize her system. "Now, you going to give me your two cents or what?"

"Fine." He tapped his cane on the wood a few times. "You just said it yourself. You're tired of running. And you should be. Running's no kind of life. You're always hoping that the next place you run off to is different. That the next town is better. Isn't that what you said?"

Alice said that it was.

"Well, maybe this is just too damn obvious, but maybe it's time to stop running, kiddo. Maybe it's time to go back home. This thing you're running from, the *real* thing, is the one thing you'll never get away from. I know. I did it, too. You can't run from that reflection that stares back at you every morning. You can't."

Alice's hand still quivered as she finished her coffee and set the mug on the deck. "You have anything stronger to drink than coffee?"

Elton nodded. "I do. Got a cabinet full of liquor bottles. But do you want it or need it?"

Alice peered down at her trembling hands. "Is it that obvious?"

"Kiddo, I might be as old as these hills, but I ain't blind. I've seen it all."

"So, I take it you won't offer me a drink?"

"I'll offer you another cup of coffee is what I'll do."

Alice clasped her hands together and pulled them tight to her chest.

"This here thing's got you pretty good, huh? Really got you by the throat?"

Alice nodded.

"You're a mess, ain't you?"

Alice started to laugh, but the tears took over pretty quickly. She tried to stop the flow, but it all needed to come out. She buried her face into her hands, embarrassed to allow herself such vulnerability.

"It's okay, kiddo. Nothing to be ashamed of. You've been through hell and back a few times. You're entitled to a few of them eye drops."

Alice still couldn't look at him. If she did, she thought she'd cry that much harder.

"Tell you what, kiddo. I'm gonna brew us two fresh cups of coffee. Make 'em nice and so strong that we'll have to chew rather than swallow. Then you're gonna tell me about that young missy that's making herself at home in my living room. I'm betting there's a story behind that one."

Alice wiped at her eyes, then cleared her throat. "There is. You've got two train wrecks staying with you."

"Everything's always better in pairs. You hold tight and I'll be back in a jiffy."

Alice watched him struggle to his feet, grip at his cane good and tight, then amble back into the house on a pair of knees that had seen better days.

CHAPTER THIRTY-THREE

Alice rolled over in the bed, couldn't get comfortable, and rolled over again. Finally, she lay on her back and stared up at the ceiling. She couldn't sleep, her mind racing like a flock of crows, wild and unpredictable. It wasn't until she got ready for bed that she remembered forgetting her suitcase back in Harrisburg—she left it in the back of Terry's truck at the train station. After packing up everything she owned, she left it all behind to be discovered. Clues and evidence that would eventually catch up with her. How could she have been so stupid?

Because you were drunk.

But the thing she was the most upset about was the fact that she left Elton's old blue T-shirt in the suitcase. She didn't care about any of the rest of her stuff, but Elton's beat-up shirt had been her security blanket for five years. The thing might be worthless—a worn-out piece of material—but it happened to be the one possession that was the most precious to her.

After a few more minutes of trying and failing to fall asleep, she sat up in bed and stared over at Delilah, curled up in a ball beside her, dead to the world. The young girl had stuck to her side all night—like she was afraid that Alice might run off. Then she'd fallen asleep almost before her head hit the pillow.

Alice hadn't been so lucky.

She pulled off the new T-shirt that Elton had given her, the material sopping wet and sticking to her skin from the cold sweats. Her hands and feet tingled and pulsated with an unwanted energy. She felt edgy and restless. Her heart pounded faster than it should. Her brain desperately wanted to shut down and go to sleep, but the rest of her body needed something else.

It had only been twelve hours or so since her last drink, but it was time to feed the beast. Being in between sobriety and intoxication was the worst—a mental tug-of-war where abstinence never triumphed. She needed to rid herself of the jitters. Block out the pain and doubt. Stabilize. She just wanted to stabilize. Maybe a shot of whiskey or a few sips of vodka or a cold glass of beer. Something to take the edge off and help her sleep.

She stood up. The wood floor creaked under her, but Delilah didn't stir. She let her feet carry her out of the bedroom, down the hall past Elton's bedroom, and into the kitchen. Elton hadn't changed a thing since the last time she was here. Same refrigerator and stove. Same kitchen table and wood chairs. Same curtains over the sink with a colorful pattern of tiny cornucopias, spilling over with fruit and vegetables.

She checked the kitchen cabinets one by one, and it didn't take long before she found what she was looking for. A bottle of rum and vodka, both unopened. A few bottles of red wine. Behind them stood the prize—a bottle of tequila. The kitchen fluorescents sparkled off the light amber liquid. Over half full. Plenty to do the trick and get her over the hump.

Stabilize. Stabilize. Stabilize.

She stared at the bottle of tequila and her throat went dry and her fingers trembled and her stomach churned, desperately wanting to feel the familiar burn. It would be so easy. Twist off the cap, tilt back the bottle, and wait. Her mind already anticipated the next few steps. The first drink would tell her it's all right, that this was the way to go, that everything would be better soon. The second drink introduced the boldness, that the process had started and that there was no turning back. The third would make her forget about even trying to stop; shutting down the voice inside her that always tried to interfere and tell her to *stop, stop, stop.* Then the rest was easy. Everything downhill from then on. The swallowing became automatic. She would keep going until the present wasn't there anymore, and the past didn't matter—the mistakes, failures, and sins hidden behind the curtain.

Alice didn't know how long she stood in the kitchen, staring at the cabinet of alcohol like it was some kind of altar. Thirty seconds? Three minutes? She finally reached into the cabinet, grabbed the bottle of tequila by the glass neck, and marched out of the kitchen with great purpose.

She slid open the glass doors to the deck, sat down in Elton's chair, and listened to the song of crickets and the low, bassy croaks of bullfrogs. Then she reached over and set the bottle on the railing, and the moonlight glimmered behind the glass. The river water gurgled past, a constant motion that would never stop.

Alice listened to all the sounds of night, smelled the river water and the leaves damp with rain, felt the moist air on her skin, and she waited to see where the midnight hour would take her.

CHAPTER THIRTY-FOUR

Phillip guided the Grand Marquis off of Highway 17 and onto Green Swamp Road. They drove for about a mile before finding a gas station—a Minuteman convenience store with a half dozen gas pumps outside and a Dairy Queen and Little Caesars inside. Both fast-food eateries appeared popular, as locals filed in empty-handed, then emerged toting boxes of mini-pizzas and Styrofoam cups of ice cream sundaes.

Sinclair examined his pack of cigarettes, silently counting how many remained. "I will be needing a fresh pack of cigarettes, please. Make it two. Might as well get me a lighter as well."

Phillip grunted his acknowledgment of the request.

"How much further?"

"Seven miles."

"Good. Very good."

Sinclair watched Phillip lumber into the mini-mart, then unbuckled his seat belt and slipped out of the car. He watched a family of five walk out of the store, clutching boxes of pizzas, milkshakes, bags of chips, and an assortment of chocolate bars. He noted that every single one of them, the mother, the father, and each of the three young kids, were the posters of American obesity. They piled into a dirty car with a rattling muffler and a bent antenna and eagerly dug into their fat-filled snacks.

Sinclair watched them pull away and glanced around at his surroundings. Not much to see. Trash littered the road. A closed tire
shop across the way. The tattered remains of a flattened woodchuck
stood in the middle of the road. Bleak and depressing.

He reached for the door handle when he heard the soft sound of
running water. He peered around, then spotted the river behind the
convenience store and listened to the flow of water, a sound that was
rather unfamiliar to him. Groups of families stood at the edge of
the water, fishing. He watched as a kid snapped his rod and reeled in
a fish that couldn't have been longer than six inches.

Sinclair approached a tall man with a beard that hung halfway
down his chest. The bearded man was filling his pickup with gasoline
and didn't notice Sinclair approach. "Excuse me. What river is that?"

The man turned and gawked at Sinclair for a moment. Looked at
him from head to toe, a little grin curling his lips at the sight of him.
"The Lockwood Folly River."

"And what kind of fish do people catch in the Lockwood Folly
River?"

The man shrugged, still grinning. "Mainly bluefish. Freshwater
drum, maybe. Why? You a fisherman?"

"I shall soon find out." Sinclair made the impulsive decision to
walk down to the river and feed the fish. He had never done anything like this before; his parents never took him fishing or hunting
or on any other kind of outdoor pursuit. He also wanted to see a live
fish close-up. "Yes. I shall soon find out."

He reached into the car, picked up his package of chocolate chip
cookies, and strode across the parking lot, stepped over a small
white fence and into a thicket of brittle, knee-high weeds. He
trudged through a patch of thick kudzu, grasshoppers taking flight
before him, snapping and swishing past his head.

The ground proceeded to get progressively softer and wetter the
closer he neared the river. His perfectly polished leather shoes sank

into the muck, and he could hear the suction of mud pulling at his every step. He continued toward his destination, pushing past weeds that grew up to his chest.

A small embankment, rocky and uneven, sloped down at a forty-five-degree angle toward the shore of the river. Sinclair selected the flattest of stones to step upon and slowly inched his way to the river's edge. The wind blew cooler down by the water, whisking in off the surface of the river and snapping at his clothing.

He watched the flow of the current for a moment before breaking off a small chunk of the cookie and tossing it into the river. The cookie bobbed and swirled on top of the water, and Sinclair waited for a fish to swim up to the surface and snatch it up. Instead, the piece of cookie got swept up in the current and quickly slipped out of view.

He tried again, but with the same result.

Sinclair neither heard nor noticed the small boy wander off from his family and approach him with a great sense of determination.

"Can I feed 'em?" the boy asked with a hopeful voice.

Sinclair glanced behind him at the small boy, perhaps five or six years old. The boy's face was dirty with ice cream, chocolate smeared at the corners of his mouth, and his nose leaked from both sides.

"Can I feed the fishes?" the boy asked again.

"It's *fish*, not *fishes*. And no, you may not." Sinclair looked down the river's edge, searching for the young boy's parents. "Where's your mother?"

The kid shrugged, then pointed to a group of fishermen sitting on some rocks, fishing rods wedged between the stones. "Down there with my papa, fishing."

"And why aren't you fishing with them?"

The kid shrugged again. "Don't like fishing."

"Then why are you here?"

"Cuz my papa likes to fish."

"I see. Well, that's unfortunate for you, isn't it?"

The boy merely stared at Sinclair.

"Why don't you run along and go play in the river?"

The boy wiped his nose on his sleeve. "How come you ain't fishing?"

"That's precisely what I'm doing. Fishing."

The kid smiled like it was a little joke. "No, you ain't. You're feeding 'em, not catching 'em."

"It is how I go about fishing. Thank you. Now please go bother someone else."

"I'm sorry."

"As am I."

Sinclair waited for the kid to scamper off. The kid did not.

"I ain't ever seen anyone feed cookies to fish."

"Is that what they teach you to say in school? *Ain't.*"

"No."

"Try using *have not*, or *will not*. That is the proper way to speak."

"Okay."

Sinclair tossed another crumb into the water and they both watched it bob and float down the river.

"Do you like fish? Eating them?" the boy asked.

"Not particularly. No."

The kid shook his head. "Me neither. I like hot dog wieners."

"I see. You do realize that hot dogs are comprised of pig parts? The hooves. The snout. Other unmentionable parts of their bodies as well."

The kid just stared at him again.

Sinclair broke the cookie in half and handed the piece to the kid. The small boy didn't thank him or say anything. Just tossed the entire chunk into the water.

"You've got to throw it out in small pieces," Sinclair said. He handed the kid the rest of his cookie. "Small pieces."

The kid moved closer to Sinclair. Pressed right to his side like Sinclair was his big brother or uncle. He picked off tiny pieces of the cookie and flicked them one by one into the water. Each chunk floated away without attracting the attention of a single fish. When he ran out of cookie, the kid stared up at Sinclair. "It ain't working. Maybe them fish don't like cookies."

"Perhaps you are right."

The kid wiped his nose on his other sleeve.

"That's all I've got. So. Off you go."

The kid did no such thing. He merely kept staring up at Sinclair with big, wide eyes. "You're small."

"I realize that."

"How come you're so small?"

"Because I stopped growing."

"Why?"

"Because I was big enough."

"You're too small. I'll be bigger than you."

"Perhaps you will be."

"I bet I'll be bigger than you one day."

"You already said that. You're being repetitive. I think it's time for you to return to your family."

They stood there for a few moments. The breeze kicked off the surface of the water and tugged at their hair.

"You like being so small?" the kid asked.

Sinclair stared out over the expanse of the Lockwood Folly River, rolling and glittering and disappearing south. "No. I do not."

CHAPTER THIRTY-FIVE

Alice pushed the grocery cart down the linoleum-tiled floor, feeling like a stranger amongst the other shoppers—a housewife with three children in tow, a bachelor loading canned soup into a handbasket, and two kids that barely passed for twenty-one, buying whatever beer was the cheapest—and she thought about the last time she came to Roberts grocery store. Mr. Roberts, the perpetual nodder, no longer stood at his station behind the register. Instead, an awkward-looking teenager with enormous ears and a crew cut that only accentuated the size of said ears worked behind the counter. But unlike Mr. Roberts, the teenager smiled and said hello to everyone and asked each customer if they needed help in finding something. Mr. Roberts was the yin to the kid's yang. Maybe Mr. Roberts finally hung up his apron and was quietly nodding to his wife and grandchildren in a recliner chair at home.

Delilah browsed ahead of Alice, pulling boxes of cookies off the shelf, and inspecting them closely, as if the decision of which brand to purchase was something not to be rushed or underestimated. The girl appeared so carefree, the weight of all the horrible things she had observed and participated in during the last few days slowly lifting off her shoulders. Alice wondered if Delilah was truly able to move past the fact that she had killed a man, and if so, she envied the girl.

Delilah finally made her cookie selection and brought the package over to the grocery cart. "You like Oreos? I do. I love these cookies. I could eat the whole box myself."

"Better grab two, then."

Delilah grinned, nodded her head, then picked up another package of Oreos.

They continued shopping, up and down the aisles, then stopped in the coffee and tea section. As Alice picked out some decent coffee, she felt Delilah's eyes staring at her. She ignored the girl, picked up a bag of sugar, but Delilah wouldn't stop gawking at her.

"What?"

"Nothing."

"Then why are you staring at me?"

"I wasn't."

"If you've got something to say, spit it out already."

"Well." Delilah now looked anywhere except at Alice. "It's just that . . . I don't know. I like it here. Elton's really cool. Seems laid back. His house is all nice and clean and everything. And it's warm and sunny here all the time. Not like Philly at all."

"Yeah. Guess it beats Philadelphia." Alice started pushing the grocery cart again.

Delilah caught up with her. A little skip in her step like she was six years old. "Why'd you leave here anyway?"

"Because."

"Come on, Alice. You never tell me anything."

"Not much to tell."

"Is it gonna kill you to open up a little? Why'd you leave?"

Alice stopped the cart and leaned over the handle. "I left because it was too close to home."

"Your parents?"

Alice said yes.

"They were looking for you?"

"Yeah. They were looking."

"Shoot. Bet my mama's not looking for me."

"Maybe you're lucky, then. If you really want to run away, it's easier if no one is looking for you."

"I guess." She broke into the package of Oreos, handed one to Alice, and then took one for herself. "Why'd you run anyway? Your parents do something?"

"No. Something I did."

Delilah waited for her to continue, but Alice started pushing the cart again.

"What happened? What did you do?"

"Nothing."

"Come on, Alice. I told you everything about me. There's nothing you don't know."

Alice hated that she was letting her guard down with the girl. "I did *nothing* when I should've been doing something."

Delilah didn't follow.

"You helped raise your little brother, right? Watched after him and took care of him?"

Delilah nodded. "Yeah. I guess."

"Well, I had a little brother, too. And I didn't do that. I didn't watch out for him when I should've."

"Something happen to him?"

"Yeah. Something happened."

"And you think it was your fault?"

"Yeah."

"But weren't you just a kid?"

"You're just a kid, and didn't you look after your brother?"

"I had to. With my mama being the way she is and all."

They found themselves standing in front of the beer and wine section.

"Parents are messed up, if you ask me. I'm never gonna end up like my mama. Never," Delilah flat-out stated.

Alice stared at the rows of beers, the bottles of amber liquid sweating and looking so damn inviting.

"I don't know, Alice, but if it was an accident, then you shouldn't blame yourself for whatever happened to your brother."

"I do anyway."

"I'm sure your brother knew you loved him. Right? You shouldn't be so hard on yourself, Alice."

"Jason. His name was Jason." Alice grabbed a twelve-pack of Michelob and put it in the cart. "And do you know what the last thing I said to him was?"

Delilah shook her head.

"He was four. He went into my room, found my fingernail polish and got it everywhere. Seemed like the end of the world at the time." She stared at the beer in the grocery cart. "So, I kicked him out of my bedroom. I yelled at him. Told him that I hated him. Then, I told him that I wished he was never born." She looked back at Delilah. "That's the last thing I said to my brother. The last words he heard before he died."

Alice glanced at the twelve-pack of beer, never wanting to drink one so badly, to feel the cold liquid spread across her tongue and roll down her throat. But one would lead to two, and so on and so on. Then, with a sense of conviction she never thought possible and not knowing how long it might last, Alice picked up the twelve-pack and returned it to the cooler.

* * *

They shuffled down the sidewalk, both toting two bags of groceries. The twelve o'clock sun beat down on them, not a cloud in the sky. Delilah had been yakking up a storm ever since leaving the store, and Alice was trying her best to tune her out.

"I dated a white boy once. Well, not really date, but kinda. In the eighth grade. Gary Mack. White as they come. Hair parted right down the middle and a big gap between his front two teeth. He used to walk me home from school a few times a week and we'd stop at 7-Eleven to share a bag of barbecue potato chips and a Mountain Dew Big Gulp."

Alice just nodded. She felt like hell. The sun was too damn hot, and her head pounded, a surging headache getting worse by the minute. Sweat rolled down her back and stained her underarms. Her palms felt slick and she had to re-grip the grocery bags before they slipped right out of her hands.

"Gary didn't talk much. He ate lunch by himself at school. Didn't really hang out with other boys and most kids left him alone. I think he might have been a little slow, but I didn't mind. The last time we went to the 7-Eleven together, we were sitting on the curb, and he leaned over and kissed me right on the lips. I didn't really care for the kiss that much, but I liked the way it made me feel."

Out on the street, a car horn blared and the droning sound went right through Alice, but Delilah kept on with her story.

"The kiss only lasted one or two seconds, but it was long enough for one of my mama's friends to see. That night, Mama staggered into my bedroom all drunk and messed up, and jumped right on top of me while I was sleeping. I thought it was Leon at first, but it wasn't. It was just Mama, pitching a crazy fit. She told me that I can't be messing around with Gary. She called him stupid. Called him white trash. The next day, when I told Gary about Mama and what she said—not the stupid, white trash part—he just kind of shrugged and said okay. And that was it. He wouldn't even look at me in the hallways anymore. How could someone be like that? One day they kiss you, the next day acting like I didn't even exist anymore?"

Alice felt a wave of nausea smack at her like an unexpected gust of wind; her stomach lurched and she thought she might vomit in the middle of Main Street. "Hold up." She set down the grocery bags and squatted on her knees and leaned against a brick storefront.

Delilah stopped and stared back at her. "What's the matter?"

"Don't feel so good."

Delilah watched Alice fumble with a pack of cigarettes, barely able to hold the flame steady enough to light one up. "Shoot, Alice. You're shaking bad."

Alice sucked on her cigarette, leaned her head against the brick wall, and exhaled slowly, waiting for the wave of nausea to lift.

"Something wrong with you? You look like you're ready to pass out. You're not having a heart attack, are you?"

Alice said no. Sucked on her cigarette a little more. "Withdrawal."

"Withdrawal? From what?"

"What do you think?" Alice snapped, the words harsh and venomous.

Delilah stared down the street. Held her head low like an admonished puppy.

Alice flicked her cigarette away. "Sorry. I just feel like crap."

Delilah set down the bags of groceries, crouched beside her, took out a pack of bubble gum, handed a stick to Alice, then popped one in her mouth. "How long does it last? The withdrawal thing."

"Don't really know. First time for me."

They sat in silence for a few moments, chewed on their sticks of gum, and watched the traffic go up and down Main Street. People parking, walking in and out of shops, running errands, and stopping to gossip with neighbors.

Then they watched as a Grand Marquis cruised past them and pulled into Lucy's Diner. After the car parked, both doors swung open at the same time like a synchronized effort, and two men that were polar opposites stepped out of the vehicle. The driver tall and thick, his big barrel-chest wider than his shoulders. He moved with little grace and looked like a professional wrestler out of his costume. The passenger's head barely came over the top of the car's roof, and he looked like an overdressed fourteen-year-old, so slight and tiny, but full of direct purpose.

Delilah smiled at the pair and nudged Alice with her elbow. "Look at those two. King Kong and Curious George."

Despite feeling like hell, Alice couldn't help herself and laughed out loud.

Both girls kept smiling and staring at the pair of men as they stepped toward the diner, a little bell clanging against the glass doors and they disappeared inside.

CHAPTER THIRTY-SIX

Sinclair felt his patience wearing thin, starting to make him irritable. He was accustomed to dealing with unpleasant situations—dealers that dip into their supply, customers that use beyond their means, avoiding narcs and undercover police officers—but never before had he been confronted with this kind of problem. A twenty-one-year-old girl taking what was his. Evading him. Silently mocking him. He imagined what he would do to young Alice. This girl he never met would learn a valuable lesson. That much he felt quite assured of.

They chose a booth in the corner of the diner, next to a window, away from other lunch patrons and inquisitive ears. Sinclair picked up a laminated menu, a few spiral pages, and perused the selection of diner food.

"It appears that this establishment is overly fond of gravy in their dishes. Biscuits and gravy. Turkey and gravy. Meatloaf with gravy. It goes on and on."

Phillip stared at his menu. "I like gravy."

"Yes. By that, I am not surprised, Phillip."

A waitress approached their table. The woman had thick ankles and a double chin that spread halfway around a wide neck. Yellow teeth and fingernails revealed that she smoked entirely too many cigarettes. "Get you fellas some coffee?"

"Decaf for me, please," Sinclair said. "Thank you."

"And for the big fella?"

"Juice," Phillip uttered.

"OJ?"

"No."

"Grape juice, grapefruit, or pineapple?"

"Half pineapple. Half grape." Phillip didn't bother looking at the woman.

"Okay. You all hold tight. I'll be right back with your beverages." She clicked her pen, stuck it in her poof of hair, and went to fetch their drink orders.

"Really, Phillip. We have discussed this many times. Manners. A simple *please* and a *thank you* go a long way. We must make attempts at being civil. Those that work in the service industry are people who have a very difficult task, working for tips, making minimum wage. Dealing with rude customers cannot be easy."

Phillip took a toothpick out of a small cup, unwrapped it, and stuck it in his mouth. "Okay." He hunched over the table, shoulders heavy, his perpetual glazed expression even duller.

"What's on your mind, Phillip? You appear a little more somber than usual."

"Nothing," Phillip muttered.

"I'm growing restless as well, Phillip. Believe me, I am. But this will end soon."

Phillip let out a long sigh. Picked at his teeth. "Maybe she's not even here."

Sinclair stared at Phillip. Watched him poke the toothpick between his teeth. "Please. That is truly a disgusting habit." He waited for Phillip to remove the toothpick, which he promptly did. "She is here. Alice is here."

"How do you know?"

"Intuition."

"I don't know. Could be anywhere. Could be dead."

"So, what do you propose? That we simply give up and return home with our tails tucked between our legs?"

The big man thought for a second before speaking. "I don't question you. Never have. Do what you ask."

"But?"

"But, maybe, we let this one go."

Sinclair stared at his manicured hands and seemed to be pondering each individual finger. "You're extremely loyal, Phillip. You really are."

The big man grunted at the compliment.

"But what you're proposing is not acceptable. Allowing someone to steal from me, and not take some kind of action, sets a precedent that I will not allow. I have taken great pains to build my enterprise, and to turn the other cheek on this matter could, and most likely *would,* have collateral damage."

Phillip played with his toothpick. "Okay."

"No, it is not *okay*. Please understand me. It is very important that we are on the same page here. This girl, Alice, did more than just steal money from me. She is responsible for the deaths of Henry and Pig. Two good men that were with me for a very long time. She has stolen quite a bit from me, Phillip, and I will not stop until I find her."

"Why don't we show people the flier then? With the picture of Alice. Ask 'em if they've seen her around here."

Sinclair took a napkin from the dispenser and wiped at a spot of grease in front of him. He scrubbed for a moment, inspected the table, and scrubbed again. He placed the napkin aside, folded his hands together, and addressed Phillip. "If you don't question me, then why do you question me now?"

Phillip shifted his gaze, staring out the window instead.

Sinclair sighed. "Don't sulk, Phillip. It's unbecoming. I will answer your question. Alice is a runaway. A young girl. If we march into town, waving the flier around in front of peoples' faces, it sends up flags. A desperate girl. Two men searching for her. People might question this. Possibly call the authorities. No. That is not the correct manner in which to find Alice."

Phillip looked back to Sinclair. "How then?"

Sinclair's jaw tensed. His face went a shade of red. "Sometimes in order to catch a rat, you need to find its nest. Determine where it scurries off to at night. That is where you catch it and kill it."

The thick-ankled waitress delivered their coffee and juice. "You all decide on something to eat?"

Sinclair painted back on a smile. "Would you recommend the biscuits and gravy?"

"That's what we're known for. Sure."

"Splendid. I'll give that a whirl. Thank you."

The waitress looked to Phillip. "And you?"

"Biscuits 'n gravy." Phillip felt Sinclair's silent scrutiny upon him. "Thank you," he said, the two words choked out of his mouth like he hacked up a chicken bone.

Sinclair took note of the waitress' name tag. "Connie, I have a question for you, if you don't mind."

She snapped a piece of gum in her mouth. "Sure, hon. Ask away."

"I take it that you're from the area here?"

"Born and raised."

"I see. I was curious, with Shallotte being so close to the South Carolina border, do you consider yourself a North Carolinian or South Carolinian? Or just a Carolinian?"

She laughed like this was the funniest thing ever to be asked. "Sweet thing, there's a world of difference between the two. I am a North Carolina gal through and through, and damn proud of it."

"I'm trying to understand the difference between the two. Why exactly is North Carolina better than South Carolina?"

She kept chuckling. "I'll give you a few simple reasons: the barbeque, NCAA men's basketball, and we were the first in flight. That's all you need to know."

"Ah. Makes perfect sense." He smiled at the woman, more from the internal satisfaction that her guard had been dropped than from what she actually had to say. "Perhaps you can help me with a small problem."

"Sure. Whatcha need, hon?"

"I recently purchased some property in the area, and, unfortunately, I have discovered that I have an infestation problem. It appears that it is overrun with rodents. Primarily rats."

The waitress didn't seem all that surprised. "We get lots of rats around here, being so close to the river and all. Comes with the territory."

"Yes. Well, I need to address the issue and I've heard a rumor that Parson's Pest Control is quite a good service. Does that name ring a bell?"

The waitress nodded, causing her double chin to expand further around her neck. "You're talking about Elton's old business."

"I guess that maybe I am."

"Sure. Elton Parsons used to be our local exterminator. He took care of everybody here in town, but he hung up his hat two, three years ago, I guess."

"I see. Does he still live in the area?"

"Sure. But like I said, he's done finished with that business of his."

"That's unfortunate. Well, perhaps he'd be able to offer a good referral."

"Guess maybe he would. He knows everything about getting rid of bugs and rats, and even opossums. He lives right outside of town here. A couple miles up the road. I could find his telephone number if you'd like."

"I'd rather see him in person. If he can't provide a referral, maybe I could convince him to come out of retirement. For the right price."

The waitress gave him a wink. "We all got our price, don't we, hon?" She picked the pen out of her web of hair and started to scribble on a napkin. "You can't miss his house. Right on the river. Real pretty place."

"Thank you, Connie."

"I sure hope you get your rat problem taken care of. I just hate those darn things."

"Me, too, Connie. Me, too."

CHAPTER THIRTY-SEVEN

Elton tinkered with the reels on three different fishing rods, one by one, checking to make sure the lines weren't tangled and that each had the proper drag. Then he grabbed a little bottle of Berkley reel oil from an old metal fishing box and squeezed a few drops on the spools and rollers and handles. He retested each line. Satisfied, he selected the proper bobber for each line and tied them off, then he set the hooks into the cork handles.

Next, he went about organizing his fishing gear. Sorting through hooks and lures, and extra red-and-white bobbers. Once he felt confident that everything was in order and in its proper place, he took a seat on the front porch, grabbed a bottle of RC Cola from a bucket full of ice, knocked the cap off against the wood railing, and took a long, deep pull. He sat for a few minutes, sipping and burping up carbonation, enjoying the sun on his face, and keeping an eye on the road that led up to the house.

With only a few sips remaining in the bottle, he spotted Alice and her young friend tromping down the dirt road, both of them toting two bags of groceries each.

"Thought you all might have gotten yourselves lost," he said.

They set their bags down in the grass and took a seat beside him.

"I was afraid that we would get lost. Everything looks the same out here. Nothing but trees and bushes and dirt roads," Delilah said.

"So says the city girl."

Delilah smiled. "Smells funny out here, too."

"That's the way air is supposed to smell."

"Like cow poop?"

"Shoot, you're just used to inhaling fumes all day from buses and factories and all that other nonsense."

Delilah shrugged. "And what do people do out here, anyway?"

"I'm not sure I understand what you mean."

"For fun? I mean, there's no movie theaters, no malls or anything, and the only good restaurant I saw was a Burger King."

Elton gawked at her like she had three heads. "I must be getting old." He gave Alice a wink, then addressed Delilah directly. "First off, little lady, I sure wouldn't consider Burger King a real kind of restaurant, serving that slop that they call food. Secondly, there's all sorts of things to do out here."

Delilah called his bluff. "Like what? Kill bugs?"

Elton let out a snort. "There's hunting and fishing. Walks along the river. Biking and hiking trails all over the place. Some folks take to bird watching. I could go on and on."

"I don't know. This town could stand a Walmart."

"Okay. I give up." He grinned over at Alice. "So, how you faring, kiddo?"

"By the skin of my teeth."

Elton grabbed two fresh bottles of cola from the bucket, un-capped them, and handed them to both girls. "Have yourself a pop. Nice and cold."

Alice sipped on her bottle, then motioned toward the fishing poles. "Going fishing?"

"Thought we all might. Nice day and all. Thought I'd take you to my new fishing spot down the river a ways. See if we can catch ourselves some dinner."

Alice looked ragged. Sweat soaked through her shirt. Face flushed. Hair sticking to the sides of her neck and cheeks. She finished off her soda in a few gulps. Anything sounded better than just sitting around feeling miserable. "Okay."

Elton looked to Delilah. "How about you, city girl? Ever been fishing?"

"Fishing? No, thank you. I don't like eating fish, so I don't think I'd like to catch them either."

"Come on. It's nice out here. What else you got to do?"

She shrugged. "Watch TV, I guess."

"The boob-tube, huh?" Elton just shook his head, then patted Alice on the knee. "Then it looks like it's just you and me, kiddo."

* * *

Elton carried the fishing poles in one hand, and leaned on his cane with the other. Alice toted the fishing box as they strolled along a narrow dirt path about twenty feet from the river, pushing past some honeysuckle and kudzu that grew wild and thick. They didn't speak—instead, both watched a pair of squirrels that seemed to be following them, running up and down trees, leaping from limb to limb, not a damn care or worry in the world.

Elton chuckled at the sight of the furry critters. "Friends of yours?"

Alice shook her head. "I don't have any friends."

"Oh, fiddlesticks. You're just feeling sorry for yourself."

"Yes, I guess I am."

"Well. At least you're honest." He handed her a handkerchief from his back pocket. "You look like death warmed over."

"Feel like it, too." She wiped the handkerchief across her forehead, then over the back of her neck.

"It'll get better. First forty-eight hours or so are the worst."

"Yeah? You've been through this?"

He swatted at a horsefly that kept going after his neck. "I have. Back when I still had hair on my head. When I was young and dumb."

"Oh. Like me?"

"Well, you're young, and as for the latter, we make our own beds and all."

The path cut closer to the edge of the river, winding its way along an outcrop of rocks that stood over the water about ten feet or so.

"You finally quit drinking?"

"I did. I made for a lousy drunk."

"Is there such thing as a good one?"

"No. I guess there's probably not, truth be told."

"How'd you do it? Quit and everything?"

"The only way you can. Go cold turkey. I didn't mess with any of that AA stuff. Way too social for me. Did it on my own terms."

The pair of squirrels finally gave up chase and flashed off into the woods.

"So, why do you still have booze around the house? You're not tempted?"

Elton pointed toward the outcrop of rocks that extended over the edge of the water, giving a perfect one-hundred-and-eighty-degree view of the river. Behind it, a clump of towering pines provided a good amount of shade from the sun. "This here's my spot."

They set everything down on the flattest part of the boulder. Some moss grew at the edge of the outcrop, making for a comfortable place to sit, and Elton went about getting their fishing gear ready.

"All that booze was Ben's. He'd have a drink every now and again. New Year's Eve, his birthday, maybe another time or two a year. There's social drinkers, then there's drinkers."

He switched lures on one of the rods, then decided to do the same with the other. "After he passed, I decided to leave all that booze where it was. It reminded me of him, and I couldn't bring myself to just tossing it in the trash can. Still got a closet and drawer full of his clothes. Sweaters, shirts, trousers, the whole nine yards. Won't fit me worth a damn, but it seemed like if I just threw all his belongings away, that I'd be throwing part of him away as well."

Alice picked up a stick and twirled it between her fingers. "How'd Ben die anyway?"

Elton's mouth drew straight and he let out a little sigh.

"We don't have to talk about it if you don't want to."

He managed a smile. Patted her knee. "No, it's good to talk about it. Better than keeping it all bottled up inside your belly." Elton took a breath. Sat up straight. "I guess it was about eight years ago. Ben started getting these headaches and felt dizzy from time to time, but he didn't like to complain. He was taking more and more naps. Chalked it up to getting old. I told him to go see the doctor, but Ben was a bit old school. Didn't like getting poked and prodded." He stopped and rubbed at his jaw for a moment. "I was busy with work. Worked too damn much back then and didn't notice how bad he was getting."

He stared out over the river. "Then one day when I got back home, Ben was on the living room floor. Thought he was dead at first. Took him to the emergency room and after a dozen or so tests, they discovered the brain tumor. They tried radiation, but it was too late. It took him quick. Six months and he was gone. Just like that."

He cast the line of one of the fishing rods and handed it over to Alice. Then he cast the second line and they both sat down on the edge of the boulder, feet dangling over the edge.

"I'm sorry, Elton."

"Me, too, kiddo. Me, too. You would have liked old Ben. He was one of a kind. The two of you would have gotten along real nice."

"You still miss him?"

"Every damn day." Elton chewed on his lower lip and his voice quivered when he spoke. "I wish . . . I wish that I would have made him go see a doctor sooner. I do."

Alice stared over at the old man. "And you still feel guilty that you didn't?"

Elton thought about that for a moment. "I managed to finally let the guilt go. Hell, it took me a long damn time. Too long. Beat myself up pretty good for years. But it was either let it go or let it eat you up alive." He gazed over at Alice. "But the sadness never went away. And it probably never will. It's all part of life, I guess."

They held their rods in silence for a few minutes.

"How old were you when you started to figure things out? When life started making some sense to you?"

Elton let out a laugh, the sound carrying across the river. "Shoot. I'll have to let you know when that day happens. Still waiting for my life to make sense."

"That's not true. You seem like you got it all figured out."

"Kiddo, just because I don't drink my worries away anymore, it doesn't mean that I don't still got a bushel full of 'em."

Alice stared down into the water, this part of the river running clean and clear. She could see straight to the bottom, at all the river rocks, some the size of watermelons, others as small as baseballs. "You think the water's cold?"

"I don't think. I *know* it's cold."

Something about the way the river sparkled under the sun and the soothing hush of water pushing over rocks compelled Alice to stand up, take off her shoes and socks, then hand her fishing rod over to Elton.

"Giving up already?"

"Going for a swim."

"In your clothes?"

"No." She moved a little closer to the edge.

"You're gonna catch yourself a cold."

"Can't make me feel any worse than I do now."

He watched as she peered over the edge of the boulder. "I sure hope that you know how to swim."

"Happens to be the one thing I used to be good at. How deep do you think it is?"

"I don't know, but not deep enough to dive in from way up here. If you're really bound and determined to take yourself a skinny dip, crawl down there to the edge of the river and ease yourself in. You break a leg out here, there's no way in hell that I'm dragging you through the woods and all the way home. I don't really like this notion at all, so be careful now."

Alice said that she would. She gave him a smile that said *Here goes nothing*, and slowly worked her way down the side of the rocks and jumped the last few feet to the edge of the river. She looked above her and all she could see was Elton's boots dangling over the edge of the boulder. She tugged her shirt and pants off, then her underwear and bra.

"Don't be looking now," she called up to him.

She heard him chuckle above her. "Kiddo, no offense, but glimpsing you in your birthday suit holds absolutely no interest for me."

Alice stared out over the river and watched the surface sparkle and churn, constant and perfect. She stepped into the water and felt the cold rush over her toes, then her feet started sinking deeper into brown silt. The shock of icy river water caused her breath to hitch in her chest, but she kept wading forward, inch by inch. Up over her knees, then past her waist. Her toes grew numb as they stepped over smooth river rocks at the bottom of the riverbed, but she kept going deeper until only her head poked out from the surface.

She floated in the current for a moment, glancing back to the shore where Elton grinned and waved and shook his head, then downstream to where the river flowed and disappeared around a thicket of pines that grew tall over the water. Then she began to swim, slow at first, her arms and legs moving in unison with nice easy strokes. She felt the tenderness in her side—the ache in her rib ever present—but the cold water dulled the pain, and she pushed past it.

The relentless waves slapped at her face and blurred her vision, and she could taste the river water on the back of her tongue, but she kept swimming. A little faster, a little harder. The current pulled at her, carrying her downstream, and she fought to swim against it the best she could. And even though it had been over five years since she last swam, Alice's instincts took over, and her body moved of its own accord, arcing and slicing through the water effortlessly.

When the thoughts of everything started to seep back into her mind—running from one place to the next; the endless cycle of drinking; the money that wasn't hers; people dying; then, finally, to where her thoughts always seemed to go, to her Jason—she swam with a renewed sense of urgency. She felt the pinch in her side but didn't slow as she made it halfway across the river, and she could hear Elton's faint voice calling after her. *Come back, come back, come back.*

Her thighs and calves began to cramp, and her arms got heavier. Both lungs, abused by too many cigarettes and lack of exercise, burned in her chest. But she wouldn't slow. She didn't know how long she swam. Two minutes? Maybe five. It didn't matter.

Let go.

The two words filled her ears like a violent clap of thunder.

She stopped and gasped for air. Her feet couldn't feel the bottom, and she squinted from the water in her eyes and the sunlight that glowed red all around her, and she stared down the river. She floated along with the current for a few moments and her breath slowly returned.

Let go.

She took in a full swallow of air, filling her lungs to their capacity, and dove under the surface. Everything was muted around her except for the rushing swish of the undercurrent. She closed her eyes, feeling the water press down on her from all sides, and she began to weep. She sank deeper, waiting for her feet to touch bottom, but they didn't find any footing and she drifted. Her mouth opened and she emitted a muffled scream, bubbles erupting in a torrent of white until they eventually ebbed away. It was then that Alice sucked in water and she felt the liquid coarse down her throat and into her belly. Her body kept sinking, slowly but surely.

She felt a wave of darkness fill her from the inside out, everything going dim.

Let him go.

Her eyes snapped back open and she peered above her. The sun was a distorted dot, shrinking smaller and smaller.

Then, just when her body began to grow numb of sensation, and all her limbs started to feel separate and far away, Alice kicked her way back up, desperate to pull herself away from the darkness that seemed determined to drag her down. It took a few frantic moments, but she finally burst through the surface of the water with a final surge. Her stomach convulsed and she retched up a mouthful of clear liquid, then took in the clean country air, filling her lungs and tasting the sweetness. She lifted her face to the sunlight that tickled at her skin and started to make the long swim back toward the shore.

CHAPTER THIRTY-EIGHT

Elton's wicker fishing basket flopped against his hip, just as light now as it was before they went fishing. He didn't catch a damn fish. Not even a nibble.

Alice watched how slowly the old man walked, putting all his weight onto his cane, hunched over, his feet barely lifting up off the ground. Seemed like he'd aged ten years since leaving the house. "You okay?"

"Too damn old is what I am. Feels like I'm breaking down piece by piece."

"This walk too much?"

"Didn't use to be."

She took the fishing poles from his hand and guided him toward a fallen birch tree that set back off the path a few feet. "Let's take five."

"How 'bout ten?"

"That's fine. I'm in no hurry to get back."

They plopped down on the tree soft with rot, and Elton let out a long sigh. "I tell you what. This getting old nonsense is for the damn birds." He looked over at Alice, at wet hair that hung down over her face, and her clothes, pretty much soaked through as well. "Aren't you cold?"

"Yeah. A little."

"Sorry you went in?"

"Nope. Not one bit."

He chuckled and gazed out over the river. "What are we gonna do with you, kiddo?"

"Got a few ideas."

"That right? That swim clear out the cobwebs a little?"

Her face grew distant, eyes wandering toward the path in front of them. "I don't know. I was thinking . . . it's just that I keep showing up here, expecting you to solve all my problems, and it's not fair. Not fair to you at all."

Elton stared at her. Waited for more. And when he didn't get it right away, he just gave her some more time to mull over her thoughts.

"I think maybe it's time to go back home."

The pair of squirrels were back, scrambling up and down some black birch trees behind them, chattering and clucking at one another. They scampered from tree to tree, thrashed in the leaves, both freezing at the same exact moment, then starting back up all over again.

Alice leaned forward on both knees and rubbed at her face. "Why can't it ever be easy, Elton?"

He played with his cane, twirling the handle between his fingers. "Sometimes we make it harder on ourselves. Making the wrong decision time and time again."

"Yeah, I've sure got that part covered."

"Seems like things usually get better eventually. Especially if you're thinking straight. Clarity sure helps matters." He dug in the dirt with the tip of his cane. "You gonna head home and try to make things right?"

"Thinking that way."

"See there. One good decision down."

"And a few others yet to make."

"You'll get there. Baby steps."

She stared into his bluish-white eyes that seemed to have gotten even whiter. "You really think so?"

"I do. If I believed in God, I'd swear to him or her right now."

"But what do I say to my parents? Sorry? Sorry that I keep breaking your heart again and again?"

"Could start with that, for sure. But seeing you, hugging you, knowing that you're still alive, all that will probably mean more to your folks than anything you could ever say."

"I don't even know. What if they moved? What if they got divorced and moved to different sides of the country?"

"You can probably find about a hundred different reasons *not* to go home, Alice, but all you really need is one good reason."

Alice grew quiet. Thought about the reality of seeing her parents again after all this time. "You know, I never tried to call them. Not once. To hear their voices or let them hear mine. To let them know that I was okay, not dead in an alley somewhere. No letter of explanation. I didn't even give them that."

"You can't look back, kiddo. If you do, it's just gonna eat you up inside. All you can do now is follow what your heart tells you to do. And I don't give a goddamn if that sounds corny as all hell."

"It does."

"Well. Fiddlesticks on that."

"Give me a ride to Wilmington?"

"I could probably manage to fit it into my hectic schedule."

The squirrels flashed past them, tails snapping, ears pressed back on their tiny skulls.

"That girl looks up to you. You know that, right?"

Alice laughed. "I'm no role model. That's the last thing I am."

"Well, you might not want to be, but you are."

"I'm a mess, Elton. Besides, she's in a lot of trouble. Even more than me, for whatever that's worth."

"Well, then, she needs your help even more. Don't turn your back on her. She's probably had a lifetime of that."

"I can barely take care of myself. How am I supposed to help her? I've got nothing to offer."

"Sure, you do. Don't sell yourself short. You can give her a little guidance and support."

Alice laughed once again. "Maybe I should just give her the money."

"You really think that's the answer to her problems?"

"No." Her smile slowly ebbed away like the image of a burst of light fading in the night sky. "I took that money thinking that it would help. Give me a fresh start. Make everything all right."

"And it hasn't done a damn thing, has it?"

She shook her head.

"Whatcha you gonna do with it?"

"Don't know exactly. How do you give back ninety-one thousand dollars of stolen drug money?"

"Shoot, Alice. I'm just an old fart. You're asking the wrong damn fella."

"You're a lot more than that, Elton." She let her head fall against his bony shoulder, allowing herself human contact for the first time in too long, and it felt safe and right and way overdue. They sat that way for a minute, both savoring the moment and the company of one another while a steady breeze played with their hair.

"Well, kiddo, you ready to head back to the ranch? I swear, the older I get, the smaller my bladder gets."

Alice smiled. Shook her head. "I'll stay here for a few minutes. See if those squirrels come back."

He patted her leg. Stood up slowly, and his knees creaked a little bit. "Okey-dokey. I'll go and see what kind of trouble that young girl is getting into. And since you're a helluva lot younger than me, I'll let you lug all the fishing gear home."

She said that she would and watched as Elton shuffled down the dirt path with his wood cane leading the way.

CHAPTER THIRTY-NINE

Alice spotted the car in the driveway as she walked up the path that crested the hill leading from the river. It looked out of place and foreign. A brand-new Grand Marquis, midnight blue, barely any mud on the car, giving it the appearance of being recently detailed. The dark-tinted windows were rolled up, making it difficult to determine if anyone sat inside.

She stopped by the mailbox but kept staring at the vehicle like she half-expected it to burst into flames, then glanced toward the house, noticing that the front door was closed—nothing unusual with that in and of itself, but something felt wrong, something off. Then she noticed an object—long and thin—lying in the gravel, right in front of the porch. She took a step forward to get a better look and noticed that it was the fishing rod that Elton had prepared for Delilah, snapped clean in half and cast aside.

Alice's head jerked back toward the Grand Marquis, and her stomach tightened like a clenched fist as recognition slowly settled upon her—it was the same car from town earlier that day.

She released the fishing poles and box from her hands simultaneously, where they clattered to the ground. Then, she made a beeline for the front porch. She ran, but it felt like a moment from a nightmare—her feet seemed to be weighed down by an unseen force, pulling her backwards instead of forward. It seemed like it took her minutes to reach the porch, her mind unspooling with dread, thinking, *knowing* something awful had happened.

She grabbed the door handle, turned the knob, but it wouldn't budge, and for some reason, she knew it would be locked anyway. She raised her fists to pound on the door, but stopped herself, reining in her fears, trying to think things through. She peered in through the window instead, but the curtains were drawn tight.

Alice slipped off the porch and sprinted down the slope that led to the back of Elton's home. She took the back-porch steps two at a time, pressed flat to the side of the house, and stared in through the sliding glass doors. The living room looked as if it had been turned upside down, like a herd of cattle had stampeded through—the couch flipped over, the glass coffee table shattered, lamps knocked down, books and vases scattered across the floor.

Next to the piano, she spotted Elton, slumped in a chair, his arms twisted behind him, and his ankles bound together with fishing line. She saw all the blood on his shirt, oozing from an open wound on the side of his head. His mouth hung open, his lips split and torn, glasses crushed at his feet.

As if sensing her presence, Elton lifted his head, one eye swollen completely shut, and he stared at Alice through the window. The old man's lips moved, words bubbling and popping out, and he shook his head. *Go. Please go.*

Alice tried to slide open the door, but the lock held secure. When she looked back toward Elton, she saw a large man approach him from behind—then she saw the knife gripped in his fist. She beat on the glass with both hands. "Stop! I'm here! I'm here," she screamed and pounded on the door again, hard enough to rattle the panes of tempered glass.

Phillip looked at Alice for a moment, his face expressionless and dull, then he loomed over the old man, pressed the blade of his knife to Elton's throat, and seemed to mumble something. Elton shook his head, thrashed in his seat, but Phillip shoved the knife tighter to the old man's naked flesh.

Alice stared at the giant. Noticed all the blood on his hands. She kicked at the glass door, screamed for the big man to stop, to leave Elton alone, but he did neither. She searched the porch for something. Anything. She reached down and picked up a terracotta pot that must have weighed fifty pounds, and barely felt her bruised rib twist and burn as she hoisted the pot above her head and slammed it against the door—the glass buckled and shattered and fell away with a piercing crack.

She didn't feel her skin slice open. Didn't feel the flow of blood spout from a dozen gashes on her arms and hands. She let the momentum carry her into the living room, the clay container still clutched in her grasp. She lunged at the large man as he pivoted toward her, and brought the pot crashing down on the crown of his head.

Alice felt the crack of his skull, heard the explosion of air choke out from his lungs.

Phillip staggered backward, chiseled arms pinwheeling until he collided with the bookshelf, sending picture frames and porcelain figurines smashing to the floor. He dropped to one knee, crimson leaking down over glazed eyes that bore a hole straight through Alice.

"What do you want?" Alice hissed, although she knew exactly why the man was there.

Phillip spat out some blood and staggered to his massive feet. "The money. Where's the money?" Before waiting for an answer, he tottered forward, the knife gripped in his paw, ready to slash Alice's throat.

Alice dove to the floor, slid through shards of broken glass, ripping open fresh cuts on her stomach. The giant was on her again.

Snatched her foot and swung her like a club. Alice collided with the legs of the piano, and the instrument emitted a mournful, distorted groan.

She spotted Elton's cane on the floor and seized it. As Phillip lumbered forward, Alice scrambled to her feet, reared back, and swung wildly at the big man, but missed her mark. Phillip slashed at her again, the tip of the blade slicing her across the shoulder. She felt the red-hot spike of pain ripple down her side, and her right arm went numb.

Phillip came at her again, the blade slashing at the air, relentless, and a primitive growl gurgled from deep inside his throat.

Alice switched the cane to her other hand and swung backhanded as hard as she could muster. She felt her bruised rib click as the ivory tip of the cane smashed the cartilage in the man's nose, fluid exploding down his chin, peppering his shirt scarlet.

Phillip teetered on mammoth feet. His eyes watered up, blurring his vision, but he kept swinging the knife.

Alice brought the cane down again. Across his jaw, cracking bone, and sending Phillip crashing into the fish tank. Glass shattered and he slumped to the floor, water and thrashing goldfish pooled at his feet as his own blood mixed in with the churning liquid.

The giant still gripped his knife, tried to stumble back to his feet, but spat out a tooth instead.

Alice let out a primal scream and kicked at the beast's face, again and again, causing the man's head to snap back into what remained of the fish tank, his neck slicing open against peaks of glass. Alice could barely breathe, her heart pounding in her chest, but she kept kicking until her foot throbbed.

The big man gurgled something, blood pumping from the side of his neck. He pressed a massive palm to the severed artery, but it did little to prevent the violent gush.

Alice backed away from the man, still struggling to draw breath into her lungs, when her feet got tangled up with something on the floor, and she landed hard on her tailbone. Her rib clicked again and a flare of pain unspooled inside her.

She stared over at Delilah, sprawled across the kitchen threshold. The girl's eyes were closed and there was a growing puddle of blood haloing the back of her head. Alice stood up too quickly, leaned against the doorframe, and felt the wave of darkness slowly squeeze out the light. She took another look at Delilah, then the warm mass rose up from her stomach and into her throat. She bent over and expelled bile all over the hardwood floor, her stomach heaving until it hurt, and all she could think was, *Delilah's dead, Delilah's dead, Delilah's dead.*

Then the girl coughed. Moaned and writhed on the floor. Alice dropped down by the girl's side and touched her cheek. Delilah moaned once again and her eyes flickered open. She stared up at Alice, her eyes glazed and dull.

"*I tried to stop him,*" the girl whispered. "*I tried.*"

"I know. It's okay, Delilah. It's okay."

"*He was looking for you, but we didn't say anything.*"

Alice stared down at the girl. Tried to speak, tried to thank her, tried to tell Delilah the way she felt, but was unable to find the words.

Then a sound came from behind her. She spun around and watched as the big man twitched, the knife finally dropping from within his tight grasp, where it rattled and settled to the floor.

They're going to keep coming.

Henry and Pig at Terry's trailer. The hulk at her feet.

She pressed her eyes closed, everything crashing down on top of her. She flashed to the images of the strangers getting out of the Grand Marquis and trudging into Lucy's Diner—they were right there in front of her, but she had been oblivious, too self-absorbed and wallowing in self-pity.

Her eyes snapped back open and she stared over at the big man. "Who the hell are you?" She stood and grabbed him by the collar of his shirt and shook him, snapping his lolling head back and forth. "Where's your friend, goddammit? Where is he?" She kept shaking the giant's head and watched as the light faded from his eyes and his body sagged as his heart finally ceased to pump.

Alice released the dead man's shirt when she heard Elton cough up something wet behind her.

"Elton?"

She knelt next to the old man, placed her hands to his face. His eyes blinked open by her touch, then flickered shut. She watched a trickle of blood seep from what remained of his left ear.

"I'm going to get you help. Okay? Just hold on, Elton. Please, hold on."

She grabbed the knife from the giant's side, sliced the fish line free from Elton's wrists and ankles, and gently eased the old man to the floor.

Alice bolted into the kitchen and yanked open drawers, sending silverware, tools, and cookware clanking to the floor. She finally found what she was looking for—she snatched up a roll of tape, grabbed a kitchen towel from its hook, then raced back to Elton's side and gently eased him up to the sitting position.

"Need to stop the bleeding."

Elton's eyes fluttered open as she pressed the kitchen towel to the wound, then began to wrap a few layers of tape around his head.

He mumbled something.

"It's okay," Alice whispered.

The old man coughed, then spoke again, his voice a raspy croak. *"Is that one of my good kitchen towels?"*

She managed to smile at the old man. "I'll buy you a new one. I swear." She eased him back to the floor, turned his head so that the weight pressed down on the makeshift bandage, and the flow of blood appeared to taper off.

Alice picked up the phone and her hands wouldn't stop shaking as she dialed 911. She gave the dispatcher Elton's home address and told them to *Hurry, please hurry.*

She went back to Elton's side, whispered into his ear that everything would be okay, then kissed him on the cheek. He tried to smile. Tried to speak again, but only managed to squeeze her hand instead.

With tears burning in the corners of her eyes, Alice began to search the giant's front pockets. A wad of cash, a lighter, a set of car keys, some folded receipts. She tried to dig into his back pockets but he was too big, too heavy. She stood up, grabbed one of his massive arms, and pulled—her rib popped and flared, and she dropped his arm with a violent gasp.

She took a breath. Tried again, and finally managed to flip the man over onto his stomach. She dug into his back pockets. No wallet. Just a slip of old, tattered paper. Before she even unfolded the piece of paper, she knew.

Hands trembling, she opened the flier and stared down at the photo of herself, the smiling image from so long ago.

They're going to keep coming.

Alice crumpled the flier in her hands and couldn't hold back the tears as she picked up the dead man's car keys.

* * *

Alice reached into a cabinet for a glass. Her hand rattled so violently that the glass slipped from her grip and shattered on the floor. She tried again. Grabbed another glass with both hands, pulled a carton of orange juice from the refrigerator, and poured some into the glass. She fumbled with the liquor cabinet door and found the bottle of vodka. Poured a few inches into the glass.

Everything was unraveling in her mind, coming apart like a papier-mâché piñata left out in the rain. She set the glass on the counter. Stared at it. Her entire body hummed with the want, the need for a drink.

She picked up the glass again.

Just one drink.

Then she stared over at Delilah, where the girl huddled against the wall and looked back at her with no judgment in her eyes.

They're going to keep coming.

From outside the house, Alice heard the faint cry of sirens break the quiet that clutched the countryside by the throat. She looked down at her drink, then dumped the vodka into the sink.

She turned back to Delilah—Alice would ask the young girl to help with one last thing.

CHAPTER FORTY

Sinclair found himself sitting alone, a circumstance he didn't particularly savor. He'd been lingering in the diner for what seemed like hours. Smoking, observing, pretending not to hear the comments his presence elicited from other customers.

He perched in the same booth, sipped on a cold bottle of Budweiser, a cigarette burning in the ashtray beside him. Outside the diner's windows, a steady rain came down, and judging from the darkened sky, it didn't appear to be letting up anytime soon. He checked his wristwatch, glanced toward the entrance of Lucy's, then picked up his cigarette.

Phillip should have returned by now, and Sinclair began to second-guess his decision in sending the big man to the exterminator's house alone. But sometimes, like with a good hunting dog, he found it best to let the man roam a bit, untethered from his leash. Men like Phillip were wired with the occasional primal need to prowl on their own, left free from scrutiny and observation. Sinclair certainly hoped that his instincts had not been wrong in this particular task.

There had been a shift change, and a new waitress stopped by his table and smiled down at him. "Get you another cold beer, hon?"

Sinclair returned the smile. "Not at the moment. Thank you." He watched her cross over to another table, examining her large back-side with a clinical scrutiny. He crushed out his cigarette, glanced at his watch again, then tapped another cigarette from the pack.

"I could use a cigarette."

Sinclair looked up at Alice. She looked like hell. Hair wild, cuts up and down her arms, her shirt dotted with blood, but her eyes were steady—focused and cold. Sinclair's eyes flashed wide, and his thin fingers fumbled with the cigarette. He opened his mouth, at-tempted to say something, then snapped his head toward the front entrance of the diner.

"Your friend won't be joining us." Alice slid into the booth across from him and placed her elbows on the table.

He stared at Alice for a moment, his lips developing a slight twitch.

"I believe you've been looking for me."

Sinclair kept staring at her, then finally extended the pack of cig-arettes toward her. "You have cuts on your hands and arms."

Alice tapped out a cigarette. "I'll heal. The same can't be said of your friend though."

She lit a cigarette and Sinclair did the same. They both inhaled deep and blew out gray clouds of smoke, staring quietly at each other, scrutinizing, waiting to see what might happen next.

"This needs to end," Alice finally said.

Sinclair forced a weak smile. "I'm not sure what you're referring to."

Alice leaned forward. "Your big friend is dead. Two other friends of yours back in Harrisburg, dead as well. I think you might be run-ning out of friends."

"I have no friends."

"No?"

"I'm simply passing through town. Perhaps you have me mistaken for someone else."

The waitress stopped by the table again. "Anything for you, sweetheart?"

"A water will be fine."

The waitress noticed the blood on Alice's shirt and arms. "My goodness. You okay, hon?"

"Been fishing. I'll clean up here in a second."

The waitress didn't seem all that convinced but placed a cocktail napkin in front of Alice and hustled away.

"Why don't you have a beer with me?" Sinclair offered.

"I'm good."

"You don't look so good."

"Neither do you."

"Not a drinker?"

"Not at the moment." Alice placed the cigarette to her lips, and her hand didn't appear to be shaking. "Why don't we just cut the bullshit?"

"Again, I'm not entirely sure what you're alluding to."

Alice sighed. "I have something you want. Unless you don't want it back."

"You're an attractive young woman, Alice. A little rough around the edges, but attractive nonetheless." Sinclair studied her face, searching for something he couldn't find. "Tell me, Alice. Why are you here?"

"Do we really have to play this game?"

He sipped his beer. "By your presence here, I'm assuming that the *friend* you keep referring to was not successful with his visit."

"Depends on your definition of success. If it means beating a fifteen-year-old girl and torturing an old man, then, yeah, he was extremely successful."

"Ah. He has a unique set of skills that are, unfortunately, necessary in my line of business. Occasionally, I'm afraid he gets a little overzealous with his technique."

"You think this is funny?"

"On the contrary. I do not."

"She's a kid."

"If the young girl was with you, Alice, then she was guilty by association."

"You're sick."

"Please. This is merely business." He tapped his cigarette on the ashtray. "You stole from me. My property. Made me chase you across four states. This is something that I don't particularly want to be doing with my time."

"So they deserved to be hurt like that?"

"To be perfectly blunt, yes. And you have good reason to be angry, Alice. As do I. But your friends were placed in harm's way because of you. You understand that, right?"

"They didn't have anything to do with this."

"Oh, but they did, Alice. As does anyone that has anything to do with you. It's very simple. You made that fatal error when you decided to steal from me," Sinclair said softly.

Alice's entire body pulsated with a dull rage, growing by each moment she sat across from this man. She dug her fingernail into her palms, trying to repress the image of Elton on the floor, hoping and praying that he would be okay.

"Again, I must ask, why are you here, Alice? I'm curious. Why haven't you involved the police in this matter—this situation we find ourselves in?"

Alice finally looked away. Just for a second. "Because I think we can resolve this between the two of us."

"Ah. You prefer to clean up after your own mistakes, perhaps?"

"Something like that."

The waitress delivered Alice's water, then quickly retreated. Alice took a sip of the cool water, then drained the entire glass.

"I don't imagine we have much time. And you better pray that my friend doesn't die."

"Praying is of little use to me, Alice."

"You think you're clever?"

"We are what we are."

"I give you back your money and all this stops. That's it."

Sinclair lit a new cigarette from the one he still smoked. "Not quite." He offered her another cigarette as well. She declined.

"What more do you want?"

"Well, simply stated, Alice, I don't fully trust you. You are resourceful. Somehow, my three best men are no longer living members of society because of you."

"Maybe you need a better caliber of people."

"Perhaps. Perhaps I do."

"You want your money back. I want this to be done. What more is there?"

"Insurance."

"For what?"

"So that you return my money. Without incident."

"And how do you propose that happens?"

"You *will* give my money back, Alice. That you will do." He reached into his jacket pocket and withdrew the photo of Alice and Jason. He slid the picture across the table and placed it directly in front of her. "Your parents seem like lovely people. They truly miss you and are sick with worry about your well-being. Apparently, you've been gone for quite some time."

Alice stared at the photo. She tried to look away, tried to force her eyes off the image of Jason—she knew that it would only make her weaker—but she couldn't. She remembered the day her parents took the picture. It was Saint Patrick's Day. Jason had just turned four and he was all amped up about eating green mashed potatoes and green chocolate chip cookies, drinking green milk, and wearing everything green right down to his socks.

She finally returned her gaze to Sinclair and watched the corners of his lips curl into a satisfied smirk. "You're an asshole."

"I've been called worse." He tapped his cigarette onto the ashtray. "Now, I realize that you came in here thinking you held all the cards, Alice, but that is not the case. While it is true that I was extremely fond of Phillip—that was the name of the man that you somehow dispatched—we move on." He picked up the picture and returned it to his pocket. "If you have lied to me and already involved the authorities, your parents will suffer. Believe me, I will make sure that they do. You will bring me the money, Alice. We will part ways, and your parents will continue to draw breath into their lungs. Do we understand each other?"

Alice felt her cigarette burn between her fingers, but she kept it where it was. She drew strength from the discomfort. "What's your name?"

Sinclair hesitated by the personal nature of the question.

"What can I call you? Give me a fake name if you want."

Sinclair finally smiled, enjoying the back and forth. "Sinclair will be fine."

"Okay, Sinclair. Here's the thing. You don't trust me. I don't trust you. But we need each other to tie up this final loose end. I think it's better for both of us if we stay in each other's company. Keep an eye on each other. I'll take you to the money. *Then* we'll part ways. That's the only way we do this."

He considered the proposal for a moment. Finally nodded. "I guess that would give us a little more time to become better acquainted. I must admit that I'm very curious about you, Alice. I'm sure you have questions for me as well."

"I don't."

"So be it. I would prefer that you drive."

"Fine."

"One more thing, Alice. I am carrying a Smith & Wesson 9-millimeter pistol. I suggest that you don't try anything foolish."

"Got it. Thanks for the heads-up, Sinclair."

He let out a sound that didn't really sound like laughter, but, in fact, it was. "It's good to keep our sense of humor in situations like these. Now, allow me to settle my tab, then we'll go and retrieve my property."

CHAPTER FORTY-ONE

The unlikely pair headed north on US 17. A fine mist dotted the windshield, but the clouds overhead, gray and menacing, threatened to crack open once again. The Grand Marquis ran smooth and powerful, hugging the road and sweeping by other cars and tractor-trailers as if they were standing still.

Alice drove, hands wrapped around the leather steering wheel, knuckles white as paper.

Sinclair perched in the passenger seat. In his lap, he held the small Smith & Wesson 9-millimeter pistol he had referred to, his right index finger snug around the trigger. A sign for the US 74/76 East whipped past the car.

"Where exactly are we headed, Alice? Where did you hide my money?"

"Someplace safe. We're very close."

"To Wilmington, I take it?"

"Something along those lines."

"Your answers are often quite vague, Alice."

"You prefer responses to be black or white?"

"Interesting. I've never considered that, but perhaps I do. It's easier to evaluate an adversary." Sinclair lit a cigarette. "Let me ask you . . . did you find what you were looking for when you ran away from your parents?"

Alice kept her focus out the windshield. Regripped the steering wheel. "Eventually."

"That's a good thing. Is it not?"

"Took me longer than I'd hoped."

"Ah. Yes. As most objectives do. They can be very elusive. Especially ones of the emotional nature."

Alice finally glanced over at him. "Like you really give a shit?"

"Language, Alice. Is it really necessary to speak in such a crude fashion?"

"The language bothers you, but you don't blink an eye at the fact that two innocent people were beaten and tortured back there? Kinda ironic, isn't it?"

"Well, unfortunately, things of that nature come with the territory. I guess I've grown a thick skin. I'm sure you find me to be quite callous."

"Doesn't really matter what I think."

Sinclair didn't argue the point. "I'm in search of a little clarity about something, Alice. Did you kill Terry?"

"What?"

"Terry. The man you stole my money from. *That* Terry."

Alice stared out at the highway. "Does it matter?"

"Perhaps not, but how does someone like you end up with someone like him?"

"Poor choices."

"I guess we're all guilty of bad judgment from time to time," Sinclair admitted.

Alice glanced over at the pistol resting on his lap, the polished black steel gleaming with oil. "After you get what belongs to you, how do I know that you'll leave my family alone?"

Sinclair gazed out the window and considered this. "It's complicated, Alice. It really is. I wish that it wasn't."

"We just want to walk away from this. Nothing more."

Sinclair nodded. "Understandable. I get that. I really do. The problem is this: you can identify me. And due to our present situation, I believe you would if I let you go. You can see the dilemma I'm in, can't you?"

Alice didn't have an answer.

"Well, Alice, all good things must come to an end, but all bad things can continue forever." He took another puff on his cigarette, then flicked it out the window.

"Thornton Wilder," Alice whispered.

Sinclair smiled at her. "I'm impressed, Alice. I didn't realize that you were so well-read."

"Used to be. Used to be a lot of things."

"Yes. Haven't we all." Sinclair watched her for a moment. "It's truly unfortunate that we met under these circumstances. Another place, another time, perhaps we could have discussed great literature, Alice."

"Why do you do that? Keep saying my name?"

"Do I?"

"Yeah. You do."

He thought about this for a moment. "Perhaps it's a means of making a connection with someone."

"Well, it feels forced. Most connections—the ones that matter—happen naturally."

"I'll take that into consideration." Sinclair lit up another cigarette and offered Alice one as well.

"So, Alice. Aren't you curious? Don't you want to know how all this will play out?"

Alice cracked the window and blew out some smoke. "No."

"No? And why's that?"

She looked over at the man, buckled securely into his seat. "I don't really like to look too far forward. Never have."

Sinclair nodded. Seemed satisfied with the answer.

"I've been running my whole life it seems like. Never in one place for very long," Alice confided. She paused. Smoked for a second. "I want this over. The money. The running."

"I understand. It can be exhausting."

Alice took one hand off the steering wheel and settled back into her seat. "My brother's name was Jason."

Sinclair listened intently. Waited for more.

"He was only four years old when he died. I was babysitting him. There was an accident. Nobody's fault. That's what everyone has always told me. But he was my responsibility. His death destroyed my parents."

"It must have been a very trying time."

She looked at him again. "I don't want to run anymore. And to be honest, I don't mind dying here today. At least it would be over. Running. From everything. But they're my parents, and they didn't have anything to do with this."

Sinclair sighed, smoke curling up from the corners of his mouth. "Yes, we owe our parents a great deal, don't we? They sacrifice so much for their children. They grant us life. Provide shelter and food and unconditional love, and how do we repay them? We leave the nest they raised us in and sometimes act as if they never existed. A thankless cycle of life."

Alice drew on her cigarette. "You know, part of the process of feeling responsible for the death of someone is dealing with the guilt. The guilt is always with you."

"I would imagine so."

"But then, after some time, the guilt begins to change. After a while the guilt shifts. I found myself going a few days, then a few weeks, forgetting about Jason. And I didn't feel guilty that I was forgetting about him. I felt guilty because I *wanted* to forget about him. Easier that way . . . but you never really forget. Not for long, anyway."

Sinclair nodded thoughtfully. "Pushing something uncomfortable from our conscience is a coping mechanism, Alice. Perfectly understandable and acceptable. It enables us to continue our lives without inflicting self-torture upon ourselves." He studied her profile for a moment. "Perhaps in actuality you didn't want to forget your brother, you merely wanted to forget his unfortunate end."

"Maybe." Alice put a little more pressure on the gas pedal.

"If I may ask, how did your brother—Jason—lose his life?"

Alice looked over at Sinclair. "Why? Why would you want to know that?"

"Because, Alice, you intrigue me. Something about you truly fascinates me. You're broken. And because of that, I want to understand you a little better. I want to understand your pain."

Alice stared forward. Watched the landscape slip past and thought about that night all those years ago. She didn't think she would respond to his question—why would she? To *him* of all people? Her mind went to Jason and that distinct thumping sound filled her ears once again, and she was overcome with a sudden, inexplicable compulsion to share the memory. "My parents went out for dinner. Jason and I were home alone. I was supposed to be watching him, but I wasn't. And I heard a sound. A sound that I can still hear—right here, right now."

"A sound?"

"Yeah. It's always there."

"I see. Sight, smell, and sound can all trigger emotionally charged memories. But with auditory perception, sounds are stored within our echoic memory. And most sound information is only maintained for a short amount of time—four or five seconds—but a specific sound resulting from a traumatic incident can remain stored for a lifetime."

"Are you talking from experience, or just something you read?"

Sinclair merely smiled. "What happened after you heard this sound, Alice?"

Alice pulled on her cigarette. "I knew Jason was making the noise, so I went downstairs to find out what he was doing. And the sound got louder."

KA-THUNK. KA-THUNK. KA-THUNK.

Alice tried to block out that awful sound, but couldn't—she knew it to be pointless. "It was coming from the basement. It was steady. Nonstop." She hesitated before continuing. "I walked down the steps. I didn't see him, but I knew something was wrong."

KA-THUNK. KA-THUNK. KA-THUNK.

"Then I looked over to where the sound was coming from. It was the dryer ... shaking and rattling." She smoked again. "Jason had climbed inside. And, somehow, for some reason, the dryer turned on."

Sinclair silently processed this for a moment. "So you were the one to make the discovery?"

Alice crushed out her cigarette and nodded.

"Disturbing. How does one recover from something like that?"

"You don't."

"Touché."

They drove in silence for a few seconds.

"Do you know what a stadiometer is, Alice?"

"No."

"Most do not." He peered out the windshield, silently composing what he wanted to say. "The stadiometer is a standard piece of medical equipment used in doctors' offices to measure one's height and weight. You step on the platform, and a sliding horizontal headpiece is adjusted to rest on the crown of your skull to determine your stature. They are cold and clinical devices." He tapped his cigarette onto the ashtray. "During my annual physical exams, my height was always taken—like it is with most children. Once a year, I would step on that platform, and the headpiece would be adjusted. Always lowered from that of the previous patient. The stadiometer would make a distinct metal clicking sound as the headpiece was lowered to rest on the top of my head. A *click, click, click.* Each piercing click went right through me. I grew to hate that sound."

He drew on his cigarette. "It reminded me of what I was . . . and would always be."

Alice offered him nothing.

"What was your sound like, Alice? With your brother in the dryer?"

Alice visibly flinched. She hadn't expected that question. But she wouldn't share this specific memory—she would not give him that piece of Jason.

She looked at the man beside her, and he held her gaze, waiting for an answer, but she went in a different direction. "Do you have any kids, Sinclair?"

Sinclair flicked his cigarette out the window. "No. No, I do not. Don't really see it in my future, truth be told."

"No? Don't want to leave a legacy behind?"

He chuckled at the thought. "I think I'll leave a different kind of legacy."

"Yeah. I'm sure you will."

"And you? You think you'll leave some lasting impression? Some mark upon the world?"

Alice adjusted herself in the seat. Put her free hand back on the steering wheel. "No. I don't think that's going to happen."

Sinclair scrutinized her for a moment. "You live dangerously, Alice. Everything about you. Right down to not even wearing a seat belt."

Alice looked over at the seat belt that hung unused by her shoulder. "Yeah. Well. We're all going to go sometime. Right?"

"But we should take precautions, Alice. That's what life is about. I've learned that over the years. It's gotten me to where I am today."

Alice glanced over at him; an odd expression—perhaps a smile—upon her face. "Maybe that's what I'm doing. Taking precautions."

He studied her for another moment, honestly perplexed by not only her statement, but by her expression as well.

"Can I get another one of those smokes?"

Sinclair handed her a cigarette, then they both lit up.

The Cape Fear Memorial Bridge loomed in front of them, and there, off in the distance, stood the USS *North Carolina*—the gray seven-hundred-foot battleship permanently docked. Alice had visited the battleship a half dozen times. With her parents on a few occasions, a school field trip, once with a group of friends.

And then there was the last time.

The last time she set foot on the battleship was with Jason. His first and only visit. He had been so excited, eyes wide the entire time, racing around, pointing at the gun turrets, touching the sides of a Kingfisher aircraft, screaming through the narrow hallways below deck. He ate it all up. Said that he wanted to be a sailor when he grew up. Her parents bought him a USS *North Carolina* T-shirt and captain's cap, both of which he wore almost every day for a month.

Alice watched as warning gates jerked and lowered in front of the bridge; lights flashing red, bells sounding. The bridge's vertical lift engaged, and the steel platform that divided the overpass started its ascent skyward, foot-by-foot.

Alice flicked on her blinker and merged into the right-hand lane.

"So, tell me, Alice. What is it that you planned to do with my money? What did you hope to achieve?"

Alice smoked on her cigarette and slowly pumped the brakes. "Achieve? I'm almost there."

"Almost where, Alice?"

"To freedom, Sinclair."

"Is that right? With me?"

"Yes. With you. I'm not running anymore. I know where I'm going. All because of you."

The Grand Marquis rolled to a stop in front of the warning gates, and the dull clanking of the bells filled the cab of the car.

"I'm curious about something," Alice said.

"Oh?"

"Do you work for somebody? Or are you on your own?"

Sinclair laughed softly. "There are people above me, of course. My product must be secured from someone, but the distribution is my enterprise alone. I prefer it that way. Partnerships can be a bit complicated."

"Makes sense." Alice almost smiled as she proceeded to unroll her window all the way down.

"Anything else you'd like to ask me? Anything else you'd like to know? I'm an open book to you."

Alice watched as the section of the bridge approached its apex, then looked toward a freight ship that loomed nearby, waiting for authorization to pass under and continue down the Cape Fear River.

"Yeah. Just one last question. Do you know how to swim?"

Sinclair started to say something, but the words weren't there. Instead, his eyes went to the river that flowed in front of them.

Alice gripped the steering wheel tight—liberation was there at her fingertips. Between her ten fingers. She slammed her foot onto the gas pedal—the Grand Marquis lurched forward, crashed through the warning gates, tires humming atop the steel grating, going faster, picking up speed.

The pistol slipped from Sinclair's hand and thudded to the floorboard. He reached forward to retrieve his weapon, but his seat belt restrained him. He tried again, but failed. Sinclair leaned back into his seat, peered over at Alice, and his face transformed as realization fell upon him. A sound escaped his lips. A single word that seemed to be etched in fear—*Alice.*

She pushed the Grand Marquis to its limit. The thundering engine and the roar of the tires upon the steel grid below blocked out everything else. For the next few seconds, the sounds proved deafening, then, as the car launched off the precipice and took flight, all went silent—an inaudible moment caught in time.

Alice glanced over at Sinclair. Feeling peace for the first time. Feeling the weight of guilt lift off her shoulders. Feeling the sense of freedom she always sought but never obtained.

Alice closed her eyes. Waited for the impact.

CHAPTER FORTY-TWO

A dozen Wilmington police cruisers, four fire trucks, and a handful of ambulances parked at the edge of the Cape Fear River, lights slashing through the gray drizzle that wouldn't cease. Yellow police tape—draped from trees, light posts, anything to tie off to—snapped in a relentless breeze, keeping reporters and a few dozen curiosity seekers back and away from the scene. Water Street had been blocked off, preventing access to the riverfront restaurants, office buildings, and tourist shops, and traffic sat in a snarl on all the streets that surrounded the area. Commuters desperate to get home laid on their horns, but aside from creating a deafening drone, their efforts did little to get the flow of cars moving again.

Nightfall approached quickly. Light dimming with each passing second. A gentle fog drifting in off the river.

Police divers outfitted in black scuba gear floated alongside the Grand Marquis as a tow truck wench methodically cranked the vehicle from the river. First the roof of the car emerged from the water like a sea turtle shell, then the hood and trunk. A few more cranks and the car completely appeared, coated with black sludge. Muddy water churned out of the car, bubbling up against the windows.

The steel cable groaned to a stop as the car eased up on the concrete shore and emergency workers descended on the vehicle like a pack of gnats—gurneys and medical packs at the ready.

On the shoreline, businessmen in suits, waiters wearing aprons, and couples out on an evening stroll talked amongst themselves. Some of them taking pictures with their phones.

One of the divers finally managed to pry open the driver's-side door with the assistance of a crowbar, and a torrent of brown water gushed out onto the shore before winding its way back into the river. A lone figure sat crumpled in the passenger seat, skin white and puckered from being submerged for so long. Many around the car thought the victim to be a child. So small. So fragile looking.

The vehicle was searched for other victims. The back seat. The floor of the car.

Then the trunk.

River water rushed from the well of the trunk, lapping over the fender and license plate, and the brown liquid, mixed with a considerable amount of blood, churned and swirled with dozens of wet twenty-dollar bills. Thousands of dollars spilled out as if dispensed from an underwater ATM. The paper currency floated atop the rushing water, then ran down the bank of the river before getting swept up in the waters encasing Cape Fear and spinning downstream.

Amidst the darkened water that remained trapped inside, a large man's body floated faceup, his neck slashed open, eyes swollen shut. It took the strained efforts of three paramedics to finally remove the dead weight from the trunk.

The body was laid out on the cold, sandy concrete. Paramedics followed protocol, but found the victim to be deceased, just as they knew he would be.

As the search continued, a police officer reached a gloved hand into the trunk and retrieved an olive-green duffel bag. The bag was turned over and stacks of waterlogged cash slapped against the ground like dead fish.

Then a team of detectives took over, scouring the car for any evidence that would determine the cause of the accident. They found and removed Sinclair's pistol. Phillip's knife was discovered strapped under the man's belt. Photographs were taken, items removed one by one from suitcases, and each article of clothing placed in plastic evidence bags. The gas and brake pedals were examined and tested for malfunction.

Amongst the detectives, there was conversation about the empty driver's seat and the opened window. More photographs were taken, flashes of white popping every few seconds.

As the investigation dragged on and nightfall settled along the river, the crowd of onlookers began to thin out one by one. Everyone getting on with the rest of their day, morbidly excited to share the story of the accident with friends and family.

A few blocks from the crime scene, a young woman stood rigid, watching closely, but keeping her distance from everyone else. She wore a sweatshirt and blue jeans, and even though all the other bystanders were damp from rain, she stood out—her clothing stuck to her skin like wet newspaper, water dripping from the cuffs of her pants and pooling around her feet. Brown hair hung over the woman's face, but her green eyes kept a steady watch.

It was only after both corpses were finally zipped up in body bags and loaded into the back of a coroner's van that the young woman began to walk away. She moved a bit gingerly—slow, easy steps with the bare hint of a limp. She didn't look back. Not once. As the woman disappeared down a side street, the rain started to ease up a little, and the wind finally tapered off until the air grew utterly still.

* * *

ACKNOWLEDGMENTS

Where to begin? Well, perhaps I'll start at home . . .

This book would not be in your hands if not for my wife, best friend, and frequent mentor, Ayn Carrillo-Gailey. She inspires me. Encourages me. Challenges me to not only be a better writer, but a better man. And all of this before she helps me craft and edit my work.

My other girl, Gray, twelve, never fails to fill me with blinding pride. Intelligent, kind, creative, and a much better speller than I.

Thank you to my mother, Deb Templeton, who instilled in me my absolute passion for the written word. I'd like to thank my sister, Robin, for her last-minute help on one of the most crucial scenes in the book, and to Geoff, for always watching out for his little brother.

I am eternally grateful to the Oceanview Publishing team for making me feel at home. To my editors, Pat and Bob Gussin, I appreciate your insightful notes. Thank you to Emily Baar, Lee Randall, and Autumn Beckett for all that you contribute in this process.

Thank you to my literary agent, Esmond Harmsworth, at Aevitas Creative Management, for his loyalty and guidance.

Where would I be without my literary manager, Amy Schiffman, at the Intellectual Property Group? You saw something in me when I was taking my first steps as a writer and have stayed by my side through each stumble and fall.

ACKNOWLEDGMENTS

I'm indebted to my French publisher, Oliver Gallmeister, *le roi du noir.*

To fellow author Matt Coyle—you may not be much of a pontificator, but you're a helluva writer and a class act.

I'd like to thank my Novel Lab students. Hopefully, I have inspired you as much as you have inspired me.

Michael Hanson—you're the champ. I believe you single-handedly purchased more copies of my first novel, *Deep Winter*, than anyone else. Keep up the good work.

A big thank-you goes to Dr. Mark Matz for his kindness and advisement.

A few of my friends deserve an acknowledgment for helping me in the writing process, whether they knew it or not: Brian Price, a gifted writer with a warped mind like my own. Christi Derreberry, who helped shed some light on the darker streets of Charlotte, NC. Jerry Abrams, a guy I've known since growing up in the backwoods of Pennsylvania, and who also happens to write the funniest damn letters ever crafted. And to Stu "Bern" Smith, thanks for making the epic trip to Orcas and reading at the eleventh hour.

Since I started my thank-yous at home, I'll end there as well. I want to express my gratitude to the folks of Orcas Island. I completed my novel on this magical Salish Sea isle. It's a special place and not just because of its majestic landscape or clean air or the fact that it's home to the Orcas Island Lit Fest and to Darvill's—one of the best bookstores on the planet. No, it runs deeper than that. This artistic community, and the new friends I've made along the way, make me realize that I finally found where I belong.